BEHOLD, A MYSTERY!

Joan Smith is the author of more than ninety novels
of the Regency period

BEHOLD, A MYSTERY!

A Regency Story

Joan Smith

St. Martin's Press   New York

Design by Judith A. Stagnitto

Library of Congress Cataloging-in-Publication Data

Smith, Joan.
    Behold, a mystery / Joan Smith.
      p.   cm.
    "A Thomas Dunne book."
    ISBN 0-312-10424-3
    1. Women detectives—England—Fiction.   2. Young
women—England—Fiction.   I. Title.
PR9199.3.S55157B44   1994
813'.54—dc20   93-40476
                                                        CIP

First Edition: March 1994

10 9 8 7 6 5 4 3 2 1

BEHOLD, A
MYSTERY!

ONE

It was the vilest trick ever played on a lady. A forced marriage could hardly be worse. Indeed what else am I faced with but a forced marriage? The only difference is that I have a choice amongst four unsuitable *partis*. Of course I shall marry Horatio. Otto would not have me as a gift; I would not have Gregory; I do not care a groat for Latin, which makes Felix ineligible, and I cannot let poor murdered Aunt Hettie's fortune go to the dog, Duke. That is the alternative. I marry one of her great-nephews, or I become a housekeeper for her hound for the next twelve months. Aunt Hettie did it on purpose to force my hand. She knew Duke dislikes me cordially, and the feeling is fully reciprocated. And now Duke has vanished.

"A shame and a caution," Horatio said when the will was understood. I do not say "read," for one reading was not sufficient to make my aunt's intent clear. We none of us could credit such diabolical chicanery.

"Intolerable!" Gregory exclaimed.

"Anguis in herba," Felix murmured.

And Otto said, with a hateful smile, "Which of us will you honour with your hand, Jessica? No, no. I did not mean the *back* of your hand!"

I had no intention of striking him. I merely lifted my hand to shake a finger at him.

It all came about at the end of December. It was the custom for Aunt Hettie Farr to recast her will at the beginning of each new year. I doubt she actually made many changes, but she used this cunning ploy to force her potential heirs to come and spend an extremely tedious and uncomfortable week with us at Downsview. Auntie's estate is a hideous monstrosity dating from the Jacobean period, done in the Perpendicular Gothic style, with strapwork, pointed arches and much misapplied classical detail. It is nestled amidst the Sussex Downs, with a view of more Downs, almost entirely lacking in features. The long row of chalk hills rises and falls gently. From the crest of a rise one may, on a clear day, catch a glimpse of the sea, or The Weald. Farms and villages nestle amidst the folds of the rolling hills. I thought it pretty when I first came, but one cannot enjoy the same view forever without wearying of it.

I had been gazing at those Downs for a decade, since coming to Aunt Hettie when I was just turned sixteen. My mama was her favorite niece. Hettie is actually my great-aunt. She was not blessed with children of her own. She, the ugliest of the Chapman sisters, had made the best match and offered me a home on Mama's death, for which I was and am grateful.

The offer was not pure charity. I worked for my keep, performing those ladylike chores a demanding old lady can always find for a poor relation. If, as my story progresses, you are left with the notion that I disliked her, you will be mistaken. There was kindness beneath her bristly exterior. She had her annoying little ways, and no doubt I have mine, but we came to respect each other, and even enjoy moments of closeness during the latter years. I sewed and did her correspondence, ran short errands and read to her in the evening, in return for which I received a roof over my head and twelve sovereigns a year, paid quarterly. Our life was not exciting, but at the end of each

December there was the annual visit of four smart London bachelors to look forward to.

We sat in the gloomy purple saloon awaiting their arrival on a dull grey afternoon. On an ordinary day, Duke would have accompanied us. He usually sits drooling by the grate, for he is old and grey like his mistress. But for this special occasion she had him banished belowstairs.

The oaken panelling consumed any wan ray of sunlight that penetrated the dust-stained windows. A few damp logs smouldered in the grate of a Tudor fireplace. Mrs. Manner sat with us. She was another poor relation, relict of a clergyman, who had already been a fixture at Downsview when I arrived ten years before. Her sole function, as far as I could determine, was to sit with Aunt Hettie and receive the old lady's insults. Auntie would have respected her more if she had defended herself, but Mrs. Manner was no adversary. If she recognized a slight, she always turned the other cheek.

She and my aunt were a perfect contrast as to type. Mrs. Manner was small and soft and round and sweet, with some remnants of beauty still in her blue eyes. Auntie was tall and tough and lean and sour. She could never have been beautiful, but I dare say she was handsome in her youth, or why would Aldous Farr, the younger son of an old and famous noble family, have married her?

Aunt Hettie wore a grey worsted gown and a grey lace cap over her grey hair, to match her grey eyes. A jabot of Belgian lace rose right up to her chin, to hide the wattles of her neck. Though she was on the windy side of seventy, she was still vain. On ordinary days, the jabot was decorated with a marcasite brooch shaped like a starfish, only I think it was supposed to be a flower. In honour of the expected company, the marcasites had given way to an impressive amethyst brooch that afternoon. On her feet she wore new black calf-skin slippers, where one was accustomed to seeing shagreen. Those were the only upgradings of her toilette.

I, being younger and in need of a husband, had made major improvements to mine. Mrs. Manner had helped me to roll my chestnut hair up in papers the night before, resulting in a riotous display of corkscrew curls that ill became my sober countenance. Like Auntie, I have grey eyes and a long, lean body. I am neither a beauty nor quite an antidote. I wore my best day frock of dark green sarsenet, with a lace collar fashioned with more enthusiasm than skill by my own hand. One end hung lower than the other, but with Mrs. Manner's assistance and a few stitches, we had evened it up. I wore my mama's string of pearls and felt very grand in all this unaccustomed splendour.

Auntie did not comment on my appearance, but only looked with her sharp, knowing eyes, and allowed a commiserating smile to move her lips. She was well aware that for nine December visits I had been putting forth my best effort, and every time it had come to nought. A perfect example of hope springing eternal.

After a long wait, we eventually heard the rumble of a coach approaching. My heart lurched, but I would not give my aunt the satisfaction of darting to the window to display my eagerness. Otto! my heart sang. Four gentlemen were coming, but any lady with blood in her veins would put Otto at the top of the heap. He was the one who made the visits special. I had about as much chance of receiving an offer from this dasher as I had of marrying the Prince of Wales, but he added a certain piquancy to the visits, with his flirting ways and heedless charm.

"Sounds like a carriage. Who is it, Addie?" Auntie asked Mrs. Manner in a calm voice, but I suspect she was looking forward to her visitors quite as much as I.

Mrs. Manner had the seat nearest the window. She glanced out and said brightly, "It is a carriage."

Auntie's lips pulled into a derisive line. "The lads decided not to walk from London, I daresay." Really, Mrs. Manner was enough to try the patience of a saint.

"Felix would not be driving a carriage," Mrs. Manner pointed out.

"His brother is the most selfish thing in nature, but I think we might count on Gregory to at least give Felix a drive," Hettie said.

Felix and Gregory Chapman were actual blood relatives of Hettie, and therefore some distant kin to myself as well. The other two bachelors, Otto and Horatio Farr, were great-nephews of Hettie's husband, and from a higher social shelf entirely. Their papa was Baron Kidd. Otto, the elder, was heir to the title. They were not called Lord Otto or Lord Horatio, however. It seems a baron's sons are only "Honourables."

"Or perhaps Felix has set up a rig, now that he has written that famous book," Mrs. Manner suggested, and smiled her sweet smile at Felix's good fortune.

"Felix did not write a book," Aunt Hettie stated firmly. "He translated some old thing from the Latin. *Plutarch's Lives of the Noble Romans,* was it? Something of the sort."

She knew perfectly well that it was, but this was her manner of belittling his accomplishment. In fact, Felix's translation had received excellent reviews from the critics, and I hoped for his sake that it would make him rich. And all the time I sat listening to their chatter with one ear while on nettles to learn which gentleman had arrived.

We were not long in doubt. The shuffling gait told the tale even before he poked his head into the saloon. It was Horatio Farr. I liked him enormously, and in fact felt he was the one most likely to make me an offer, because he had a heart made of melted butter, and felt sorry for me. There was enough of Otto in him to make him physically appealing. He was tall with black hair and kind blue eyes, yet they were not eyes to set a maiden's heart aflutter. He was a blurred, faulty copy of Otto, and rather foolish to boot. It was unkind of nature to give the elder son and heir the brains and looks of the family as well.

Horatio entered at his habitual gait, with his head inclined forward, perhaps because of his height. "Ladies," he said, making a sort of general bow. Then he went to Aunt Hettie and did the pretty before folding his long body into a seat by the smouldering grate.

"A nasty day," he said. "I expect you feel the cold here, Auntie."

"I like it," she replied. "Jessica has managed to get herself a cold. She'll pass it to all of us before the week is out."

Horatio inclined his head towards me. "Sorry to hear it."

"And you are not wearing your woollen shawl, Jessica," Aunt Hettie said, skewering me with one of her knowing smiles. My woollen shawl is old and tatty. She knew why I had discarded it, despite the sore throat.

"Cook is preparing her cold mixture," I said.

"A cold syrup won't keep you warm," my aunt pointed out. "You ought to run down to the kitchen and see how the brew is coming along. I'll take a bottle of it upstairs myself tonight. I am not feeling any too stout." Then she turned to Horatio and said, "How are things at the Elms? I hope you are keeping up that little property your Uncle Siberry left you."

"Just dandy. That is to say, the roof is falling apart."

"The roof perishing, and you with five thousand a year! That is inexcusable, Horatio. You owe it to your future sons to keep it fit, and expand the acreage if possible."

"I have the roof lads there this minute looking it over."

"I should hope so." She turned to me. "Why are you sitting there staring, Jessica? I told you to see how the cold medicine is coming along. You'll have ample opportunity to roll your eyes at Horatio over the next week. Tell Cook not to forget the raisins. And use rum instead of wine."

Horatio cast a pitying smile at me as I left.

The kitchen was awash with a variety of delightful odours, for Hettie did not stint on her meals. A joint was roasting, a plum-cake sat steaming on its dish, and at the stove, Cook stirred the simmering cold medicine. Linseed and liquorice, raisins and lemon juice, water and pounded sugar, rum, and belladonna to suppress a cough, combined to create a strong odour.

Cook's face was pink and moist from her job, and her figure was full, as a cook's should be. "I heard a carriage. Does she want tea served?" she asked me.

"We'll wait until the others come. I'm here to see how the cold medicine is coming."

"And to remind me to use rum instead of wine. As if I didn't know! This is done. I'll set it aside to cool and fill the bottles later. How's the sore throat, dearie?"

"Scratchy. I'll gargle with brine. I find that better than anything, if you catch it early."

She made me up a brine solution, and I took it to my room to wash my throat. When I returned below, Felix had arrived.

He is pale, tall and slender, with rusty hair the color of a fox. There is something of the fox in his sly face too. He is fair-looking, but he takes no notice of how he is turned out. His blue jacket was shiny at the cuffs, and his cravat looked as if he had knotted it in the dark. Unlike the other gentlemen, he did not travel with a valet. It seemed he had acquired a carriage, however. He was discussing it with Horatio.

"Just a plain black carriage and team. It is light; it has no need of four nags to pull it. Now that my labours are beginning to pay off, I can afford the luxury. It is my only one. Fortunately I am not afflicted with *amor sceleratus habendi*."

Horatio said, "Eh?"

"The accursed love of possessing," Felix translated.

"What you ought to put your blunt into is property," Hettie declared. "Horses and carriages are just an expense; an estate makes money."

"What would I want with an estate?" Felix said, staring as if she were mad. "I haven't time for such things. My books, my research, my translations . . ."

Mrs. Manner cast an admonitory glance at him, and he began backtracking himself into Auntie's good graces. "Unless it were a splendid estate such as Downsview, of course. Naturally I would hire a steward to look after it—if I had such a place."

Auntie looked from Felix to me. I don't know how she did it, but that look managed to convey that I must be taken along with the estate. Felix, who was quicker than I expected at grasping her meaning, said, *"Domus et placens uxor."*

"I wish you would speak English, Felix," she said testily.

"Home and a good wife, Auntie," he replied, his clever eyes smiling at me. "Naturally a man needs a wife."

Horatio became frightened and erupted into speech. "Good Lord, have you offered for Jess, Felix? I hadn't heard of it."

"No, he has not," I said firmly.

"No one has offered for Jess," Auntie agreed, then added, "unfortunately." I sat feeling like the unwanted runt of the litter.

Horatio said merrily, "Can't think what ails all the lads hereabouts. There cannot be a prettier gel for a mile around."

To take the palm within such a small circumference was hardly flattering. There was no other gel of any sort within a square mile, but I appreciated his moral support.

Auntie disliked to serve tea before the whole crew had arrived, but the evening shadows were closing in, and if she felt as hungry as I, she was more than ready for her tea.

She soon gave the faded bell-cord a yank to summon the butler. Juteclaw was an ancient skeleton of a man, but spry for his eighty years. He appeared at the door with his wisps of white hair in wild disarray.

"Are ye ready for your tea, madam?" he asked.

"At once," Aunt Hettie said, and he left with a bob of his head, at the same lively gait. She had been trying for a decade to teach Juteclaw to wait until he was spoken to before speaking, but it was a lost cause.

We waited, making desultory conversation as daylight faded to dark, and Juteclaw came to holler, "Shall I light the lamps, madam?"

He did, and we all sat on, waiting for the diversion of the tea-tray.

TWO

Before long, Juteclaw returned, bent under the weight of the heavy silver tea-tray. Horatio, always the perfect gentleman, took it and placed it on the sofa table. I was the official pourer, since my aunt could not lift the pot and Mrs. Manner had once dropped it, doing considerable damage to the sofa and carpet, but more to her self-esteem. She was never allowed to forget it.

Gregory Chapman arrived just as I was pouring. Being the elder of the brothers, he had inherited his papa's estate, but it was a small one. Its income was certainly not enough to support the lavish style of life he had adopted. I expect he had mortgaged Hanshurst to the chimney. Gregory had rooms in London at the Albany, where bachelors of the ton lived. He enjoyed horse-racing, cards, balls, and the company of ladies. His only hope of indulging in such frivolities after he lost his estate, as he inevitably must, was to marry a fortune. He had sufficient looks and charm that he might very well succeed.

In appearance, he was not much like his brother Felix. He was a bigger man, both taller and broader, with a fine set of shoulders. His hair was chestnut like mine, but his eyes were green like Felix's, set in a pleasantly masculine face. His toilette was the epitome of elegance. There was no lack of nap on his blue superfine jacket. His cravat was a marvel of intricacy; his biscuit trousers were spotless, and his Hessians gleaming.

He rushed forward and placed his two hands on Hettie's shoulders as he leaned down to kiss her cheek. "Aunt Hettie! How do you do it, old girl? I swear you become younger and prettier with every passing year."

Her stiff old face creased into smiles. It was well-known that Gregory was her favourite. She had once told me Gregory reminded her of her papa. What she could not like was his spendthrift ways. If he would only remove to the country, run his estate at a profit and visit her oftener than once a year for the short remainder of her life, he could be assured of inheriting the bulk of her fortune. But that was Gregory all over. He could not curtail his immediate pleasures, even for such a prize as Downsview.

"Flattery will get you nowhere, Master Jackanapes," she said, but she said it with the air of a coquette. "Jessica, pour Gregory a cup of tea. And a slice of that plum-cake. Or perhaps you would prefer sherry, Gregory?"

The other gentlemen had not been offered sherry.

"Both! I shall have both," Gregory declared. He briefly acknowledged the rest of us, then drew a chair close to Hettie, where he proceeded to beguile her.

Hettie sent Mrs. Manner off to oversee the preparations for dinner, and I had the other two gentlemen to myself. We instituted some chatter amongst ourselves, but between lapses I caught the gist of the other conversation.

"Have you given any thought to standing for Parliament, as I suggested?" Hettie asked Gregory.

"You may be sure I have, Auntie. The devil of it is, Lord Basingstoke picks the man for our constituency, and always sends a dashed Whig up to Parliament."

Aunt Hettie was a confirmed Tory. They discussed this for

a while, with Auntie suggesting other constituencies he might stand for. When I caught another fragment, she had switched to chiding him for running his estate into the ground.

"Cut that stand of oaks! Gregory, you must not think of it! They are the making of Hanshurst. The place would look desolate without them."

"I agree. It breaks my heart to do it, but I need five hundred pounds."

"Gambling debts, I suppose?"

"If you want to call a business investment gambling," he said, in an injured tone. "I was given every assurance that the company—"

Horatio tugged at my elbow. "He's bamming the old gel," he said in a low voice. "He's already cut those oaks. I noticed at Christmas when I was driving home to visit the folks. I happen to know he dropped a bundle at Mrs. Hennessey's gaming hell. The old girl will fall for it and give him the five hundred."

"He can always bring her round his thumb," I agreed.

"I mean to have a go at her m'self. The roof at the Elms is full of holes."

"Horatio! I hope you have not fallen prey to this vice of gambling too!"

"Nothing of the sort. I lent Cousin Ralph a few hundred. He got married at Christmas, you know, to that nice Jennie Huddlestone. I no sooner did it than the water took to gushing into the attic. Always the way, ain't it?"

"Could your papa not help you out?"

"Don't like to ask Papa. Cuts up stiff."

"What about Otto?" I was eager to bring Otto into the conversation, to hear how he was doing.

"Bad time for poor Otto."

"Poor Otto? He must be rich as a nabob by now. One sees his journal everywhere."

"Lawsuit. The *Clarion* made some nasty comments about

Prinney. Mean to say, what other sort *could* they make, and folks do like to read about him. The fellow's costing the country a fortune."

"Was that what Otto wrote?"

"Not this time. 'Twas about Prinney's new mistress, Lady Hertford. All to do with Prinney reneging on Catholic emancipation. Used to be for it, then he takes up with Hertford, and suddenly he changes his coat. Grey and Grenville was in on the attack in the *Clarion*. All Prinney's old Whig friends are on the outs with him. They hoped to seize power, but of course old Perceval was brought back in. Prinney is claiming the story was next door to treason, and has set up a lawsuit for five thousand pounds."

"That much!"

"It'll kill the *Clarion*—and Otto. He ain't foolish enough to hit Hettie up for the money. She would never spend a sou on a Whig cause, so he'll play the thing up for all it's worth, to rile her."

"Yes," I agreed. There was a deal of mischief in Otto.

"Putting her in a pelter won't do *me* any good. My roof, that is to say."

It seemed unfair that Gregory could lie his way to five hundred pounds to throw away on cards or light-skirts while Horatio, whose only sin was generosity, would get nothing. I was more concerned for Otto, however. He had been a little wild before starting up the *Clarion*. Gambling, women—the usual vices of the aristocracy. But when he had instituted his newspaper three years before, he had thrown himself into it with such vigour that he had no time for dissipations. It had been his salvation, and if he lost his journal, he might revert to his old ways.

Gregory suddenly rose. "My usual room, Auntie?" he said, with such a doting smile that I knew he had weaseled the money out of her. "I shall have a lie-down before dinner."

Felix immediately took up Gregory's vacant seat beside Aunt Hettie. As Gregory was walking to the door, Felix called, "How is Mrs. Rampling, Gregory?"

Gregory stopped dead in his tracks and turned around slowly. A pink flush crept up his neck and coloured his cheeks. There was murder in his eyes as he glared at his brother. "Very well, thank you, Felix. So kind of you to ask."

"Mrs. Rampling?" Hettie demanded at once. "And who, pray, is Mrs. Rampling?"

"Why, she is Gregory's new—er, friend," Felix said, with an air of innocence. "I made sure that was what he was whispering in your car, Auntie. So gay and lively. Quite the life of the town, one hears."

"A divorcée?" Hettie exclaimed, aghast. "Surely you are not seeing a divorcée, Gregory?"

"Of course not," he said. "Mrs. Rampling is a widow."

"Indeed she is," Felix agreed. "Her late husband was recently shot in a duel defending her honour."

"Gregory! That is not the sort of lady—"

"She is only a friend, Auntie," Gregory said. "I helped her handle a little business when her husband died. We are just friends, nothing more." He turned and resumed his departure, at a noticeably stiffer gait.

"Shame on you, Felix, frightening me for nothing," Aunt Hettie said. "But enough of that. Tell me all about your little book."

"Actually it is rather a large book. I have brought you a copy, Auntie. I left it with Juteclaw." He drew a sheaf of reviews from his pocket, and for the next moments the air rang with a recitation from them. "A truly remarkable work, showing a breadth and depth of knowledge astonishing in one so young. It is helpful for each age to take its own look at the classics, and we have not had a good translation of Plutarch's *Parallel Lives* for nearly half a century," he read. "That is in the *Edinburgh Review*.

And Coleridge says, 'Mr. Chapman's translation has the lively style of Sir Thomas North's version, with the accuracy of the Langhornes's.' North and the Langhorne brothers were two earlier translators," he explained. "And that, *in nuce,* was the conclusion of all the scholars. The work took five years of my life, but it was worth it."

"And what will you do next?" she asked.

"*Pro tempore,* I shall concentrate on—"

"Might I suggest you concentrate on learning English, Felix," Hettie said. She never really cared for Felix, but when she saw his hangdog look, she softened. "You have done very well, my dear. We are all proud of you. Quite an ornament for the family tree."

"Actually there is some rumour of a knighthood," Felix said. He got all the praise he could want from Hettie then. Gregory had not received a more doting welcome. Felix had lived too long amidst his books. He hadn't sufficient experience with people to realize the glitter of a knighthood meant more to Hettie than any scholastic achievement.

"She likes that," Horatio said aside to me. "Felix may get a leg up on Gregory now that he is on his way to fame."

"Is he really becoming famous?" I asked.

"Rumour has it he will be offered a post at Oxford. A tad young for the Chair of Classics, but that will come in time. They say the book is a wonder. I never cared for Greeks and Romans m'self. A bloodthirsty lot."

There was a knock at the front door, and I felt a gush of excitement. Otto! But when Juteclaw appeared, he said, "A Mr. Weldon, for Mr. Felix Chapman."

"Weldon, my neighbour? How did he know you would be here, Felix?" Hettie asked.

"He wrote to congratulate me on my book, and raised a few points he wishes to discuss. I wrote and arranged to meet him here. I hope you don't mind."

"It is news to me that John Weldon is interested in anything but dogs and horseflesh." Weldon bred and trained dogs. Hettie had got her Duke from him. "Are you sure you are not thinking of his papa? Doctor Weldon died two years ago. He used to tutor old Lord Handley's lads. Handley had a high opinion of him."

"I realize Doctor Weldon is dead," Felix said. "I considered him a friend. Do you not recall I attended his funeral, Auntie? I stayed with you."

"So you did. Bring Weldon in," Auntie said to Juteclaw.

"You will not be interested—" Felix said.

Juteclaw took his orders from Hettie. He nodded and leaped out the door. In about ten seconds John Weldon was shown in. He had a Spanish look about him, with his swarthy complexion, black hair and eyes, and small, muscular build. I knew him slightly from the village and local assemblies. His reputation was such that my aunt did not encourage the acquaintance. And as I did not care for him, I did not make an issue of it.

He behaved like a gentleman, however. He made his bows to the ladies and said "good day" to Felix and Horatio.

Auntie quizzed him for a few moments about his farm and his mama, but when he proved taciturn, she suggested he and Felix remove to the study for their discussion. Felix was not slow to get away. I was surprised he did not use this visitor as an excuse to expand more on his *magnum opus,* but perhaps he realized Aunt Hettie was not really interested in it.

"Five-thirty, and still no sign of Otto," Hettie said. "What can be keeping him? When I extend an invitation to tea, I expect my company to be here for tea."

"It would be the *Clarion* that's holding him up," Horatio said, in an apologetic way. "Nothing else would keep him away."

That was typical of Horatio's kind nature. Either Gregory

or Felix would have taken advantage of the other's tardiness to turn Hettie against the culprit. You would think brothers would be kinder to each other.

Auntie said, "I shall go to my room to rest before dinner. We dine at seven, Horatio. City hours, for you city bucks."

Horatio assisted her from her chair and walked her to the door. As soon as she was gone, he poured us two glasses of sherry and we settled in for a good chat. As he refilled our glasses, he said, "Felix and Weldon would appreciate a gargle of this. Excellent stuff! I'll take 'em the bottle."

When he returned from the study he said, "They are hot at it. Don't it beat the Dutch how scholars can come to cuffs over something written hundreds of years ago? Weldon had his notes with him, arguing till he was blue in the face about Pericles. Would he be the fellow who built the Parthenon?"

"I have no idea," I admitted, and we spoke of more contemporary things until it was time to change for dinner.

Mr. Weldon was just leaving as we entered the hall. "We'll continue this discussion tomorrow, Mr. Chapman," he said, with a challenge in his eyes.

Felix replied placatingly, "I look forward to it, Mr. Weldon. I believe you have a point."

He bowed civilly; Weldon made a jerky bow, and left.

We all went upstairs. And still Otto had not come.

THREE

Mrs. Manner came to help me with my toilette for dinner. With her assistance, I had re-fashioned my deep-blue evening frock, ruching up the hem and adding velvet bows. She helped me tame my corkscrew curls to a more civilized do, and pulled two strands to the back, decorated with one of the left-over skirt bows, in what she called the *corbeille*.

My room was a shambles when I was ready to descend. Auntie had not shuffled me off to any inferior cubby-hole when I came to her. I was given a fine bedchamber with lofty ceilings and elegant gold-coloured brocade window hangings to match the canopy on my bed. What I especially treasured was the vanity table with the mirror above it. I felt quite a lady of fashion when I sat there, using Mama's chased silver brush and comb. I never had such a room when Mama was alive.

It bothered me to see clothes strewn on the chairs and bed of my cherished room, but I had heard Otto's voice echoing in the hallway, and wild horses could not have held me back. A last peek in my mirror showed a flush on my cheeks and a glow of excitement in my grey eyes. He, Otto, had once called my eyes stormy grey. We had been arguing at the time. I daresay he did not even mean it as a compliment, but I treasured the description. At least he had looked at me, and seen what he was looking at. Poor relations are so often looked past, rather than at. But then Otto was bound to look at any lady younger than forty, unless she was a positive antidote.

"You look just lovely, dear," Mrs. Manner assured me.

"So do you," I replied.

She, too, had taken pains with her toilette. In Mrs. Manner's case, taking pains means shifting from her grey cap to her ecru one with the blue satin ribbons, and puffing her grey hair in little buns over her ears. And of course wearing the pretty opal ring her late husband had given her. It is small, with chips of opal and seed pearls and rubies resting in an oval platform. She calls it "your ring," meaning my ring, as she has left it, her dearest possession, to me in her will.

"I hope we don't all come down with this cold that is threatening, and destroy the yearly visit," she worried.

My scratchy throat no longer bothered me. The dryness in my mouth was due to pure anticipation of the evening ahead. "Take the cold medicine. Auntie says it is a preventive, as well as a cure."

"Aye, but it is the rum she likes."

Mrs. Manner does not usually make sly comments. I put it down to her excitement. We went together, nervous as a pair of debs, to the great staircase. It has a narrow brass banister worn silk-smooth by generations of fingers, and bronze fretwork below. The stairs are broad and shallow, with a great sweeping curve in the middle. A marvellous staircase for making a grand entrance to the rose marble floor below. I peered over the railing, and was disappointed that no one was waiting in the hall to admire our descent.

A blending of polite voices issued from the saloon. We would make our grand entrance into the purple saloon instead. I stopped a moment at the doorway, revelling in the view that greeted my eyes. Four young gentlemen of fashion, wearing black evening suits; Auntie sitting in state by the grate; an unaccustomed number of lamps casting puddles of light in the gloomy chamber; and Juteclaw passing a tray of wine. No marvellous sight for most people, perhaps, but at Downsview it was something quite out of the ordinary, and my blood warmed even before Otto turned to welcome us. He was the first to spot us; my fond imagination decided he had been waiting impatiently for my arrival. Something in his smile suggested it—a look of long anticipation satisfied.

To describe him is to become mired in cliché. He was tall, dark and handsome. But it was neither his height, his colouring, nor his well-formed face that lent him that particular air of distinction. It was his liveliness, and his charm. Half of London was running mad for him; how should a mere provincial miss not be bowled over? His dark eyes danced with pleasure as he came forward and placed a lingering kiss on my warm cheek.

"You are one of the wonders of the world, Jess," he said, looking deeply into my eyes. "You never change. Happy New Year." Then he turned and said substantially the same thing to Mrs. Manner, only in different words. He cupped my elbow firmly in one hand, Mrs. Manner's in the other, and led us into the saloon. "Let the party begin. The young ladies have arrived," he announced. He handed us a glass of wine and saw us seated.

I saw at a glance that Aunt Hettie was in the boughs about something. I thought at first she disliked Otto's intimation that the party must wait for anyone but herself, but her next speech enlightened me.

"Just what one might expect of you, Otto, to insult and humiliate the royal family. Upon my word, I think the Prince of Wales was kind not to throw you in the Tower. He will certainly win his lawsuit. All you have accomplished by this ill-bred piece of impertinence is to bankrupt yourself. Don't look to me to pay the cost. I am ashamed to claim any kinship with you."

"We are not actually kin, but only connections. Kith, perhaps," was Otto's reply to her tirade.

"Eh?" Horatio said. "Ah, kith and kin. Just so."

"Would you like me to leave, Auntie dearest?" Otto asked blandly. He had not taken a seat. He lounged by the fireplace in an attitude of casual ease.

"I cannot turn my late husband's nephew from the door. That is all that restrains me. I should not be at all surprised if this prevents Felix from winning his knighthood."

Otto turned to Felix, his eyebrows lifted in surprise. "A knighthood! Well done, Felix. I have bought your book—as you failed to send a copy to the *Clarion*—and begun to look into it. From what I have read, it lives up to its reviews. That, in itself, is amazing. That is not a denigration of your work, by the by, but of critics' taste—or veracity. As to my squib at Prinney lessening your chance of a knighthood, that is sheer nonsense. I doubt Prinney realizes we are connected. I shall see that he is informed."

"Otto!" Hettie exclaimed.

He raised a finger and shook it at her. *"Honi soit qui mal y pense, ma chère tante.* What could be a finer gesture of Prinney's fair-mindedness than to bequeath honours on the kin—or even kith—of the man he is prosecuting? It would shout from the pinnacle of Carlton House that he is above petty considerations. I consider that knighthood as good as yours, Sir Felix."

I noticed Aunt Hettie was glancing at a journal she held in her lap. She began reading aloud from it. "This is monstrous, Otto. 'It surprises no one that the Prince has traded in his Whig jacket for Tory blue; he is well known for his facility at turning his coat. What does cause surprise is that he is now sporting a petticoat in lieu of trousers. The donor, of course, is Lady H***, informally known to her host of detractors as The Old Lady of

Manchester Square. Her opposition to Catholic emancipation is well known. We smell something fishy here." She looked up, frowning.

"Lady Hertford's son, Lord Yarmouth," Otto said, "is active on his mama's behalf. It is not really the article that insensed Prinney so much as the cartoon. Cruikshank outdid himself. An amazing talent for caricature in one so young. Have you seen it, ladies?"

He took the journal from Hettie and passed it along to Mrs. Manner and myself. The cartoon was a ridiculous drawing of the Prince of Wales wearing a voluminous petticoat and a baby's bonnet. Lady Hertford wore the trousers. While she dandled the Prince on her knee like a baby, she was snatching from him a rattle bearing the words "Catholic Emancipation."

"It is very humorous to be sure, Otto, but is a laugh worth five thousand pounds?" Mrs. Manner asked.

Otto considered it a moment, then said, "No joke is worth more than one thousand, but Catholic emancipation is worth any sum. What price can be put on freedom? Only see where the lack of it leads. I am referring, of course, to the revolution in France."

"This is the most arrant nonsense. We are not Frenchies," Hettie said angrily. "Really, Otto, your actions defeat comment."

"That is not the impression your tirade gives, Auntie. If it takes such crude reminders as this to shame the Prince into keeping his promises, then so be it."

"But will it mean you lose the *Clarion?*" I asked.

He seemed pleased at the question, or at my concern at least. His voice, when he answered, was almost tender. "I shan't be left to bear the full brunt of the fine. I have colleagues—or do I mean cohorts?" he added, with an impish grin.

Felix cleared his throat and said, "You might have made

your point in a manner less degrading to the Prince, Otto. You should have some respect for the position, if not the man."

"I consider this very much an attack on the man, not the monarchy," Otto said. "We have never done anything against mad old King George the Third. As he cannot help his condition, it would be mean-spirited to make fun of him. Prinney, on the other hand, has thus far escaped being declared *non compos mentis*. Until such time, he must be judged as a sane man."

Gregory stirred to life. "They say he spends every afternoon at Manchester Square, with his head on her breast."

"And his ear at her mouth, hearing things he shouldn't," Otto added.

Auntie called them to order. "You will please remember there are ladies present."

Juteclaw appeared at the doorway and hollered that dinner was ready. Gregory and Felix darted to assist Auntie from her chair and escort her to the dining-room, one propping her up on either side. Horatio offered me his arm.

Otto strode forward and said, "You have had your turn, Horatio. Now it is mine." So saying, he placed my fingers on his arm and patted them.

Horatio latched on to Mrs. Manner, and I finally had a moment's private conversation with Otto.

"Would it help if you apologized—publicly I mean, in the *Clarion?*" I asked him.

"I have no idea, nor am I interested. It would be hypocrisy to apologize for the truth."

"But what will you do if you lose the *Clarion?*"

"Then I shall open a new journal, and call it something else. The *Phoenix,* perhaps, as it will rise from the ashes of its former self. My list of subscribers would swell as a result of the scandal. You never want to underestimate the drawing power of scandal, Jess." He inclined his head close to mine and added, "Now if you would just smarten up and make a scandal of yourself, you would have the gents bursting down your door."

"It is not easy to institute a scandal in this house."

"I beg to differ! I accomplish it every time I come, and you know what an unexceptionable fellow I am."

"No, you accomplish it in London, and flaunt it here. What do you suggest I do?"

"You could take off your clothes and take a stroll into the village. Let me know when you want to do it, and I shall see that Cruikshank is here to sketch you *au naturel*. We'll give you space on the front page. Let us say, about May. December is not the weather for it."

Auntie would have swooned if she had overheard that conversation. I daresay it was a trifle broad, but that, too, was a part of Otto's charm. He never went over the edge into licentiousness, however.

At dinner, Auntie had Gregory at her right hand, although that honour should have gone to Otto as the only one with any claim to a title. Otto sat on her left, and I sat across from him. We had a lovely dinner with two courses and two removes. The turbot did not taste too fishy, as it sometimes does. The roast beef was pink and succulent. For that interval, all troublesome conversation was set aside and we simply gossiped about family matters. Auntie liked to keep abreast of all that was happening. Our wineglasses were kept full. When dessert was served, I felt quite giddy and refused the rum-cake.

This white sponge cake with raisins, served with a jug of hot sugared rum, was Hettie's favourite. She poured the syrup over hers until the cake was soaked. Horatio and Felix had fruit and cheese instead. After dinner, the gentlemen cracked walnuts for us with their bare hands, except for Felix, whose fingers were not strong enough. Mrs. Manner complimented them on the strength of their sinewy fingers, and Horatio said it was riding and driving that developed the muscles. When Aunt Hettie rose to lead the ladies to the saloon, the gentlemen all stood up and bowed.

"Don't dally over your port. I am fagged, but I would like to see you all for a moment before I retire," Auntie said.

Within thirty minutes they rejoined us, and we had some pleasant conversation over the teacups. This was the crucial hour. Tomorrow Auntie would call her solicitor to discuss her will, so any good impressions to be made must be made before she retired. Felix spoke of his new book; Otto unwisely spoke of his journal; Horatio yawned, and Gregory just looked smug. The name "Mrs. Rampling" did not arise. At nine o'clock Aunt Hettie yawned and said she was for the feather tick.

"You will not want to stay up late, Addie," she informed her companion. "Ten o'clock is plenty late enough. Naturally you will bring Jessica upstairs with you. You might bring me up a bottle of my cough syrup when you come."

"Juteclaw has already taken it up."

"A piece of the rum-cake then. I read for an hour to encourage sleep. I shall see you all tomorrow morning. Breakfast is at eight."

The atmosphere changed the minute she left. All the play-acting could be dropped, and the gentlemen were at their ease. Juteclaw brought a bottle of sherry to replace the tea.

"You are looking mighty smug, Greg," Horatio said. "She gave you the five hundred?"

"She is going to, tomorrow. I want to thank you for not telling her those oaks are already cut. I realized, when you were squinting at me, that you would have seen it on your way from Cleremont."

"You cut that stand of oaks!" Felix exclaimed.

"Not to worry, young brother. Hanshurst *does* belong to me now, you know."

"Was wondering," Horatio said, "think there's any chance she might dip into her purse for me? Five hundred . . ."

Gregory just shrugged. Otto asked Horatio what he needed the money for.

"If she doesn't come across, I'll see what I can do," Otto said, when Horatio told him about the wedding gift, and the roof.

"Can't ask you at this time," Horatio objected.

"I haven't lost the case yet," Otto said airily. "Libel involves not only attacking a man's reputation, but making unjust, i.e., untrue, statements. I printed no more than the truth. If he goes after me for treason, he'll be laughed out of London. This suit is no more than an attempt at intimidation, to make us all tuck in our tails and be good boys."

"But if worst comes to worst, the Whigs would kick in and help defray the cost?" Horatio asked.

"That is our understanding. They would also raise the mother of ruckuses in the House. *Entre nous,* we are hoping the case does go to court."

"Then it won't," Gregory said, and laughed.

Otto shrugged. "It might. Bread and circuses—that is what the public want, eh, Felix? And it will be a fine circus, I promise you."

"This is *amabilis insania,*" Felix said tolerantly, then went on to hint for a review of his book in the *Clarion.*

"I have every intention of reviewing it myself, as soon as I have finished reading it," Otto assured him. "Unlike some journals, we make it a habit to read books before reviewing them. From what I have read thus far, I can tell you the review will be favourable. Are you not ashamed to write so well?"

Felix blushed. "Oh, I would not say that! Really, you are too kind."

Otto, for some reason, looked first surprised, then embarrassed. "You have made great strides since that translation of Cicero you did—when was it—five years ago?"

"I cringe to think of that! I rushed into print to try to make a name for myself, and only did myself discredit. I have slaved for five years over Plutarch."

"It must have been pleasant slaving, though, for a scholar," Otto said. "There is such a wealth of anecdotage in Plutarch. I had forgotten all those jokes about the size and shape of Pericles's head. I wonder Teleclides was not threatened with a libel suit for that poem about 'Fainting underneath the load of his own head.' Obviously Pericles had a better sense of humour than certain rulers who shall be nameless."

"Oh yes, a long-headed fellow," Felix said. "That is why he is usually depicted wearing a helmet, to conceal his disfigurement. He was a marvel—a supreme tactician at war, a wise and able ruler, a patron of the arts."

"Not to forget a famous lover," Otto smiled. "I am referring, of course, to Aspasia."

Felix nodded. "And a tolerable musician as well, a pupil of Damon."

Otto looked at him in that same surprised way he had looked earlier, when he asked if Felix was not ashamed to write so well. "It is spelled 'Damon,' but pronounced 'Dammon,' is it not? I seem to remember reading it in your own book, Felix. I chuckled to myself, thinking they were as bad as we English in that respect. What poor student of English would ever suspect 'Saint John' was pronounced 'Sinjun,' or 'Leveson' as 'Loosen'?"

"You are quite right. I had forgotten that detail," Felix smiled.

"Ah, well," Otto said, "we cannot expect an eagle to bother himself with flies. I am enjoying your translation immensely."

"Perhaps Otto would like to meet John Weldon," Mrs. Manner mentioned.

I thought Felix would enjoy to have his audience widened, but he frowned. "The fellow is a bit of a bore, to tell the truth.

A quibbler. But I must be polite to my readers. I have told him I'll see him again tomorrow, but I shan't subject you to his ravings, Otto."

"I have other plans for tomorrow," Otto said, and turned a questioning look on me. "I am hoping to beguile Jessica away from Downsview for a drive into the village. She has to select a route for a certain pilgrimage she is to make in May."

I ignored the curious stares of the others, and said I would be happy to go with him. Otto usually managed one private outing each year—the best part of the visit to me. He moved from his chair and sat beside me for ten minutes before we ladies retired. He spoke of the new London fashions and the plays and parties he had attended.

"It sounds lovely," I sighed. "Coming to Downsview must be a dead bore for you."

He flicked a curl over my shoulder and said, "Downsview has its own rewards. It is the only time I get to see *you*."

"It is the only time I get to see anyone," I complained.

"Ah, and here I thought you were going to say it was the only time *you* got to see *me*. That will teach me to take you for granted. Who is my competition? Gregory?"

Otto was an outrageous flirt. Of course he was smiling, but I soon imagined there was something more than mere flirtation in his dark eyes. "Oh no, he is Auntie's flirt."

"Is she hatching a match between the pair of you?"

"She would like it, I think. She puffs him off a good deal, but she has not actually suggested I marry him. I doubt he would agree to it."

"There is no accounting for taste," he said, with a shake of his head. "That is a compliment to you, my pet. You are worlds too good for him. Of course Hettie is too clever to actually say what she means. I wonder, though. Greg is looking mighty smug."

"He got the promise of five hundred pounds."

"It's no secret she favours Greg. She also likes you, and must feel some responsibility to see you provided for. Perhaps she has some fond and foolish notion that you could settle him down. I should dislike to see you in his hands. He'll run through the fortune in jig time. Then what becomes of you?"

"If she mentions such a scheme to me, I shall scotch it."

"Good girl," he said, and gave my hand a little squeeze. "And now it is ten o'clock. Even Cinderella was allowed to stay up until midnight. Auntie is very clutch-fisted with your time— but then our moments together seem more dear for being limited." He rose and assisted me from the chair. "*A demain*. We shall have more privacy for a good cose tomorrow during our drive. There is something—"

Mrs. Manner rose and came towards us. Otto wore an air of frustration at the interruption.

"Ten o'clock," she announced. "I'll remind Juteclaw about the rum-cake. Good night all."

Otto waited at the foot of the stairs until Juteclaw brought the cake and a posset, but with Mrs. Manner present, Otto could not give me any idea what the "something" was that he had mentioned. I was thus allowed to take my imagination to bed with me, and imagine all sorts of impossible things.

It was the last happy evening I was to enjoy for a long time. In the morning, Aunt Hettie was dead.

FOUR

Duke took to fussing during the night. He sleeps in Aunt Hettie's room on an old patchwork quilt in a basket beside her bed. I could hear movements from the room; something was knocked from a table, by either the dog or my aunt while trying to quieten him. The guests sleeping in the west wing would not have heard him but we permanent occupants sleep in the east wing. The dog was old and not well. He was jealous of Hettie, and resented being separated from her for most of the day, or perhaps his arthritis was acting up on him. He continued whining occasionally through the night, but neither Mrs. Manner nor I thought anything of it.

I rose at my usual seven-thirty, full of excitement because of our guests, and especially my drive with Otto. A glance out the window showed the first rays of a golden dawn lighting the darkness of the winter's sky. The jagged tops of fir trees bucketed in the wind, promising a chilly drive. I dressed with care in the same green gown I had worn the day before, but with my woollen shawl to ward off the cold. I was just putting the finishing touches on my hair when Mrs. Manner came pelting in. She usually knocks, but she just flung open the door and stood, silent as a flower, but looking as if she'd seen a ghost.

"What is it, Mrs. Manner?" I demanded, with an awful premonition that something was going to rob me of my drive with Otto, and already resenting whatever it was. Her reply knocked all such selfish thoughts from my mind.

"She's dead!" she exclaimed, clutching her heart. "She must have died in the night. I heard Duke making a racket but I never dreamed—"

"Dead? Aunt Hettie?" a strained voice exclaimed. I hardly recognized it for my own. "No, you must be mistaken." My head felt as hollow as a drum. This could not be happening. Oh, but it was. It *was*.

"Come, Jessica."

She latched on to my arm for support as we ran down the hallway and into Hettie's room. It was dark as pitch, with only a triangle of illumination from the doorway pointing to the canopied bed. I flung open the draperies, and the morning flooded in to light her chamber, all baroque grandeur, with scarlet window hangings and a matching canopy on the ornate bedstead. Heavy old furnishings from the last century were all carved and inlaid with rare woods and mother-of-pearl. An ormolu mirror cast an image of the room back at me.

Duke was there, forlorn in his basket. He rose and looked up at the bed, then turned an accusing eye on us, whined deep in his throat, and trotted out of the room. Juteclaw would let him outdoors. I went to the bedside, but I knew at a glance that she was dead, because her eyes were open and staring at the ceiling. In death, the pupils had become enlarged. She had a pained expression on her poor withered face, and her hands clutched at the bedclothes, which she had been trying to rip off.

The carafe of water she kept by her bed had tipped over on the floor, wetting the pillow and my aunt's flannelette night-gown, but they were nearly dry now. The red patterned carpet was darker where the water had spilt from the mouth of the crystal carafe. That was what I had heard fall in the night. If only I had come to help her!

"She died in her sleep. That is a blessing at least," Mrs. Manner said. But that agonized expression and the spilt water did not suggest a calm passing. Mrs. Manner murmured on in a soft voice, "I see she ate her rum-cake. See, the empty plate is on the table." I glanced at the plate and fork. The cold medicine was there too, as was the book my aunt had been reading.

A huge lump grew in my throat. It was like the end of the world for me. For ten years Aunt Hettie had been my nominal mother. She had a sharp tongue, but she had been kind to me. And now it was all over; she was dead. I did not think, yet, what would become of me. That would come later.

"We had best call the doctor and Vicar Jennings," I said. I stood a moment, just gazing at Hettie's pain-clenched face, while a thousand pointless memories drifted through my mind. What had all her pride and peevishness amounted to in the end? She was gone. She had had so much in the way of worldly goods, but for as long as I had known her, I don't think she had much enjoyed life.

"I'll stay with her," Mrs. Manner said. "A dead body shouldn't be left alone. Could we cover her face?"

I drew the sheet up to hide the awful sight. It didn't seem real. This was not really happening. In a daze I went downstairs and spoke to Juteclaw.

He stared as if he did not believe me. "She's never dead!" he exclaimed. "The old malkin? I made sure she'd bury me. You leave me without a word in my cheek, miss."

"It was very sudden. You'll send for the doctor and Vicar Jennings."

"That I will, and get out the hatchment for the knocker. Lord A'mighty, I couldn't be more shocked if it was yourself, missie. Her never sick a day. Have you told the lads? It'll pound the sugar out of them."

"I'll tell them when they come down to breakfast."

I went into the cold purple saloon and sank onto a sofa to think. That tenebrous chamber seemed a suitable spot for reflecting on the awful mystery of death. I was glad her nephews were there to help arrange the funeral. They would all have come anyway, but I was glad they were here now, to help us. There would be no drive with Otto that afternoon after all, and no visit from the solicitor to discuss the will. It would remain as it had been last year. Aunt Hettie would not see Felix become a knight, and Gregory would not get his five hundred pounds.

When I got around to thinking of Mrs. Manner and myself, I rather thought we would remain at Downsview. It was unlikely that whichever of her nephews inherited the estate would actually live here. He would visit, of course, and oversee the running of the farm, but I felt Auntie would have stipulated that we could stay here as long as necessary.

Gregory was the first one to come down. He found me in the purple saloon, sitting alone in the cold dark chamber.

"Mrs. Manner told me," he said in a suitably subdued voice, but it was a stage voice. Young nephew grieving death of beloved aunt. He sat down beside me. "This comes as a bit of a shock, I must say."

"She was old, but in good health. I am simply astonished."

"No idea what caused it?"

"At her age, I suppose it was the heart."

"She didn't change her will?"

I did not try very hard to conceal my dislike of that question so soon after her death. "No, she didn't get to speak to the solicitor this year."

"I fancy she never changed it much from year to year. Just a little tinkering with small bequests. It was a sham to keep us in line. The fortune is to be split evenly five ways, amongst you and us nephews. I, as the elder, am to get a few extra trinkets—the jewelry and so on."

"How do you know that? She always made a secret of her will."

"I weaseled it out of her two years ago," he replied.

"How can five people inherit a house?" I asked in confusion.

"We'll have to sell."

"Sell Downsview? Surely that is not what she wanted! She was fooling you, Gregory."

He frowned, but soon decided my opinion was worthless. "That is what she said. We'll sell; what else can we do with it? If anyone wants to buy me out, I am more than agreeable. There are her investments besides. That will amount to something in the neighbourhood of ten thousand each."

I was shocked out of my disgust with Gregory at this news. "Ten thousand pounds!"

"Plus your share of Downsview. You'll be rich, Jessie."

"Good gracious!" I felt quite giddy at his news. "What of Mrs. Manner?"

"She was in for five thousand, last I heard. I fancy she'll still get it. What will you do?"

"I have not even begun to think of the future yet. Perhaps I shall share a place with Mrs. Manner."

"You ought to run up to London and make your bows. You'd nab a fellow quick as winking."

It seemed disrespectful to be speaking of such things. "Let us have a cup of coffee," I said. "I feel so cold."

"Of course," he said, resuming his doleful face. He offered his arm to escort me to the breakfast parlor.

Otto was just passing through the hall. He levelled a peculiar look on us. I dashed up to him. "You've heard?"

"I have. I fancy the whole house knows by now. This is a great shock for you, Jess. I am so very sorry."

His kind words brought a tear to my eyes. He handed me

his handkerchief and I dabbed at my tears while the gentlemen discussed it between them.

"A shocking business," Gregory said in his stage manner.

Otto said, "What happened to her? Was it her heart?"

"Juteclaw told me she died in her sleep," Gregory replied. "The doctor will tell us what caused it. Good timing for you, Otto. She hadn't time to cut you out of her will. She would have done, you know. She wasn't a bit pleased about those slurs on Prinney."

"A good thing she wasn't murdered, or I would be the prime suspect," Otto replied, and we continued along to the breakfast parlor.

I had the feeling Gregory could scarcely contain his glee. He didn't care a groat for Hettie. He just wanted to get his hands on his share of her fortune. He helped himself to gammon and eggs from the sideboard and ate a good breakfast. Horatio and Felix joined us a few moments later, both suitably sober in the face of death.

There was talk of the funeral arrangements. The gentlemen would stay on until it was over. Otto was going to write to inform his parents, but he did not expect them to come. His father, Lord Kidd, had been feeling poorly at Christmas. Someone would have to remain with the body until the doctor came. Mrs. Manner would probably want to do that. I would write notes to relatives and a few neighbours, and arrange for Mrs. Wiggans to attend to the laying out. Felix offered to notify the local journal, and assist with her obituary.

"Don't forget to inform the solicitor," Greg reminded him.

Felix gave him a rebukeful look. "Our aunt has just been taken *ad patres,* Gregory. A little respect, if you please."

Gregory set down his cup and smiled. "You no longer have to impress her, brother. She's dead. You can speak English. Your fine book and your knighthood come too late. You'll not cut the rest of us out, so you can quit shamming it. None of us liked her. She was a sour, manipulative old bint, so let us not mince words. The sooner we get her buried and get the solicitor here, the sooner we can take our money and go back to London."

Every face in the room looked at him with disgust.

"And call on Mrs. Rampling," Felix sneered.

"I shan't have to go to London to do that. She is visiting relatives nearby. I dropped her at her aunt's house on my way down. A pity you hadn't known, and you could have told Hettie *that*." Then he rose and swaggered out of the room, revealing the tawdriness of his mind to all.

"Allow me to apologize for my brother," Felix said. He was pale and looked strained. "I shall take my coffee to the library and work on the obituary. If Mr. Weldon comes—never mind. I'll speak to Juteclaw."

"You could drop a note and tell him you cannot see him today," I suggested.

"That might be best," he said, as he rose and left.

"I'll see if Juteclaw has some mourning bands," Horatio said, and followed Felix out.

I was alone with Otto. "What will you do now, Jessie?" he asked. "Or has Gregory already been offering you his help?"

"He told me Auntie's fortune is to be split evenly amongst us all. If we have to sell Downsview, then—"

"Sell Downsview? She would never set her will in such a way that Downsview left the family."

"But that is what Gregory said. She told him two years ago. If it is true, then you won't lose the *Clarion* if you lose your lawsuit."

He looked doubtful. "I would not place too much reliance on what Auntie told Gregory. She is—*was* full of mischief."

Juteclaw appeared at the doorway and ushered in Doctor Culpepper. He was our family doctor at Downsview, an elderly, kindly man with no airs or graces about him, but a good doctor.

"I am sorry to hear about your aunt, Miss Greenwood."

I thanked him and introduced Otto, who went off to attend to his business while I accompanied the doctor abovestairs. Doctor Culpepper went immediately to the bed, where he drew back the sheet and began examining Hettie. Mrs. Manner and I shrank against the farthest wall, as though death were contagious. Culpepper asked a few questions about what time Hettie had retired, and what she had eaten. He picked up the plate that had held the rum-cake and smelt it, then put his finger in the remains and tasted it. Next, he espied the bottle of cold remedy and uncorked it to have a taste.

"Was Mrs. Farr suffering from a cold?" he asked, frowning at the bottle.

"No, but I had a sore throat yesterday, and she asked for a bottle of the syrup," I replied. I noticed she had taken about a quarter of the bottle already.

"Have you taken any yourself, Miss Greenwood?" he asked.

"No, I washed my throat with a brine solution, and it seemed better."

"Don't take any of it," he said.

"Is there something wrong with it?" I asked at once.

"There is something very much amiss somewhere. That spilt water, the dilated pupils, and the bedclothes all yanked off—it looks very much like an overdose of belladonna. She used it in her cold medicine. I told her repeatedly it was only to be used as a cough suppressant."

"Are you saying Cook's medicine killed her?" Mrs. Manner asked. Her eyes were like saucers, and her chin trembled in dismay.

"I wish I had seen her before she died. We medical men have a saying for an overdose of belladonna: Hot as a hare, blind as a bat, dry as a bone, red as a beet, mad as a hen. You see she was overheated, for she has pulled her coverlet off. She was reaching for water, which suggests she was dry, and as she spilt it, it seems her eyesight was fading. Her flush has faded, but when you throw in the dilated pupils, it is hard to come up with anything but poisoning by an overdose of belladonna."

"But Hettie took the medicine every year. It never hurt her before," Mrs. Manner said.

"There must have been a massive overdose in the bottle, obviously."

"I helped Cook brew it myself," Mrs. Manner said. "There was no overdose, I assure you."

"Then it was added later. We'll compare her bottle with the rest of the batch. And you'd best send off for the constable."

Mrs. Manner went white as snow. "Are you saying it was—murder?" She looked puzzled, as if she could not quite grasp such an idea.

"Accident, very likely, but accidents have to be looked into as well. Now don't get yourself all het up, ladies. I am not suggesting you killed her." He essayed a nervous little laugh.

I was aware of a dead weight dragging at my side, and when I looked, I saw Mrs. Manner sliding to the floor in a swoon. It was only my body that held her up. I felt like swooning myself.

Doctor Culpepper flew into action. Between us, we got her along the hall and into her bedroom. He gave her a paregoric draught to calm her, and when she was resting he drew me into the hallway for a private word.

"Poor Mrs. Manner is a nervous soul, Miss Greenwood. It will be for you to run the ship here during this difficult time. I am sorry to have to bring the constable down on your head in the midst of your grief, but it cannot be helped. I do not see how such a massive dose of belladonna could have been administered by accident. Was your aunt depressed recently?"

"On the contrary. She was happy, with all her nephews coming to visit."

"Not suicide then, I take it."

"She would never take her own life! She held very strong Christian beliefs in that respect."

"I never took her for a suicidal type. Well, it looks bad. Mind you don't take so much as a drop of that cold medicine until it has been examined. Get hold of the whole batch and lock it up tight. Where would such chemicals as your belladonna and laudanum and so on be stored?"

"My aunt kept them in the cheese-room upstairs, to be out of the way of servants."

"Is it kept locked?"

"No. They are on the top shelf of a cupboard. You have to use a stool to reach them."

"Lock the door until the constable gets here."

"My aunt keeps the keys to the house. They would be in her room."

"Best get them."

How I dreaded to go back into that room. It was like a cave at the best of times, with the heavy furnishings and blood-red hangings. I snatched the key-ring up from the bedside table and went to the door of the cheese-room. I had to try a dozen keys before I found the right one. My hand was trembling so that I could scarcely turn it in the lock. The dreadful word kept whirling in my brain—murder, murder, murder—as I darted to the kitchen to secure the bottles of cough medicine.

Cook locked them in her cupboard for safekeeping. She was subdued in the face of death. "The old malkin, killed to the bone," she kept muttering, as if she could not believe it.

I thought, too, of Gregory's ill-concealed glee at the prospect of inheriting. But, he could not be that bad. It must surely have been an accident.

FIVE

It was Doctor Culpepper who gave the local constable an outline of Hettie's death when Hodgkins arrived an hour later to begin his investigation. We all gathered in the saloon.

Hodgkins was a simple, ill-educated man of middle years with curly brown hair just silvering around the ears, and wearing a mildewed blue jacket. In an effort to intimidate the local youngsters, he kept his lips pulled so tightly together you had to look twice to find them. His usual duties were to lock drunkards in the round-house until they sobered up, chastise the youngsters who filched sugarplums from the sweet-shop, and intervene on those occasions when domestic violence rose to such a pitch that it bothered the neighbours. He was also responsible for keeping an eye on gypsies and other "foreigners" who visited the village with the apparent intention of leaving it poorer than they found it.

This amiable soul was completely intimidated to find himself in a house of the gentry, and was so frightened of giving offence that he might as well have stayed in the village. Really it was left almost entirely to Doctor Culpepper to manage things. He suspected that Auntie's cold medicine did contain a lethal dose of belladonna and that the rest of the batch, including my bottle, was not similarly adulterated. Cook assured us the bottle of belladonna was still half-full when she used it for the cold medicine the day before. It was empty when Hodgkins examined the cheese-room.

It was unlikely that Aunt Hettie personally had climbed to the cheese-room, tottered up on the stool and emptied the bottle into her own medicine. The conclusion was inevitable: some person or persons unknown had added the poison to Aunt Hettie's cough medicine.

"In other words, you are saying one of us murdered her!" Gregory exclaimed, full of dudgeon. "This is outrageous!"

Constable Hodgkins blushed and said, "Nothing of the sort, I do assure you, sir."

Felix said quietly, "As Cicero so wisely asked, *'Cui bono?'* Whose purpose does it serve?"

"Yours as well as mine, and Otto's and Horatio's too," Gregory retorted. "And let us not forget the ladies. It is Jessica and Mrs. Manner who had to live with her."

Culpepper whispered something in the constable's ear. Hodgkins cleared his throat and asked timorously, "Would it be possible to hear which of you knew where the medicines were kept?"

"We all knew," Otto said, looking around with a challenging light in his eyes. "We have been coming here for years, often to spend a month in the summer when we were younger. We all had equal access to the poison—and if Gregory is to be believed, equal reason, insofar as financial gain is concerned."

Felix looked dissatisfied. "If it is an argument *ad crumenam* we are talking about—"

"Speak English, for God's sake!" Gregory snapped. "We are not all scholars, Felix."

"If we are talking about money, you said yourself I would have done better after the will was changed," Felix pointed out.

"Aunt Hettie might have looked more leniently on me as a result of my book's success. The knighthood is what I mean."

"And less favourably on you, Otto," Horatio mentioned. "Not that I mean to say you had anything to do with it, of course," he added hastily, when Culpepper's head slewed in Otto's direction.

Otto just rolled his eyes to the ceiling and said, "Thank you, Horatio, for that vote of confidence."

Hodgkins cleared his throat again and said to Otto, "I am sorry to interrupt your conversation, gentlemen, but perhaps if you would explain that statement, Mr. Farr."

Otto explained brusquely that he had offended Mrs. Farr by writing against the Prince of Wales. Mr. Hodgkins took this sorely amiss. His ire lent a touch of authority to his humble manner. "It ill becomes a man to bite the hand that feeds him," he said stiffly.

"I am not accustomed to receiving any crumbs in the way of perquisites from the Prince, if *that* is your meaning," Otto said, high on his dignity.

I doubt Hodgkins was even aware of such things as royal perquisites. I don't know what he meant, except that he admired the royal family, and took any word against them for high treason. His anger fired him up to demand Otto's whereabouts last evening. With Culpepper's help, this eventually led to the revelation that none of us could prove that we could not have found ten minutes to dart up to the cheese-room, down to Aunt Hettie's room to doctor the medicine, and back up to return the empty bottle to its shelf. Cook, when questioned, said she had sent the bottle of cold medicine up to Juteclaw before dinner, and he had taken it to Auntie's room at once. So it had been sitting on the bedside table for several hours, where anyone might have seen it and tampered with it.

After another whispered colloquy with Doctor Culpepper, Hodgkins asserted that as we all had the time and the means and the reason, what he must do was "look into it." This he did by descending to the kitchen for a cup of tea with the servants.

Culpepper shook his head in dismay and said, "Hodgkins will be making his report to Croton, our local Justice of the Peace, as soon as he returns to the village. I will be giving evidence at the coroner's inquest, of course. There is little doubt as to the outcome. Croton will have to appoint someone to investigate all this, as it is a case of some importance. Perhaps he will send to London and ask Townshend for assistance. A Bow Street officer might be sent down."

There was a general sound of protest from all the gentlemen. Culpepper was not cowed. He said severely, "If you do not all want a cloud hanging over yours heads for the rest of your lives, you ought to welcome it, gentlemen."

"We do not want that kind of fuss," Gregory said angrily.

"Is there some special reason you do not wish to discover who murdered your aunt?" Culpepper asked curtly.

"She is dead. A scandal is not going to bring her back."

"You understand, of course, that her fortune will not be disbursed until this matter is settled," Culpepper told him. "The law prohibits a criminal from gaining by his crime. Until we know who is the criminal, I doubt anyone will be given his blunt. It is up to you. I am only a doctor, but if she were my aunt, I would not leave it like this, with a cloud hanging over you all. Good day, gentlemen, Miss Greenwood. I shall see you all at the inquest."

He strode from the room. After the front door slammed, we all looked at each other in a frightened way. For a moment, there was not a sound in the purple saloon but the snapping of the logs. The unspoken idea had taken wing—one of us had killed her. Which one? The question hovered in the very air we breathed.

Then Gregory said, "For God's sake, let us have something to drink," and went to the wine table to pour himself a full glass of claret. "Otto, does that demmed fool doctor know what he is talking about? Can they keep our money from us until this thing is solved?"

"I rather think they can," Otto answered.

I decided we all needed bracing, and served wine to the rest of us. Everyone, including myself, took a long deep draught and sighed in dismay.

"Thing to do," Horatio said, "send off for Bow Street. Look odd if we don't. Don't want a dashed cloud over our heads."

"That will be for Croton to decide," Otto said. "I doubt he will do it against our wishes. Let us put our minds to the problem. I cannot believe any of us poisoned Hettie. It must have been an accident. Or had she any enemies in the neighbourhood, Jessie?"

"She hardly even had friends. No one called yesterday."

"Mr. Weldon called," Horatio said, and received bewildered looks from all of us.

"Weldon did not leave the study. He was with me all the time," Felix said. "Besides, what reason could he possibly have for harming Auntie?"

"He was a caller is all I'm saying," Horatio pointed out. "Jessie said there were none. Any others, Jessie?"

"Perhaps Cook received someone in the kitchen. Hettie had ordered in special supplies from the village for this visit, but I cannot think a merchant murdered Aunt Hettie."

"Let us get back to the idea of an accident," Otto said.

"Cook did not send any servants up to the cheese-room," I reminded them. "She got the belladonna herself, and left the half-full bottle on the shelf. She brought down the Stilton for dinner while she was there, so there was no reason for anyone else to go up. Cook certainly has no reason to kill Auntie. She will be out of employment if we sell Downsview."

"Mrs. Manner might know something," Otto said.

"When she awakens, we shall ask her if she sent anyone to the cheese-room. She might have sent off for headache powders, or some such thing."

I shook my head. "The headache powders were not kept there. Just the dangerous drugs—laudanum and so on."

"Who took laudanum?" Otto asked with quickening interest.

"It was only used for emergencies—a toothache or some such thing. No one has a toothache at the moment."

"Still, we should speak to Mrs. Manner before letting Croton send for Bow Street," Greg said. "No point making a mountain of a molehill. They would have to give us our money if we could make them believe it was an accident."

"Are we not trying to discover the truth?" I asked him. "You sound as though you want to fool the authorities."

He looked around the room slowly. "It's pretty clear one of us did the old girl in. What's done is done, and I for one do not wish to look a gift horse in the mouth. She cannot be brought back to life, but we can all be dragged through the mire if we don't get our heads together and come up with a good story. Now, say Aunt Hettie had a ripping headache, and went up to get the laudanum. By candle-light, she might have mistaken the dose."

"Really, Gregory. I am ashamed of you," Felix scoffed.

"It could have happened that way for all we know," Gregory said.

"She died of belladonna poisoning, not laudanum," I said.

Gregory dismissed it with a wave of his hand. "Culpepper is a simple country sawbones. What does he know?"

"Gregory's suggestion would certainly simplify things," Otto said pensively. I was disappointed in him. When he saw my frown, he did not push this notion any further. "We shall speak to Mrs. Manner before proceeding. Are we all agreed on that?"

Everyone agreed, but I think in our hearts we knew Mrs. Manner did not hold the answer to this problem.

I went upstairs to see whether she was awake yet. She heard me enter her room, but she was still drowsy from her draught. "I had such a horrid dream, Jessie," she mumbled, trying to sit up. Then she noticed she was fully dressed. I watched as her vague blue eyes darkened with memory. Then her eyes closed and she lay down again, moaning in her grief. "Poor Hettie." It was a soft croon, as if she were already wafting off to sleep.

"Do you know if anyone went to the cheese-room yesterday afternoon or evening, Mrs. Manner?" I asked.

"Cheese-room," she said, in a muffled, sleepy voice. Her eyelids fluttered. "Oh yes—I remember." Her voice was fading away as sleep overtook her once more.

"Who? Who went to the cheese-room? Was it you?"

"I saw . . . him."

"*Who?* Who did you see?"

She stirred restively, but did not reply. I nudged her shoulder. "Who, Mrs. Manner? Was it Gregory?"

"He—murdered— "

I shook her shoulder, trying to rouse her from sleep. But it was too late. She was past hearing. I knew she had not even heard me say the name Gregory. But she had seen someone at the cheese-room, a man. One of the four nephews. Gregory, Felix, Horatio, or Otto. One of them had murdered Hettie, and I had to go below and face them. I did not have to tell them what Mrs. Manner had said, however. She had been drowsy. She had probably not heard me, or understood my question. I would say nothing until she was fully awakened, and had given an account of what she had seen.

For one weakening moment, I almost thought Gregory was right. The thing was done. Why stir up a hornet's nest by insisting it was murder? Then I remembered Otto's unexpected words, "It would certainly simplify things," if we all got together and pretended it was an accident. Surely it was not Otto? That was when I knew the investigation must proceed. We could not all go through life with people saying, "Surely not Otto; surely not Horatio; surely not Jessica Greenwood." We who were innocent deserved the truth, and so did Hettie.

SIX

I returned below and told the gentlemen only that Mrs. Manner was still sleeping. They seemed almost relieved.

"Let her rest," Otto said. "It is the last peace she'll have for some time, poor girl."

Felix said he would return to writing the obituary, and went to the library. Gregory said, "I need a breath of fresh air," and also left the saloon.

Horatio waited until Gregory had got beyond sight, then said, "He'll be jogging into the village to see Rampling, I daresay. There'll be no mourning in that quarter." He refilled his glass and settled in at the grate with a recent journal.

Otto gave me a commiserating smile. "Our drive must be postponed until another time, Jessie."

I no longer saw any charm in him. His dark eyes were not glamorous, but dangerous. Like everyone else, he was tainted with suspicion. "Why did you not want a Bow Street officer sent down, Otto?" I asked.

"For purely selfish reasons. A suspected murderer will not receive a fair hearing at my upcoming trial."

"All the more reason to clear your name, then."

"The *Clarion* trial begins next week. From the shambles we are faced with here, I doubt any conclusion will be reached in that time. But you are right; we must find out what happened to Aunt Hettie."

I did not think Horatio was even listening, but he said over his shoulder, "Gregory did it. Stands to reason."

"He is the obvious choice," Otto agreed. "Do you have anything concrete to go on, Horatio?"

"Mrs. Rampling. 'Twas Gregory instigated that duel, though he did not fire the killing shot. Stands to reason he ain't above murder."

As this sounded like an interesting tale, Otto and I joined Horatio by the fireside, and he continued. "I heard the story at my club half a year ago. She had been seeing another chap, young Henredon, a month before. Then she met Gregory and dumped Henredon. She stayed out all night, or until five o'clock in the morning, with Gregory. Her husband was waiting up for her. Went storming over to Henredon's place and challenged him. The duel wasn't fought for another twenty-four hours, but neither Mrs. Rampling nor Gregory said a word to save Henredon. They just let the duel go forth. Henredon shot Rampling, and Gregory waltzed off with the widow. Henredon ran to ground at a friend's place in the Cotswolds until things cooled down."

"What an awful thing to do!" I exclaimed.

After a frowning pause, Otto said, "That speaks to Gregory's character, or lack thereof, but does it have any immediate bearing on Hettie's death?"

"He needs the blunt, doesn't he?" Horatio asked in a rhetorical spirit. "He won't hold on to Anita Rampling long if his pockets are to let."

"Hettie had promised him five hundred," I pointed out.

Horatio gave a mirthless snort at my naïveté. "Five hundred ain't ten thousand. Anita bankrupted her husband. She would go through five hundred in a week—or a morning, if she was let loose on Bond Street. She'll beggar Gregory, then toss him aside like an old shoe."

"Someone should warn him!" I said.

"I expect he is acquainted with the lady's ways," Otto said with a shrug. "They are no secret."

Auntie's murder was sitting like a thunder-cloud over our heads. "I shall go and speak to Cook about lunch," I said. "I suppose we must eat, even if—" A sob caught me unawares.

Otto placed a comforting arm around my shoulder. "Why don't you go upstairs and have a good cry?" he said gently. "You'll feel better for it."

I dabbed at my moist eyes. He took out his handkerchief and blotted away the incipient tears. When I rose, he accompanied me to the hallway. "I must notify my lawyer of this turn of events," he said. "Hansard won't like it. He most particularly warned me to stay out of trouble, and thought Downsview the best place for me. Of course that is not the only reason I came." His look was not exactly quizzical, but it seemed to imply some special reason.

"You always come for the New Year."

"True, but on this occasion I had an excellent excuse to beg off, had I been looking for one. I most particularly wanted to come."

"I cannot imagine why."

"Can you not, Jess?" he asked softly.

His dark eyes lingered on my face in a peculiarly tender way. It was the sort of look that had often caused my heart to flutter in the past, but after ten years I had learned it meant nothing except that Otto was a flirt. This did not seem a proper time for flirtation.

"Downsview is coming to seem a horrid place," I said, and went upstairs—not to cry, but to see how Mrs. Manner was. I was surprised to see Gregory in the east wing.

"What are you doing here, Gregory?" I asked.

"I was looking in on Mrs. Manner. She is sleeping soundly."

"We thought you had gone to see Mrs.—that is, to the village."

"Is that what the delightful Farr brothers have been telling you?" he asked. There was an angry glint at the back of his pale eyes, though he was smiling. "As I told Auntie, Mrs. Rampling is a friend, nothing more. I had no intention of calling on her. Let me take you out for a spin, Jess. You need to get away from this wretched atmosphere for an hour."

"I could not possibly leave. With Mrs. Manner unwell, I must look after her, and the house."

"Let me help you. What can I do?"

"There is nothing you can do, Gregory. You might as well have your spin."

He reached out and touched my cheek. "I would rather be here, with you," he said, in lover-like accents. This was such a startling change from his usual manner that I could only stare in wonder. "Poor Jessie," he said. "I wish I could take you away from all this unpleasantness."

"I am fine," I said stiffly, and hurried away from him.

I watched from Mrs. Manner's door as he turned the corner to the stairway. I wanted to see for myself that she was sleeping. It occurred to me that Gregory might be eager to hear what she had to say, if he was the one she had seen at the cheese-room. A terrible alarm seized me. He might want to do more than hear her story. He might want to prevent her from telling it! I flung open the door and went inside. Mrs. Manner was sleeping peacefully.

My imagination had momentarily convinced me I would find another corpse, but if Gregory meant her any harm, he had had a chance to silence her, and had not taken it. The possibility was still there, however, that someone might silence Mrs. Manner before she could speak, and I rang for a servant to sit with her. It was Mary, the upstairs maid, who was free at that hour. I found her just finishing her work on the guests' rooms. I remained with Mrs. Manner myself until Mary could speak to Cook, who was more or less in charge of the girls' time. Mary was a good, sensible girl who knew how to look after herself. She was pink-cheeked and bright-eyed, and as strong as most men. I suggested that she keep the door locked, and pull the bell-cord to summon help if anyone but myself tried to get in.

"Lordie, you don't think someone will try to kill her too?" she asked, eyes goggling.

"I shouldn't think so, but it is best to take no chances at this time."

"He'll have to kill me first!" she said, and picked up the poker from the grate to defend herself and her charge. Mrs. Manner was a great favourite belowstairs.

When I went to speak to Cook, I found Hodgkins tucking into a piece of apple tart and a wedge of Cheddar, discussing not the case, but Henry Milliner, who had beaten his wife the night before and was sobering up in the round-house. Doctor Cull-pepper was right. We required a proper investigator.

We settled on a cold nuncheon and a bowl of Cook's beef-and-barley ragout "to warm our vittles," as she put it. I kept thinking of Gregory's sudden change in attitude towards me. Was it possible he wanted two shares of Auntie's fortune? Was he making up to me? I did not know whether to laugh or be angry. I was curious to test my theory, and went back to the saloon to see if he had gone off to visit Mrs. Rampling.

He had not. He sat in the saloon with Horatio. They were not talking, but sat apart, Horatio still reading, Gregory doing some ciphering on a piece of note-paper at the secretary desk in the corner. He immediately put away the paper and turned a smile on me.

"Have you changed your mind, my dear? Shall we have our spin after all?"

Horatio looked up from his reading and cast a surprised glance at me.

"No, I have not changed my mind," I said curtly.

I was about to turn and leave the room when Otto came back. "I mean to run this letter to Hansard into town at once. Is there anything else that needs posting, Jessie?"

"No, thank you. We have not gotten around to writing the notices for the relatives yet."

"Would you like to come with me, to get a breath of air? There is time before lunch."

I wanted to go, but as I had twice refused an outing with Gregory, civility prevented my accepting. I did accompany him to the door, however, using the excuse of asking him to pick up some black-edged cards at the stationer's shop.

Weldon and Felix came down the hall from the library as I spoke to Otto. Their smiles indicated they had reached agreement on whatever point of Felix's translation they had been quibbling over. I was surprised Felix had kept the appointment at this time, but perhaps Weldon had arrived before he could be put off.

"I take it you scholars have settled your differences?" Otto said. "Tell me, what was the subject of dispute? I always like to stick my oar into an argument."

"We were just discussing a passage in my translation of the life of Caesar," Felix said.

"What passage was that?" Otto persisted, turning to include Weldon, but it was Felix again who replied.

"Mr. Weldon questioned my interpretation of certain words—I used the phrase 'broke out in tears,' in the passage comparing the accomplishments of Caesar and Alexander. Mr. Weldon felt it too strong. He suggested something along the lines of 'drew a deep sigh' might be more realistic."

"One can hardly picture Alexander the Great breaking into tears," Mr. Weldon said with a laugh.

"Nor Caesar either," Otto replied with a bland smile. "Can I give you a lift, Mr. Weldon? I am going to the village."

"I rode, thank you all the same, Mr. Farr."

Otto said adieu to me and to Felix, and held the door for Weldon. As they went out, Duke came in. He usually used the kitchen door, but today was a day like no other. I felt sorry for him, and patted him a little.

I overheard Otto say, "Tell me, Weldon, what do you think of that story in the life of Pompey—"

Felix suddenly remembered something and called Weldon back. "I was going to loan you my translation of Cicero," he said. "Better not wait, Otto. The book is in the library."

Otto left, Weldon came back in, and Felix darted back to the library to get the book. Duke recognized his former master and demanded a little attention. Weldon had a way with dogs. Duke became quite frolicsome. When he began barking in pleasure, Juteclaw took the dog away. I invited Weldon to wait in the saloon, but he preferred to remain in the hall. He said a few words in commiseration of my aunt's death, then Felix returned and gave him the book.

"Thank you. I look forward to dipping into this, Mr. Chapman," Weldon said, and left.

Felix strolled into the saloon to chat to his brother. I was surprised that Weldon had an interest in scholastic matters, although his papa had been quite an expert, so I ought not to have been.

I went to the dining-room to see that the table was properly set up, as an excuse to keep away from Gregory. I did not want him making advances to me. The table was fine, and I went to the library to think and grieve in solitude until it was time for luncheon. The reek of cigar smoke lingered on the air. Weldon smoked cigars. Some ashes were in a dish on the table.

The library was a sober and fit place for entertaining my grief. The dark leather bindings of a thousand books stood sentinel down the length of the long chamber. Stately busts of old Romans and Greeks looked down from the top of the bookshelves. The only illumination came from the French doors at the end of the room. Yews beyond the door dripped with moisture onto the sodden grass. It had rained in the night. The sky was a cold, silvery white. It occurred to me that I ought to be wearing a black gown. As I did not possess one, however, my dark-green and dark-blue must do until I could get one made up. That meant a note to the modiste, Mrs. Maherne.

I went to the writing-table and wrote a brief note requesting her to make me up a plain black bombazine as quickly as possible, using the pattern of my navy sarsenet. With half an hour until lunch, I picked up a book that lay on the table. It was Felix's youthful translation of Cicero, the book he said he was going to fetch for Mr. Weldon. Perhaps this was the copy Felix had given to Aunt Hettie five years before. Very likely he had taken it down to show Weldon. I opened it and looked at the flyleaf. It bore Felix's own name, nothing more.

Curious, I went to the bookshelves. Auntie had a special row for books given to the family over the years and signed by the author. Her copy of Felix's translation of Cicero was there. What book had Felix given to Mr. Weldon then? Surely Felix did not travel with several copies of his own translations? That whole business of Felix's detaining Mr. Weldon began to seem suspicious. Almost as if he did not want Otto to be alone with him . . .

I shook away the wisp of thought. I was becoming overly suspicious. Felix had been in a hurry; he had obviously picked up the wrong book to give to Weldon. I had thought Gregory might have murdered Mrs. Manner too, but she had been sleeping peacefully. There was no liquid by her side that he could have tampered with. I must not let these suspicions turn me into a frightened spinster, looking under her bed before retiring.

I took the letter to leave on the silver mail salver in the front hall. Juteclaw was just putting up the mourning hatchment, and wrapping the door-knocker in crape.

"These are sorry times, missie," he said, shaking his head. "Like a birthing, they'll get worse before they get better."

I hadn't the heart to chide him for calling me missie. "We must be brave, Juteclaw. How are the servants taking it?"

"Nervous as hens at setting time, with the poor mistress killed to the bone. Sally says the girls will all sleep on the floor in Cook's room till the villain is caught."

I thought it an excellent idea, and wished I could do the same. But I was mistress now; it was for me to show fortitude and set a good example. I decided I would share Mrs. Manner's room until the gentlemen left, as a precaution for her safety as well as my own. At least no one was trying to kill me.

I would soon be disabused of that heartening notion, but at that time I had no fear for my own safety.

SEVEN

Murder, especially by poison, has a strange effect on a household. Over lunch, I found myself wondering at every bite if I was ingesting poison. To judge by the wary faces at the table around me, the others felt the same way. We would each take a bite of ragout, testing it for a foreign flavor, peering at the barley to be sure it was barley, and glancing at our companions, wondering if they noticed anything amiss, or if they were abstaining from eating altogether, which would suggest a knowledge of poisoned food.

At length Horatio said, "Dash it, this food came straight from the kitchen. We are all partaking of it, including whoever slipped the belladonna into Auntie's bottle, so it must be safe."

His blurting out what was on all our minds had the effect of loosening our tongues. Nervous tension dispelled itself in an untimely but brief eruption of merriment.

"Eat, drink, and be merry, for tomorrow we die," Gregory said, lifting his glass. "Who said that, Felix? One of your Roman friends, no doubt."

"Perhaps you are thinking of Horace: *Carpe diem*. Seize the day," Felix replied.

"You may be sure I am not thinking of Horace," Gregory said with a grimace. "It is probably Shakespeare."

"I believe your quote comes from the Bible, Gregory," I mentioned.

He smiled at me as if I were a wizard. "I might have known *you* could tell me, Jess. It is amazing how well-informed you keep yourself."

I blinked at this ill-advised compliment. I had never laid claim to any intellectual endeavours. Novels, poetry, the journals and ladies' magazines had been my sole vehicles of learning once I left the schoolroom.

"Have you switched to blue stockings, Jess?" Otto asked with a satirical smile.

A moment later Horatio said, "Actually I told a lie, about all of us being here. Mrs. Manner is not with us. You don't suppose she—"

Our forks returned quietly to their plates. Gregory paused a moment, then said, "Mrs. Manner has the least of any of us to gain. Only five thousand."

"How do you know that?" Felix demanded at once.

"I was closer to Auntie than the rest of you. She mentioned it once, some time ago."

"But she changes the will every year," Felix said.

I lifted a forkful of ragout to my mouth, to show my confidence in Mrs. Manner. Such nonsense! She hadn't a sly bone in her body.

Our wary lunch was soon over. The afternoon was busy with calls from the near neighbours offering help. Word had spread, perhaps through Vicar Jennings, to whom we had written a note. Culpepper and Weldon also knew. My aunt's death would be a matter of interest in the neighbourhood, as it meant a new owner of Downsview. None of us were prisoners yet, and we had the freedom of the house. We did not all remain in the purple saloon all the time by any means. Juteclaw brought the black armbands and hatbands down from the attic, and the gentlemen went off to arrange their mourning tokens. Felix spent some time in the library, and Otto went to his room to do work on a column for the *Clarion*. Horatio, who is interested in antique weapons, spent an hour in the armaments-room.

We had a call from Vicar Jennings to express his condolences and inquire about funeral arrangements. Gregory offered to drive into the village to order a headstone. Downsview did not have a mausoleum, or even its own graveyard. Hettie's coffin would be placed in the mausoleum of St. Alban's Church until spring, at which time her mortal remains would be placed beside those of her husband in the graveyard.

Gregory did not invite me to go with him, for which I was happy. I wondered if he meant to call on Mrs. Rampling while he was at Littlehorn.

Before Gregory left, Doctor Culpepper returned to confirm that the chemical analysis of the cold medicine in Auntie's bottle showed a lethal dose of belladonna. The larger batch was not overdosed, nor was my bottle. Her death was now officially not a death from natural causes.

"An inquest will be held to determine whether the belladonna was administered by accident, or by design," Culpepper informed us.

He had brought a note from Sir Aubrey Croton, the Justice of the Peace, informing us that Doctor Culpepper would be representing the law on an *ad hoc* basis in this matter for the time being, and we should give him every assistance in his investigation. Croton obviously knew the job to be beyond Hodgkins's capabilities.

"You may proceed with your funeral arrangements and the reading of the will," Culpepper said. "As I mentioned, the disbursement of the monies must await the outcome of the inquest at least. Your solicitor can arrange for the forwarding of whatever small sum is necessary to see to the running of Downsview—servants' salaries, and so on."

I was surprised that Gregory did not offer to call on

Auntie's solicitor while he was in town. It was Felix who suggested it, and Gregory was not slow to take him up on it. In fact he left at that time.

I ordered tea and Culpepper put forth once more the idea of calling in Bow Street.

"We agreed, *entre nous,* to wait until we heard what Mrs. Manner might have to say," Otto told him.

"About Mrs. Manner," Culpepper said, "I should like to have a word with her myself."

I told him she was still sleeping the last time I looked.

"It is four o'clock. She ought to be awake by now," Culpepper said.

I was surprised it was so late. The day had seemed endless, yet with the many interruptions I had not found time to look in on her again.

"I hope you have not left her alone," Culpepper said with a minatory look. I knew at that moment that he also feared for her safety.

"A servant is with her," I replied. I was suddenly overcome with anxiety, and ran straight upstairs to see how she was.

From two rooms away, I saw that her door was open. I ran as fast as my legs could carry me the last few yards. My heart was pumping wildly, and my head was full of horrible visions. Her bed was empty, and carefully made up. Of Mary and Mrs. Manner there was no sign, but neither was there any indication of a struggle. I ran down to the kitchen by the shortest route, the servants' stairs, and flung open the door. There at the table sat Mary, enjoying a cup of tea and a plate of toast.

"Where is Mrs. Manner?" I demanded in a tense voice.

"She is fine, Miss Greenwood," Mary assured me. "She was feeling peckish when she woke up, and had a snack in her room. That put her back on her pegs. She wanted a breath of air, and went out for a walk—oh, just around the park."

"Alone?" I asked. "Why did you not tell me?"

My sharp voice brought a guilty flush to Mary's cheeks. "You had company in the saloon, miss. I didn't like to disturb you. I offered to go with her. She said she wanted to be alone to think. She took Duke with her, so no one . . . he's a good guard dog."

Duke was better than nothing. He is old, but his hackles can rise menacingly when he senses danger to his household. "Did she say where she was going?"

"She didn't say, but she always goes to the belvedere, doesn't she, to look down the road to Littlehorn?"

"How long ago did she leave?"

"I couldn't say for sure. About half an hour, wouldn't you say, Cook?" Cook agreed.

"Even half an hour is too long to suit me."

The belvedere was Mrs. Manner's favourite walk. Having lived a long time at Bath, she disliked the isolation of Downsview. She liked to see the carriages even if she could not speak to the occupants. If she had reached the belvedere, she should be safe. It sits at the top of a rise, looking down to the road below. The belvedere is visible for some distance, and thus an unlikely location for murder. My greatest concern was that, to reach it, she would have to pass through an isolated and less easily seen valley.

"I must go to her." I did not stop to get my own pelisse, but threw on Cook's rough woollen shawl. "If I am not back in ten minutes, Cook, tell Doctor Culpepper where I have gone."

Perhaps my fear for my friend's safety showed on my face. I looked an invitation to Mary.

"I'll go with you, miss." She jumped up, leaving her tea and toast on the table, and snatched up her shawl.

I was thankful for her presence as we left the security of Downsview and entered the park. In the short days of late December, twilight had already fallen. Complete darkness was not far off. It was a cold, blustery day. The white sky had not lightened to blue, but turned a dull silvery grey. Long, boat-shaped clouds of a darker grey were gathering in the west. The tall pines moaned, and the stark branches of leafless trees whipped in the wind. Mrs. Manner disliked such blustery days as this. She usually only walked in milder weather. It almost seemed as if she had wanted to escape the house. Well, that was understandable. She had a secret, and she would want peace and privacy to weigh whether she should reveal it, and to whom.

She had a scrupulous conscience. She would want to do what was right nearly as much as she would dislike to make trouble for any of the young gentlemen. And she must know that if she had seen one of them loitering about the cheese-room door, they had been up to no good. I wished she had confided in me.

The grass had grown long. It wrapped itself around our ankles and wet our slippers and skirt hems as we hastened to-wards the belvedere. From the park, only its roof was visible. From the higher level of the family quarters within the house, the upper half could be seen.

"I should of gone with her," Mary lamented.

"She said she wanted to be alone," I reminded her.

"She did. Mind you, I sensed she was frightened."

"How? Did she say anything?"

"Just asked where all the gentlemen were, and I told her they were all inside the house. I wondered at her going out the back door, for she usually uses the front. I had the notion she didn't want to be seen."

"Did she mention seeing any of the gentlemen around the cheese-room door yesterday, Mary?"

"No, miss."

I did not wish to frighten Mary, and decided to wait until I caught up with Mrs. Manner to satisfy my curiosity on that crucial point.

But when we found her it was too late. We would never learn her secret. She was dead.

EIGHT

We nearly missed seeing her. We were hastening past a clump of holly bushes that grow in a low-lying valley where, two weeks before, Mary and I had come with one of the footmen to cull greens to decorate the saloon for the Christmas season. It had been a happy day, Mary flirting with Crump, and myself anticipating the annual visit. Today, the mood was quite otherwise. It was in the path skirting the hollies that Mary spotted one of Mrs. Manner's stout laced walking shoes. It looked such a pathetic sight, that little black shoe, tipped over on its side. I think I realized at that moment that we were not going to find its owner alive.

Fear blocked the air in my lungs and quickened my heart-beat until it pounded in my ears. I looked at the shoe, then I looked at Mary. Her large eyes stared back at me in mute fear. The sudden silence was shattered by the chirp of a bird in the bushes, displeased at our presence.

"We had best go back to the house and ask for help," I said in a hollow voice. I was mortally afraid to go one more step forward. Yet darkness was falling; if we did not find her now, we might not do it until morning.

I felt a tugging at my sleeve. Mary pointed to the base of

a holly bush, where the heel and sole of the other shoe were visible. An empty shoe would not sit perfectly upright on its heel. It would fall over. Mrs. Manner's foot was still in the shoe, then. Her other leg was flung out to the side, shoeless. Cold terror gripped me. Was it possible she was still alive? If so, she must be unconscious, for she would not remain pushed into a prickly holly bush if she were able to move. The lower branches grew very close to the ground.

"We must pull her out, Mary," I said.

Mary whimpered. Tears were flowing down her cheeks, but she nodded her agreement. It seemed a horrible way to treat a body, to take hold of the ankles and drag it along the ground, but to crawl on my belly under the sharp branches was the only alternative. Even then, I doubt if I could have done it. It had taken considerable force to ram Mrs. Manner under those low-growing branches. Her face must be horribly scratched. We drew her forth slowly, with as much care as possible, already knowing in our bones it was a dead weight we were dragging.

Her pelisse and the skirt of her dress caught on the holly leaves and stayed behind while her body came forward. I pulled them free and settled them decently around her legs. There was no sign of ripping or blood on the clothes, but some mud from the wet ground stained them. She still wore her tan leather gloves. We pulled a little more, and her shoulders came into view. I dreaded to see her face. We pulled again, gently, and slowly her bonnet appeared. She was lying on her back, but her face was completely covered by her plain black round bonnet. It had got pulled over her face and caught on her chin. I gently eased it back and gazed at her.

Her face was not disfigured, but the horrified expression frozen on it was disfigurement enough. I knew it would haunt my memory for many a long day. The bonnet had protected her face from scratches, but a trickle of blood oozed from her left temple, matting her hair and collecting in the pocket of her ear.

I leaned forward and saw a deep, straight gash, with something whitish-blue that might be skull-bone protruding through the skin and blood. I took several deep swallows of air to keep down the wave of nausea that rose up in me. She had been struck forcibly by a hard, straight-edged object, a brick perhaps. Sweet little Mrs. Manner, who had never hurt a fly in her whole life.

Mary was kneeling, swaying back and forth, with her two hands rammed against her lips, while a keening sound came from her throat. I knew exactly how she felt. I could not ask her to remain with the body while I went for help, and I was also afraid to stay alone myself.

"Come," I said, and drew her up. "We'll go home, Mary."

I put my arm around the poor trembling girl's shoulder and we hastened back through the gathering dusk, huddled together for comfort. The massive hulk of Downsview loomed before us. Where the rooms were lit, the pointed windows formed an abstract pattern against the stone wall. Juteclaw had lit the lamps in the saloon, of course. The armaments-room was shrouded in darkness, as it usually was. Above, in Aunt Hettie's room, a single light moved surreptitiously. Culpepper, at the scene of the first crime? He had wanted to speak to Mrs. Manner, and must have gone abovestairs to find her. He would be wondering what had happened to her, and to me. I had not given him another thought since I had seen Mrs. Manner's door ajar. It seemed a lifetime ago.

When we reached the kitchen, Cook took one look at us and reached for her cooking sherry before saying a word. She pointed us to a couple of chairs and we sank gratefully onto them. Before I caught my breath, Mary said, "Mrs. Manner's murdered! He stuffed the poor soul under a holly bush." Then she burst into racking sobs.

Cook's face was as pale and flaccid as the unbaked bread that sat on the table before her. "Is it true?" she asked me.

I took a gulp of sherry and said, "Yes, I'm afraid it is."

"Under a holly bush!"

"Yes."

"There's bad luck in hollies, always has been."

"With one shoe off," Mary said through her tears. "I'm leaving, Cook. If you're wise, you'll do the same. This place isn't safe."

Cook gave her a chiding look. "Hush up, you foolish girl. Who'd be bothered to kill the likes of us?" she asked rhetorically. "It's the money that's at the bottom of this blood-letting, mark my words. Who ought to get away till it's cleared up is yourself, Miss Greenwood. Is there any place at all you could go for a bit?"

How I wished there were! Yet as I sipped the sherry, I tried to console myself that I was safe. Aunt Hettie had been killed for the money, and Mrs. Manner because she knew who had done it. But until the will was read, it was unsure that I had any money, and I did not know who had killed Hettie.

"I'll be all right, Cook," I said wanly. I finished the sherry and rose. "I must tell Doctor Culpepper what has happened."

"Why they set a doctor to catch a murderer is above and beyond me," she scolded, "though Hodgkins is about as much use as a cold in the head."

"I fancy Sir Aubrey will send off for a Bow Street runner now."

Before I left, Cook reached out and removed her shawl, which still hugged my shoulders. "I just sent up tea. Mind you have a cup, Miss Greenwood. You look next door to a corpse yourself."

Culpepper was on his way down the kitchen stairs as I went up. "Where is Mrs. Manner?" he demanded. "I waited an age for you to come back, Miss Greenwood, and finally sent a servant after her. She is not in her room."

He stopped and stared at me, realizing from my looks that

something was very much wrong. "What is it? She's not . . ."

"She is dead, Doctor Culpepper," I said.

"Good God! Not another."

"Let us go someplace private to talk."

I took him to the morning-parlour and we sat at the small table while I opened my budget. I told him everything: that I thought Mrs. Manner had seen one of the nephews around the cheese-room, what precaution I had taken for her safety, and so on. "We must bring Mrs. Manner home at once. We cannot leave her lying in the park," I said when I had finished.

"Whatever possessed her to go out alone in the park in the dark?"

I looked at the window, and saw darkness had fallen. "It wasn't dark when she left. It wasn't even dark yet when I went after her. And she wasn't alone. That is, she took Duke with her."

"Where was he, then? How did he come to let anyone at her?"

My mind gave a lurch. Until then, I had forgotten all about Duke. "I don't know. There was no sign of him. Perhaps he is dead too."

"The first item is to get the body indoors before the ferrets discover it," he said.

The very thought made me feel extremely ill. "Do it, at once. She is lying by the stand of hollies in the park. I expect you'll want to take the gig, and a blanket. I'll ask Juteclaw for a blanket."

"And a brace of stout footmen. I am too old to be hauling bodies about."

"Very well."

I was glad to have something to do to dispel, temporarily, the awful image of Mrs. Manner's face, frozen in its mask of horror, and of that one small shoe, sitting forlornly in the path.

I told Juteclaw briefly what had happened. His eyes stared

in disbelief, and his lower lip trembled. He bit it to steady it, but I could see his teeth chattering still. "There's a devil let loose in this house," he said, and crossed himself to ward off further evil. Then he quelled down his feelings and said in a quavering voice that he would call for the gig and footmen, and get the blanket.

I was curious to know what Culpepper had been doing in Aunt Hettie's room, and asked Juteclaw if he had said anything. "Doctor Culpepper did not go upstairs at all, miss," he said. "In fact he asked me to lock the mistress's door to keep everyone out, which I did."

"When was that, Juteclaw? Just a moment ago?"

"No, miss. He told me when he first came in, over an hour ago. He showed me the letter from Sir Aubrey making him in charge of us all, so I had no excuse to refuse."

"You didn't happen to leave a lamp on in her room by accident?"

"Oh no, miss. I didn't go in the room at all, and besides it wasn't dark yet. I had set young Jenkins to guard madam's body for a corpse should never be left alone, and in all the commotion you forgot to do it. I sent Jenkins off and locked the door."

"I see. Thank you for your help, Juteclaw. I should have seen that my aunt was not left alone."

"You're only human, after all, missie, and not used to such weights bearing on your young shoulders."

I was grateful for his pardon, though I could not quite pardon myself. It seemed a locked door did not mean much in this house. Someone had entered Hettie's room after Juteclaw locked it. He was obviously looking for something. The first one who popped into my mind was Gregory, having a snoop about for money. He would have found nothing there but the few pounds and pence she kept in her reticule. Her cash-box was kept locked in the safe in her late husband's study. But in any event, Gregory was in the village.

While Culpepper was awaiting the gig, I drew him into a corner of the hallway for a private, whispered conversation. I told him of the light in Auntie's room. "Were the gentlemen in the saloon with you at that time?" I asked.

"Only Horatio Farr was there. Did Mrs. Farr keep her valuables there, her jewelry and so on?"

"No, they would be in the safe in the study, along with any significant quantity of cash she kept in the house. Her nephews would be aware of that."

"And the safe was locked up tight. Whoever it was could not have got much then. Perhaps he was after a look at her will."

"That could be it. She took it to her room earlier this week for its annual review."

"No real harm done, it seems. What is in the will won't be a secret for long."

Juteclaw came with the blanket, and told Culpepper the gig was ready. My heart sank to my boots as I watched the doctor hasten down to the kitchen. The gig would be at the back door, for easier access to that area of the park where the hollies, those ancient harbingers of ill luck, grew.

I was now faced with the unpleasant task of informing the household of Mrs. Manner's death, and sending off once more for Mrs. Wiggans, to come and perform another laying out. I would tell Horatio, and let him inform the others. It would be for Juteclaw and Cook to tell the servants. My fortitude was at an end. I wanted to go to my room, lock the door and roll up in a ball beneath the counterpane. I wished I could set the clock back to before murder struck. My easy assurance to Cook that I was in no danger had deserted me.

It was well to be alert, because if Aunt Hettie had included me in her will as Gregory said, then I did now possess money. I had not made a will of my own. Very likely my money would be disbursed amongst the others. Or perhaps only to the Chapman brothers, as my kin. I was not a blood relation of the Farrs.

I decided that if Hettie had not entailed my share of her fortune back to her family, I would ask the lawyer to make me a will when he came tomorrow. Whom would I leave my share to? I had no one really close to me now, with Hettie and Mrs. Manner gone. It made me aware of how alone I was. I would will the money to the church.

This decided, I turned to the saloon to tell Horatio the sad news. At least Horatio was safe. I would not be afraid with him. He had not killed Mrs. Manner. Though she had actually been gone from the house for well over an hour now. Horatio had not been in the saloon all that time. None of us had. It would not take long for a grown man to cut through the park, armed with a brick or a sharp rock, and beat the life out of Mrs. Manner. And there was Duke, who had disappeared. I hadn't a doubt in the world that he was dead as well. Duke was familiar with all the nephews. He would not attack any of them. Not at first, in any case. In his innocence, he would let them get close enough to pat him—with a brick!

I shook away the dreadful image and went to the saloon.

NINE

Horatio sat alone by the fire enjoying a cup of tea and the journal. He looked up with a smile.

"Ah, there you are, Jess. I was wondering where everyone's got to. You look like death, old girl. Come and have a cup of tea."

He looked so safe and normal, and it was such a relief to be back to normal, that I suddenly burst into tears. Horatio leaped up and put his arms around me awkwardly, drawing my head to his chest. "Now, now, what is all this?" he demanded in a hearty voice that did not conceal his lack of ease. "It is nerves. I am as nervous as a tick myself. I shall pour you a nice glass of sherry."

I lifted my head and tried to speak, but could not get a word out for the racking of my body. I wished that I had gone to my room to suffer this breakdown in private. It was embarrassing. Aunt Hettie had always told me ladies did not make a display of their emotions in public. It was vulgar.

Horatio stroked my head, much as one would stroke a well-loved dog. "Have a good cry then," he said, resigning himself to my fit of hysterics.

I looked up with a watery smile of gratitude and saw, over

his shoulder, Otto. He was standing silently in the doorway, watching us. A cynical smile decorated his handsome face. "Am I interrupting something?" he said, stepping in. "How extremely tedious of me. You will both be wishing me at Jericho. But lovers, you know, ought not to indulge themselves in public rooms. That is what the bedchamber was created for."

Horatio released me at once. "Mind your manners, Otto," he said gruffly. "Can't you see the poor girl is done in?"

I began wiping at my tears. Horatio handed me his handkerchief, then turned to his brother. "Jessie has cracked under the strain of all this business," he explained.

"And who shall blame her?" Otto replied in a voice noticeably void of pity.

I glared at him and said, "Mrs. Manner has been murdered. I found her body in the park."

His body gave a convulsive jerk. "What!"

Horatio's eyes bulged in astonishment. "Egad! We're none of us safe. The sherry, Otto. Get the poor girl a toothful of wine."

I received all the sympathy and attention I could want then. Between them I was assisted to the sofa, handed a glass of sherry, and when I could not hold it for trembling, Otto held it to my lips.

"Drink it up," Horatio ordered. I gulped it down and felt somewhat better, but whether it was the wine or the solicitude that did it, I could not say.

When I could speak coherently, I outlined what had happened.

"You should not have gone to the park alone," Otto said angrily. "Are you trying to get yourself killed? Why did you not call me?"

"Or me," Horatio added.

"I took Mary. It is Mrs. Manner who should not have gone with only Duke for protection."

"Is Duke all right?" Horatio asked. He was inordinately fond of dogs.

"He's missing. Perhaps Culpepper will find him."

Otto refilled my glass. As I sat in front of the warm grate being pampered by two handsome gentlemen, my tensions eased away, to be replaced by a languorous glow, no doubt increased by the unusual quantity of wine taken within a short space of time. I felt this was how the annual visit should have been. The feeling of well-being played havoc with my discretion, and before long I found myself telling the Farrs things I had meant to keep to myself, or share only with Doctor Culpepper.

"But why would anyone kill Mrs. Manner?" Horatio asked.

"Because of what she must have seen," Otto said. "That is why we were waiting for her story, before calling in Bow Street."

"She did see something," I told them. Both heads turned eagerly to me. "She saw someone outside the cheese-room, where the belladonna was kept. She was half-asleep when I spoke to her, but—"

"Who was it?" Horatio asked.

"I don't know, she didn't tell me, but whoever she saw was afraid she would tell, and that is why she was murdered."

After a frowning pause Otto said, "Make sure you announce loud and clear you don't know whom she saw, or our murderer might have you next on his list. And be sure you lock your door at night."

"I don't know anything. And what good does locking a door do? He can walk right in—as he did at Aunt Hettie's room this afternoon."

"You mean last night," Horatio said.

"No, this afternoon. There was a light in her room as I came home from the park. Culpepper had had the room locked, but someone was in it. Was it you?" I asked Otto, as Horatio had been downstairs with Culpepper.

"What the devil would I want in her room?" Otto said.

"Maybe to get a peek at her will," I suggested.

"I can wait until morning."

Horatio said, "Who is itching to get a glimpse of it is Gregory."

"Don't be too quick to accuse Gregory," I said, thinking of his visit to Mrs. Manner's room, when I had suspected him of harming her.

Horatio, never one to bother with subtlety, asked, "Is he making up to you? Mean to say, called you 'my dear' this afternoon. Invited you for a drive. Never did that before."

"Yes, I believe he is," I said, and laughed. "Perhaps he wants my share of the money, and is even willing to marry me to get it."

"You have a low opinion of yourself," Otto said, examining me closely. "Though perhaps in Gregory's case, the money would be the main attraction. He is not known for his refined taste in ladies."

Horatio began fidgeting. "I wonder if Duke got away safe," he said. "Believe I'll go out and give a whistle. He might have managed to crawl home. A shame to let him die like a dog on the doorstep."

"Go ahead. I shall look after Jessie," Otto said.

"See that you do," Horatio said with a commanding look, then he hastened from the room. A moment later, the front door slammed.

"Horatio is very nice," I said, smiling fondly at the memory of his kindness.

"Even if he were not my brother, I would have to agree with you. He is almost too nice. Beggaring himself to keep his friends supplied with blunt verges on the foolhardy."

"It is hard to find fault with an excess of generosity. Of all the nephews, he is the one I cannot find in my heart to suspect of these murders."

"Indeed!" Otto exclaimed. "Then I am left with the conclusion that you *do* suspect *me*."

"I did not mean that!" I said at once, though I daresay that was exactly what I did mean. Otto lacked his brother's generosity. Like most wealthy bachelors, I think he was more interested in himself than the world at large. "I do not say you would murder anyone, but you have not Horatio's generosity."

"Well, upon my word, you are hard on me. Have I not put my newspaper—you might as well say my life—on the line for my beliefs? The whole reason I created the *Clarion* is to fight for justice for the common man. At the moment, I am fighting for the religious rights of Ireland. Otto only lent Ralph five hundred pounds to buy a cottage."

"The *Clarion* is for you yourself, Otto. It is your toy; you enjoy it. I think you even enjoy all the commotion you are causing."

"I enjoy my work immensely," he conceded, "but I purposely chose a 'toy' that is useful as well as amusing."

"You need not have libeled the Prince of Wales—and risked five thousand pounds."

"If you are implying I need my share of the fortune, I admit it would come in handy, but I assure you I did not hasten either Hettie's or Mrs. Manner's demise to get it," he said stiffly.

It pleased me that I could rouse him to anger. "Who do you think did do it?" I asked.

"You know who."

"Gregory."

"I am already being sued for libel. I shan't add to it by spreading slander, but I believe we understand each other. Don't be taken in by him, Jess."

"I am not that easily gulled."

I noticed Otto looking towards the doorway. I turned to see what he was looking at just as Felix stepped in.

"Where is everyone?" he asked, glancing around.

"Why, I am here, Felix," Otto replied, in the satirical way he has. Felix saw no humour in this sally. "I suggest you arm yourself with a glass of wine and take a seat, Felix. We have more bad news."

Felix just stared, as if frozen. I think he had some intimation of what was to come. "Not—not another death," he said. His tongue flicked out and touched his lips.

"It is Mrs. Manner, Felix," I said. The mood of golden languor had dissipated. I don't know when it happened, for I was still sipping sherry. In fact, my head felt quite light.

"Oh my God! The poor woman." He sank onto a chair and covered his eyes with his hand. In a moment he looked up. "How did it happen? When?"

I told him. He listened intently, with a sad, dark look in his eyes. "It is hard to credit it," he said when I had finished. "While I was working in the library, that poor woman . . . Why would anyone do such a thing?"

Otto looked at me, then said vaguely, "Perhaps he was afraid she saw something, or knew something. If that is the case, we shall never know what it was she saw, or knew."

"Is something being done to bring her home?"

"Culpepper is taking care of it," I said. "He should be back any moment. I shall go downstairs and see if I can be any help when he comes in."

"Where are Gregory and Horatio? Do they know?"

I let Otto answer the question. I went downstairs and was just in time to see Mrs. Manner being brought in the kitchen door on a litter, with a blanket covering her. The servants stood in a flock, staring silently. The girls were holding on to each other, some of them weeping. The footmen tried to look brave, but they were saddened too, and afraid.

"Send for Mrs. Wiggans, Cook," I said. "We shall take Mrs. Manner to her room for the nonce. I shall remain with her until Mrs. Wiggans arrives."

"That you will not, Miss Greenwood," Cook said firmly. "You are worn to the socket. Tell her, Doctor. We don't want another corpse on our hands."

"You had best let someone else tend to it, Miss Greenwood," he agreed. "You have taken quite enough for one day. I shall leave you a sleeping draught for tonight. And I shall speak to Croton about getting Bow Street down here as well. This business has gone beyond my help. We need a professional to sort it out."

Culpepper accompanied the footmen up to Mrs. Manner's room. I remained below with Cook for a moment, to discuss dinner. No one would be able to eat much, but it seemed important to maintain some semblance of normal life. It would be good for the servants to have their regular chores to perform, to keep them from becoming obsessed by the murders. The pantry was loaded down with all the dainties prepared for the nephews' visit, so arranging the meal did not take long.

"Just something simple but hot," I said. "In such weather, cold mutton is unappetizing."

"I'll carve the roast then, but not bother with the turbot," Cook said. "A pity, for the fish looked especially fine. But there you are, this is no time to be setting a feast on the board."

I ran up the back stairs to see that Mrs. Manner was laid out on her bed with all due ceremony. Culpepper was alone with her, examining not her body, but her clothing. He was looking through her pockets.

"I hoped she might have a note on her. It is possible, you know, that someone asked her to meet him at the hollies. They provide excellent concealment from the road and the house. He had her to himself there, the villain."

"I doubt she would have kept any such appointment,

Doctor. She must have realized the danger of her position. You did not find a note?"

"No, and there was no point looking either. Whoever did this to her"—he gestured to her head—"would have looked to see his note was not left behind." He shook his head. "Such a gentle creature she was."

"She did not deserve this," I agreed. "You saw no sign of Duke?"

" 'Twas nearly dark by the time we got there. We could hardly find Mrs. Manner. I'll be back out in the morning. He'll turn up, but not alive."

"I shall be in my room for the next half-hour if you need me, Doctor. Will you stay to dinner?"

"I would rather not. No offence, Miss Greenwood, but I do not enjoy eating in a house of death. My good wife will have my mutton ready for me. You and I shall have a chat tomorrow. I'll leave your sleeping draught with Juteclaw."

"Thank you. I shall be thankful for any help you can give me. Sleep will not come easily tonight."

He patted my arm. "We'll get to the bottom of this, my dear."

I went to my room and lit one lamp. Then I just sat in the slipper chair by the window, looking out into the blackness beyond, thinking. I would not make an occasion of dinner this evening by dressing for it. There was no pleasure in knowing that I shared my mutton with a murderer.

TEN

When I went belowstairs for dinner, I stopped a moment at the top of the curving staircase, as I had done the night before. Only twenty-four hours ago Mrs. Manner and I had stood on this same spot full of delightful anticipation, while Aunt Hettie had sat below, enjoying her visitors. Now two of us three were gone, and I was faced with such profound changes as usually only occur over the space of a whole lifetime. I had lost my closest family, as well as my dearest friend—lost them in the cruellest, most brutal way imaginable. And I now had to confront the guests, wondering in my heart which of them had murdered two helpless old ladies.

How I longed to run back to my bedroom and hide under the covers. But I would not let myself give in to such paltry cravings. I would face the nephews, and keep my eyes and ears open for the false move that might reveal the culprit.

They were all four in the saloon, all of them changed into black evening suits. The mourning bands on their left arms, scarcely visible, seemed superfluous. I had received a note from Mrs. Maherne that my mourning gown would be finished by tomorrow. She was to give it precedence over all her other work, and had even hired an assistant to help speed the job. As

I entered the saloon, it struck me that the mood was more hostile than sad.

"Completely inappropriate!" Felix said to his brother.

"He's right," Horatio said. "Don't you agree, Otto?"

After a moment's consideration, Otto said, "Mrs. Rampling is hardly the optimum choice, yet some lady must be found, and in very short order. Preferably this evening, in fact."

"Here is Jessie. Let us ask her opinion," Gregory said, and came to meet me. "We have just been discussing your chaperone, my dear. We cannot leave you here unattended with a houseful of bachelors. Not that your virtue would be in danger, but for the sake of Mrs. Grundy, as you might say."

"Who?" Horatio asked. "What the deuce has a Mrs. Grundy to say about it I should like to know."

"For the looks of it, Horatio," Gregory explained.

"Are you suggesting bringing Mrs. Rampling here as chaperone?" I asked, incensed at the idea of being chaperoned by Gregory's mistress.

"Just for the nonce, until we can ship in an aunt or some such thing," he explained.

"Would a neighbour not be more appropriate? The vicar's wife, perhaps," Otto suggested.

"Jennings is a widower," I said. "But Mrs. Culpepper, or Mr. Weldon's mother might—oh dear. Mrs. Culpepper has her sick mother to look after."

"You would hardly want Mrs. Weldon," Felix said. "I mean to say . . . I met her when her husband was alive. She could curdle cream at sixty paces."

Mrs. Weldon was an austere old Methodist. I did not look forward to having her to deal with at this trying time. And besides, she was crippled with gout. I could not think of anyone else close by. We lived quite independent of society at Downsview.

"You will like Anita," Gregory said. "I shall dash her off

a note at once. She will be here within an hour. She is the most obliging creature in nature."

"So one hears," Otto murmured in his satirical vein.

Gregory coloured up angrily, but he did not make any retort. "Has anyone a better suggestion?"

"Might we not remove Jessica to a hotel in Littlehorn?" Otto said.

"Not alone, surely," Felix said uncertainly.

"I could not possibly leave at this time!" I pointed out. And Otto knew it. "There is too much to be done. Very well, invite Mrs. Rampling, Gregory, but pray make it clear it is only an emergency for one night, until we come up with someone else."

"I shall ask Juteclaw to send the carriage for her at once," he said, smiling, and darted into the hallway.

Otto hunched his shoulders. "At least she is pretty, and a lively lady, one hears."

I gave him a look laden with contumely. "That would appeal to you, Otto, but it is hardly a recommendation for a house of death."

"You forget there are also a few of us still alive, my pet. We must warn Mrs. Rampling it is the ladies who are in particular jeopardy at Downsview." I felt there was a warning in the look he directed at me.

Gregory soon returned. He took up a seat beside me and discussed Mrs. Rampling until dinner was announced. He assured me she was charming and considerate. Once I met her, I would not be in a hurry to have her replaced. As it seemed this paragon would keep Gregory from dangling after me, I was not entirely unhappy at the prospect of her arrival.

Dinner was a dismal affair. We pushed our food around on our plates. The gentlemen drank a considerable quantity of wine. I had a headache from the afternoon's indulgence, and drank water. Horatio asked the footman if Duke had turned up.

Gregory said he was not likely to "turn up." They would have to continue searching the park for him.

"For God's sake, can we not talk about something else?" Felix snapped.

I was glad when the meal was over and I could escape, leaving the gentlemen to their port. Mrs. Wiggans had arrived and was tending to the laying out of Mrs. Manner abovestairs. I had selected her best gown, the pretty blue silk, and the ecru bonnet with blue ribbons. I arranged her hair myself, with the little buns over her ears. The hair was still wet; Mrs. Wiggans had had to wash the blood out. This was the last thing I would be able to do for my old friend, who had done so much for me over the years. She was always there to comfort me when Aunt Hettie was in one of her moods. She was as willing as a girl my own age to discuss gowns and beaux and such things that could not really have interested her much. Really she was my best friend, and I could not hold in the hot tears that slid down my cheeks as I bid her farewell. I had not felt this bad since my mama's death ten years before.

At least Mama's death had been expected, and peaceful when it finally came. She had declined over the space of ten months. Hettie and Mrs. Manner had been wrenched away so rudely. As I stood gazing at that sweet face, I made a silent vow that I would do all in my power to bring her murderer, and Hettie's, to justice. I assumed the same man had killed them both.

"What do you want done with her ring, Miss Greenwood?" Mrs. Wiggans asked, pointing to "my" opal ring.

"She has left it to me in her will."

"Why don't you take it now, while you think of it?"

I slid it from her cold, lifeless finger and put it on my own, happy to take this reminder with me as I went to have a room turned out for Mrs. Rampling. I put her in the east wing, away from the gentlemen. Without her, I would have been alone in

the east wing that night, except for whoever was to sit with Mrs.
Manner. That would be a job for the nephews to share. Horatio
had decreed I was to be spared that ordeal. Tomorrow Aunt
Hettie was to be laid to rest. A few neighbours would drop in
afterwards.

Vicar Jennings had arrived when I returned to the saloon.
He was wearing a solemn face and looking very much at home
in it. Gregory and Otto discussed the funeral arrangements with
him. Later, Sir Aubrey Croton paid us a darting visit to discuss
the feasibility of sending for Bow Street.

Croton's prosperity has gone to his stomach and his back.
He is stout, and takes a keen interest in his attire. Ever on the
run (he is an aging bachelor, and dines out six evenings out of
seven), he wore black evening clothes and could spare us only
a moment. Otto briefly outlined the recent happenings at
Downsview.

"Culpepper has been at me about sending for Bow Street,"
Croton said to the gentlemen. "Bit of a nuisance, what?"

No one disagreed with him, which encouraged him to
continue. "I mean to say, it seems Mrs. Farr was killed for her
blunt, and her companion because she saw something she
shouldn't ought to have. That should be the end of it. Am I
wrong?"

"I should be happier with a Bow Street officer in the
house," I informed him.

He gave me a tolerant smile. "Are four handsome young
gentlemen not enough for you, Miss Greenwood? Heh-heh. I
trust I can rely on you lads to look after Miss Greenwood?"

"I really do think, Sir Aubrey—"

He cut me off with a flap of his hand. "Doctor Culpepper
has more wits than you are likely to find at Bow Street, my
dear."

"But he has his own work to do. He cannot spend much
time with us."

"You have only to call him if you need help."

"Is he likely to hear me from over a mile away if I am attacked?" I asked sharply.

"Heh-heh. In that unlikely case, you have your four body-guards," he said, nodding to the nephews, who smiled back in agreement. "I am promised to Lord Thorpe this evening for a round of whist," he said, and rose to take his leave.

That is how the safeguarding of Downsview was left. In other words, we were to look after ourselves.

I was in charge of the callers who would drop in after the funeral tomorrow, and to check on this, I went to speak to Cook about refreshments. For such a small funeral, we decided a cold nuncheon would suffice, with of course tea and wine to ease the chill of winter.

"I've all manner of food prepared, so there will be no shortage," Cook said.

Her eyes were red from crying. Several of the girls were weeping openly. I noticed Mary had been talked into staying with us. Good positions were hard to come by, and Hettie had been a fair employer. It was all so different from how I had been imagining these last days before the New Year. Who ever thought the feast prepared for a jolly visit would be served at a funeral?

When I returned to the saloon, Gregory immediately came to me and began talking about Mrs. Rampling again. I was already tired of her before she arrived, but when she appeared in person, she was better than I expected. She was quite strikingly beautiful. Still nominally in half-mourning, she was dressed in a violet silk gown that any lady would envy, but it was her manner that surprised me more. She seemed nice. And best of all, she was no older than I, perhaps even a few years younger. I had been picturing a more formidable lady altogether.

Gregory presented Mrs. Rampling to us. It seemed she had already met Otto. She was a petite blonde with pretty brown eyes and a warm manner. Before she had spoken three sentences, I realized she spoke in italics.

"My dear, how *horrid* for you!" she exclaimed, seizing my two hands and squeezing them. "I came dashing the *instant* I received Gregory's message. You must forgive me if I am dressed inappropriately. I cannot even *begin* to imagine how you must feel, losing your two companions so suddenly and unexpectedly—and in such a *brutal* way. It is almost beyond belief."

"Yes, I have not begun to grasp it myself."

"Let us sit by the fire," she suggested, urging me closer to the grate. Felix rose to give us the sofa. "There is something comforting in a fire, is there not? And perhaps tea. Am I being a pest? I did not take time for my tea, but dashed the *minute* I had your summons."

I called for a fresh pot, and for the next half-hour we sat talking, quite ignoring the gentlemen. Felix soon wandered back to his books. Horatio took a turn abovestairs with the death vigil, and Otto kept Gregory from bothering us.

After we had discussed the murders for a while, Mrs. Rampling decreed a change of topic, or we would not sleep a wink for worry. I found myself describing to her the sort of life I had been leading. She was quite simply amazed.

"My poor child! You have been virtually buried *alive!* It is *monstrous!* What was your aunt thinking of? She should have presented you at St. James's. You would have been a great hit, I promise you."

"I had no dowry, Mrs. Rampling. I would have been ineligible."

"I daresay you are right. And now you are, perhaps, just a *little* old, but that is not to say you should remain here. Really, London is the only place for you. After your mourning is up, you must come to visit me. I *insist*."

It was kind of her, but really I could not see myself staying with such a dashing creature, whose husband had been killed in a duel while defending her honour. Still, she lent my thoughts a less lugubrious turn. My life was not over. With whatever competence Aunt Hettie had left me, I would make a new life for myself somewhere else. I would not remain buried at Downsview.

When I finally rose to show Mrs. Rampling to her room, she said, "You go on ahead, Miss Greenwood. The servants will show me to my room. Ten o'clock is a little early for me. I shall have a chat with Mr. Farr, and Gregory."

She turned her sparkling eyes on Otto. He heeded their mute summons at once, as quickly as if she had actually spoken. I realized, then, that he had been listening to her every word.

"It is very kind of you to come to our assistance, Mrs. Rampling," he said.

"I am glad I could be of help. You must not believe all the *horrid* things you hear of me, Mr. Farr. I *do* have a heart, you must know."

I looked to see how Otto reacted to her coquettish manner, and saw him smiling. "I assure you Gregory has been saying nothing but good of you, ma'am." Then he turned to me. "Are you retiring now, Jessica?"

"Yes."

"I shall accompany you to the stairs," he said, and took my arm.

When we were beyond the door he said, "Well? What is your opinion of your new chaperone? You seemed to hit it off remarkably well with her. I am amazed."

"She seems very nice and friendly," I said, though it bothered me a little that she was equally friendly to Otto.

"Perhaps she will provide the diversion you need to keep from slipping into melancholia. Shall we bother looking for a replacement, or will you be comfortable with her for the nonce? It hardly seems worthwhile to go scouring the country for an eligible relative when you shan't be here long. At least . . ."

"I don't know, Otto. Let us wait until the will is read, and see how things have been arranged."

"That might be best." He gave a "tsk" and added, "What a wretched turn-up this is. As if being sued by the Prince were not bad enough, now we are confronted with murder. Be sure to lock your door."

I nodded and left. When I was alone in my locked room, I found myself re-thinking the evening. It was Gregory's idea that Mrs. Rampling come, but it was Otto who had first agreed to it. Felix and Horatio had objected. And now Otto had suggested she should remain, that it was hardly worthwhile to find someone else. He had certainly been listening to her every word, and she had certainly smiled more warmly at him than at Gregory. He had admitted knowing her before. I wondered just how well he did know her.

Juteclaw had brought up the sleeping draught Doctor Culpepper had left for me. It was on my bedside table—as Hettie's cough medicine had been on hers last night. I was afraid to take it, and had trouble getting to sleep.

ELEVEN

The morning was a chaotic affair, made worse for me by my lack of sleep the night before. Doctor Culpepper, the county coroner, had arranged the joint inquests for both Hettie and Mrs. Manner for eight o'clock in the morning at the Coroner's Court at the local inn, as he knew we had the funeral to contend with that same day. Otto accompanied me on this sad journey. As I had found both bodies, I was required to give my testimony. It was mercifully brief, with a verdict of death at the hand of person or persons unknown in both cases. I had a nagging headache when I returned, and noticed that all the nephews looked hagged. Except for Mrs. Rampling, we were a sorry-looking lot. It was an unworthy and vain thought on my part, but it bothered me that she was allowed to look charming in a lutestring gown of gold and mauve stripes, while I must play the carrion crow in my mourning gown. The black bombazine had arrived, as promised. My contrived curls had dwindled to listless waves, and without dear Mrs. Manner to help me, even the waves were but indifferently arranged.

Mrs. Rampling continued as warm and friendly and as full of italics as ever. "My dear, you *must* excuse this gown I am wearing—so inappropriate. Gregory told me only that I was needed, and I just snatched up whatever was at hand. I look a *quiz,* I swear."

I was happy for her presence, but I also kept an eye peeled to see how she and Otto behaved with each other. I sensed some effort to attach him on her part, and Otto was never reluctant to make eyes at a pretty lady. But overall it was clearly Gregory who was her particular friend. She treated him with a conjugal offhandedness that betrayed their alliance.

We ladies were spared the funeral. I said my last farewell to Aunt Hettie in her room, just before the coffin was removed. That lifeless face did not look much like the Hettie I had known. It might have been one of Madame Tussaud's wax figures I had heard about; the features were those of the original, but without the spark of animation—the pride and sharp temper—that were so much a part of her. It was Mrs. Manner who looked more like her old self. In death, they were finally equal.

We knew that Mrs. Manner wished to be buried beside her late husband at Bath. Her coffin was to be removed that afternoon, but I would come and make a separate farewell to her later. When the men came to remove Aunt Hettie's coffin, I went to my room. I did not want to see the sorry sight, but I saw it in my mind's eye all the same as the heavy tread of their footfalls struggled down the great staircase with their burden.

Mrs. Rampling was waiting in the purple saloon when I returned below. She came to me and put her arms around me. "Poor Jessie," she murmured. "Do you mind if I call you so? You need a friend at this time, and a friend would not call you Miss Greenwood."

"Of course," I mumbled through my tears. It was a comfort to feel the warmth of a human touch. I did need a friend. Her words reminded me of how very much alone I was.

"And you must call me Anita," she said at once.

Such a rushing forward of the intimacies of friendship was

not in the best of taste, but the unusual circumstances made it seem natural.

While awaiting the return of the funeral party, we sat by the grate and talked. Mrs. Rampling—Anita—apologized again for not having proper mourning clothes. When I volunteered the use of Aunt Hettie's black shawl, she accepted gratefully.

"I have half a dozen black gowns at home," she mentioned, "for my husband passed away recently. I only switched to half-mourning at Christmas. Perhaps Gregory mentioned my situation?" she said, and looked at me closely.

"Yes."

"I hope you did not—but of course Gregory would not have told you those *malicious* rumours." I looked encouraging, and she continued. "Certain people have been saying my late husband died defending my honour. It was a *lie*. George and I were *very* much in love. George's duel was fought over a card game. A Captain Sharp was using marked cards, and George accused him of it. The man called him out, and George was killed. When a younger lady is married to an older gentleman, that sort of malicious scandal is only to be expected. My friends know it is untrue. They have all stood by me. Gregory was a *great* help to me in handling all the business of settling the estate."

The story from the lady most intimately involved was at variance with the rumours Horatio had related. Naturally I did not challenge her. I thought the truth probably lay somewhere between the two tales. It seemed plausible that she had been carrying on behind her elderly husband's back, and when he was killed in a duel, the gossip-mongers invented the rest of it.

"The reason I mention it, Jessica—"

"You don't have to explain things to me, Anita. That is none of my concern."

"But I *want* you to know! You must not think too badly of me," she said cajolingly. "When you come to stay with me in London, you must not think you will be ostracized from decent society. I have *dozens*—nay, *hundreds* of friends. I am out every night. The theatre, routs, balls. Gregory will be our cicisbeo. I have no doubt Otto will be happy to squire us from time to time as well. I have been feeling him out in that respect, and he seems agreeable. He could be a *great* help to you. He has the entrée everywhere. There would be *no hope* of attaching him, of course. With his expectations he will marry some well-dowered noble daughter, but his friendship could be very useful."

"You forget I am in mourning, Anita," I said, astonished by the tenor of her conversation.

"Of course," she said at once. "I was speaking of next year. In fact, it might be a good idea for us to travel a little during your year of mourning. Something to pass the interval in an interesting manner. With Boney bestriding Europe, it is difficult. Ireland, perhaps . . ."

I had no intention of making Anita such a bosom bow that we set off on a year's travel together, and said vaguely, "I daresay there will be business to tend to here in England."

"We shall wait until the will is read before deciding *exactly* what is to be done. But you must not forget you are to come to me. *That* is settled."

It was settled in my mind that I would do nothing of the sort, but I worded my intention less sharply. "I have not really decided yet, but I thank you for the offer, and shall keep it in mind."

Before long the mourners arrived. A fair number had turned out for the occasion. Vicar Jennings and Doctor Culpepper came, along with Aunt Hettie's solicitor, Mr. Ogilvy, a dark and dapper man from Littlehorn. Mr. Walgrave, her man of finance, also came. John Weldon and some of the other neighbours were there as well. With the four nephews, it made a decent showing. Wine was served first, followed by tea and the cold lunch Cook had prepared. The guests spoke respectfully of Hettie, and mentioned Mrs. Manner. As if by tacit consent, the subject of murder was avoided, but it was there, the uninvited guest at the feast. I noticed Culpepper's sharp eyes darting hither and thither, and knew he was looking and listening, as I was, for a false move.

He took up a seat beside me before leaving and expressed his dissatisfaction with Croton for not sending for Bow Street. He inquired why Mrs. Rampling was here. I explained she was acting as chaperone for the time being.

"She looks young for the job. Is there no decent local lady you could hire?"

"She is not indecent, so far as I know."

"Lord, Miss Greenwood, I thought you had more sense. You don't know a thing about her except what young Gregory has seen fit to tell you. She might be his accomplice, for all we know."

"Accomplice?" I leaped on the word. "Are you saying you have discovered something that proves Gregory—"

"No, no," he said at once. "But we know it was one of the lads. Why take chances? You must stay here until the will is read, of course, but after that, I think you should get away for a while."

Horatio came ambling up to us and our private talk was finished. Culpepper moved away, but he had left me with something to think about.

"Well, that is over, thank God," Horatio said. "How are you making out with the widder, young Rampling?"

"She told me that her husband's duel was over a game of cards, Horatio. Where did you hear *she* was the cause?"

"You may hear it anywhere. It was a great secret. The whole town was whispering about it."

"You don't actually know it was true then?"

"Not for a fact. No smoke without fire though, eh?"

"She invited me to stay with her in London."

He looked positively alarmed. "You mustn't think of it! You might never leave the place alive. Even if you did go, no one decent would receive you. No, no, my girl. Put that notion out of your mind."

"I did not tell her I would go, but she invited me."

I noticed, of course, that Horatio's mind was running in the same groove as Culpepper's. He suspected Gregory too. I think I suspected him myself, but Anita Rampling was not his accomplice. She had been at Littlehorn when both murders occurred. Whatever her sins, I rather liked her.

When Horatio left me, he walked straight to Otto and whispered in his ear. Within a minute, Otto came to join me. He just shook his head.

"I thought you had more sense, Jess."

"Horatio told you."

"He did, and I agree with him—the idea is preposterous. You'd be eaten alive by Rampling's crew."

"I know she is not quite the thing, but I rather like her. She is lively and amusing."

"All the more successful light-skirts are. That is what makes them successful, but I had not realized they could enchant ladies as well as gentlemen."

"You are the one who said she should stay on."

"Only for a day or two. I had no idea she worked so quickly. You have not agreed to join her in London?"

"I haven't agreed to anything, but I obviously must go somewhere if Downsview is to be sold."

"I don't believe for a moment Hettie put that in her will. One of us will get it. Probably Gregory . . ."

"Well then! I don't suppose you are suggesting I stay here with him."

"He won't make Downsview his home, but I don't suggest you stay if he inherits. He will, no doubt, come from time to time to see what depredations he can make on the estate in the way of cutting timber, or selling paintings, or selling off parcels of land. If you must leave, and I agree it would be advisable, you have connections you can go to."

I noticed he did not say "relatives." My connections were the Farrs. I looked a question at him, but he did not pin-point what connection he had in mind. I felt it could only be his mama.

The guests began to leave, and we went to the saloon door to see them off. Horatio joined us. "Are we calling that bite of cold mutton lunch?" he asked.

"Yes, we want to get on with the reading of the will while Ogilvy is here."

"Business before pleasure," Otto said.

The atmosphere at Downsview had been oppressive since my aunt's death. It grew almost unbearably tense as Juteclaw ushered the last guest out the door. Now we would hear the will read. Hettie's fortune was the reason she had been murdered. We were all on thorns to hear the will, but did not wish to reveal our eagerness.

Mr. Ogilvy, the lawyer, looked around and said, "Shall we begin now, Miss Greenwood?" I was surprised that he put my opinion over that of the gentlemen. Little did I suspect the reason!

Mrs. Rampling darted up to me and squeezed my fingers. "Good luck, Jessica. Let me know how it turns out." Then she left before I could reply.

As everyone was eager to hear the news, I led Ogilvy to the study, with the others following like sheep. He opened the door, and we saw Felix and John Weldon sitting in the study. In my excitement, I had not noticed Felix was not with the other nephews. He sat behind the desk, Weldon in front of it. Scholars, it seemed, could not be distracted from their arguments, even by death. That they were, or had been, arguing was clear from their postures and sharp expressions.

Felix looked sheepish to be caught out in this slight to Hettie's memory, and coloured up. "Is it time already?" he said. "I fear Weldon and I got carried away over a point of translation. Another time, Mr. Weldon."

Mr. Weldon said, "Another time. But let us make it very soon, Mr. Chapman." He rose, bowed curtly and left.

"What a fellow," Felix said, with a shake of his head. "He has got it in his bonnet that I traduced the memory of Crassus by overemphasizing his greed. The facts speak for themselves. If I erred, it was a *culpa levis* on my part."

"Yes, yes, Felix. Never mind that now," Gregory said impatiently, and Felix moved away from the desk to allow Mr. Ogilvy to use it.

The lawyer took a folder out of his case and spread it on the desk as we all settled in. Gregory drew a chair for me beside himself. Otto sat on the other side, with Horatio hovering over my shoulder. Felix stood behind us, as there were not enough chairs.

Ogilvy cleared his throat and began the reading of the formal document. "I, Hettie Elizabeth Farr, being of sound mind and body, do hereby—"

"Do we have to bother with all that?" Gregory said.

"You want to know who gets the estate and money," Ogilvy said with a certain distaste. "Very well then . . ." And he immediately reverted to more unintelligible mumbo-jumbo about estates and chattels. The facts were slow to penetrate, but after a few repetitions and several questions, Hettie's intentions became clear.

"Yes, Miss Greenwood is the major beneficiary, providing she marry one of you four gentlemen within twelve months of Mrs. Farr's demise," Ogilvy said in plain English. "If at the end of twelve months she has not married, or if she has married someone other than one of you, the estate is to be divided evenly amongst the five of you. In the case of her demise before the twelve month period, the estate is to be evenly disbursed amongst the nephews. There are other details: in the case of the demise of any of the nephews, the estate is to be divided evenly amongst the remaining heirs. There are some smaller bequests. Mrs. Farr's dog, Duke, is to remain at Downsview with Miss Greenwood during the next twelve months if she does not marry. Mrs. Manner was to be a beneficiary, and of course the servants. A thousand for the church, and so on."

"Intolerable!" Gregory exclaimed, but he did not seem so angry as I would have thought. In fact, he did not even seem surprised. His face lacked that stunned expression of the other nephews.

"Anguis in herba," Felix murmured softly.

Horatio said, "Eh?"

"A snake in the grass," Felix explained.

"Where?" Horatio demanded, looking about him.

The others spoke too, but I scarcely heard them for the humming in my ears. She had left it all to me! I was rich beyond the dreams of avarice. Downsview, the money, the lot. But there was indeed a very large snake in this new Eden. In order to inherit, I must marry one of these four gentlemen—and one of them was a murderer.

TWELVE

We thanked Mr. Ogilvy. He asked me to remain behind a moment, after the others left, and told me he would be happy to assist me in any way he could. He explained that I was to receive the year's income for Downsview and be responsible for the running of it until such time as I chose my husband. He assumed I would choose from amongst the four. As I had never looked beyond that little circle for a match, I did not find this strange. I asked him to tell the others I wished to be alone for a moment, and he was very happy to oblige the potential heiress of Downsview.

I sat on alone, looking at the astonishing document Aunt Hettie had left behind. Whatever had induced her to create such a monstrous piece of mischief? And why had she not warned me of it? After the first bout of disbelief I tried to think rationally, for there must surely be a rational explanation.

I thought she wanted to be fair to us all, yet did not want to see Downsview sold to strangers. She knew the money should revert to the Farrs, as the estate had been Aldous Farr's to begin with, yet her own inclination was to leave it to her kin, the Chapman side of the family, which included me. Over the years she had come to place some trust in my common sense. At the bottom of her heart, she knew Gregory to be unreliable, yet she did not much care for Felix. Unable to reach a compromise without selling Downsview, she had dumped the matter in my lap. But she had not foreseen the complication of murder.

Of course she hoped I would choose Gregory, and ride herd on him hard enough to keep him in line. Blinded by his superficial charm herself, she thought I must admire him too. He would be my last choice. He had been behaving in a worryingly lover-like way during this visit. Had Auntie told him what was in this will? Why else had he suddenly begun courting me? He had told me a quite different story about the will; that it was to be shared amongst us. Had Hettie misled him? No, he must have known the truth. But if he planned to offer for me, why had he imported Mrs. Rampling?

He had not made up to me when he first arrived. His advances only began that day in the hall upstairs, when I feared he might have done Mrs. Manner some harm. He said he had gone to the east wing to look in on her, but Auntie's bedchamber was close by. Had he slipped into her room and found her will? I knew she had had a copy of it there to review while planning her annual revision.

I felt certain that was it. That was when he learned I was the major beneficiary, providing I choose one of the nephews. He was trying to inveigle me into choosing him. Mrs. Rampling had come to Littlehorn with him earlier, before he read the will. Yes, that would explain her presence close by.

Hettie was clever enough to know I had a tendre for Otto, but she must not have thought he would ever offer for me, even with the added inducement of Downsview. He would inherit Cleremont; he had no need of her estate and money. She did not know about his lawsuit when she made this will, of course. Things might be different now . . .

My thoughts turned eagerly to Otto. He might very well have me now. But it was small consolation to nab a husband who needed my money, and had no use for me myself. I thought of Horatio—he was kind, and he liked me. I would have accepted him had he offered anytime over the past ten years. Felix? I hardly considered him at all, really. He was a book in breeches, and a book in a foreign tongue at that. There was nothing in him to turn a lady's head. With his new success, and with his knighthood in the offing, he was a more attractive *parti* than before from a worldly point of view, but I had never had a hankering for worldly honour and glory.

Of course I could always refuse to marry any of them, and in one year we would divide the estate. That seemed the fairest course, except that it meant selling Downsview, and that was not what Hettie wanted. She had no right to rule my life from the grave. The only consolation in the overwhelming problem was that it did not demand an immediate solution. I would remain at Downsview for the meanwhile, which meant hiring a companion.

A light tap sounded at the door. Before I could reply, the door opened and Anita Rampling popped in, wearing a smile. "Gregory has just told me the news, Jessica! Is it not *marvellous?* I could not *wait* to congratulate you."

"Thank you."

"I have sent Juteclaw for a bottle of champagne. We are going to celebrate, you and I, and decide which lucky gentleman is to win the prize."

I would have preferred to be alone, but could not be rude to a guest. I was also curious to hear what she would have to say. Juteclaw arrived hard at her heels, carrying a bottle of champagne and several glasses.

"May I congratulate ye, miss," he said, smiling. "The cat's amongst the pigeons now. Ye'll have more offers than ye know what to do with."

"Thank you, Juteclaw. Perhaps you would open the wine for us."

He struggled with the cork, and eventually poured the wine and handed us each a glass.

"To Jessica, and her *mari*," Anita said, playfully touching her glass to mine.

We sat in front of the desk, using it for a table. "Gregory tells me you get the income from the estate during the year," she said. "That will be *more* than enough to hire a mansion in Ireland. You can live in a grand manner cheaply there. Dublin, of course, is where you will want to go. I have many friends there."

"Under these new circumstances, I don't plan to leave Downsview," I said firmly. "I am in charge of running it."

She looked quite taken aback. "You have a steward. Mrs. Farr did not actually run the place herself. Why, you will be bored to *flinders* here, Jessica. Oh, *I* will come and visit as much as I can, of course, but really, you know, the deep country is *not* my style."

"I would not dream of dragging you away from London, Anita," I said quite cordially, but with enough firmness to let her know she was not going to bearlead me.

She adopted a moue and tossed her curls. "I am only thinking what is best for *you,* my dear. If you think to nab Otto now that you are an heiress, I wish you luck, but I would *not* bet on your chances. He is practically engaged to a *very lovely* heiress, you must know. Lady Mary Swanson, Lord Edgeworth's daughter. One sees them *everywhere* together."

This news smote me like a physical blow to the heart. I realized then where my heart, and hopes, lay. I had always known Otto was above my touch, but when did that ever stop a maiden from loving? There was no reason to doubt Anita's claim. It was easy to believe. The only surprise was that it had taken him so long to reach the sticking point. Pride demanded a denial of Anita's suggestion. It also demanded that I not reveal my true feelings.

"Otto?" I asked, and gave a little laugh. "Where did you get the notion I favoured him?"

"Then it is Gregory after all?" she said. Her eyes were bright with curiosity, but not with pleasure, I thought. She disliked the idea, and well she might if she loved him herself.

"No, not Gregory."

"Who, then? It cannot be Felix. *Horatio!*" she exclaimed. "But *he* does not come into any title, you must know. Of course he is well-connected. You would have access to all the *best* people. But really, to have to be bedded by *Horatio!*" she said, and laughed. My mouth flew open at such blunt speaking.

Anita rushed on to excuse herself. "I forget you are not an old married lady, like most of my friends. You are not quite a *child,* however. These missish airs paint you as a *provincial,* Jessica. I am only trying to hint you into a more acceptable style. At *your* age, a touch of town bronze will be expected. What I said is true. There is more to marriage than walking down the aisle and being called 'Mrs.' "

"I am well aware of that. I happen to find Horatio attractive."

"Really?" She looked dumbfounded.

It was not long before there was another tap at the door, and Gregory came in. "I hope I am not interrupting you, ladies," he said with an ingratiating smile. Just so had he been smiling at Aunt Hettie for ten years. That smile was nothing less than an insult.

"You will *never* guess what, Gregory. She plans to marry *Horatio!*" Anita said, and laughed as though it were an uproarious joke.

"Good God!" he exclaimed. Gregory was not laughing. He looked alarmed, and almost angry.

"I did not say I wished to marry Horatio, Anita," I said stiffly. "I was merely correcting your assumption that I wished to marry Otto."

Anita poured Gregory a glass of champagne and he dragged a chair to the desk. "Jessica feels she cannot leave Downsview, now that she is in charge of it," she explained to Gregory.

He assumed an avuncular tone and began a new role. "Quite right. Hettie knew she might depend on Jess to do the proper thing. As Hettie's closest kin, naturally I shall do all I can to help you," he began. "A young lady would have very little idea how to deal with the steward and tenants and so on."

"You cannot stay here, Greg," Anita pointed out. "Unless Jessica hires a companion. I daresay you *will* be doing that right away, Jessica?"

"Yes, as soon as possible, but I shall not require help in running Downsview, Gregory. I have a very good idea how Hettie managed her affairs. I have been doing her correspondence for her the last five or so years."

"Still, I fancy you will want a little company—family is the best company, after all." We sipped our champagne a moment in a silence that was not one of those comfortable silences. Far from it. I wished they would finish their wine and go.

"If it is not Horatio, and it is not Otto you plan to marry," Gregory said, "then who . . . ?" He cast a speaking glance in Anita's direction. It was as transparent as glass. He was urging her to leave, so that he might have me to himself.

"It is quite possible I shall not marry anyone, Gregory. The fairer course would be to wait and split the estate evenly between us all. That is the other alternative the will provides."

"But that would take a year!" he said.

"You have waited all these years. Surely another twelve months is not beyond your patience."

He looked frustrated, but mumbled something about its being up to me. "You haven't forgotten she promised me that five hundred? As you speak of fairness, I am sure you will want to honour her intention."

"I shall have a look at the books early in the New Year," I said vaguely.

Anita was becoming restless. "Let us all go out for a drive," she suggested.

"You go ahead," I replied. "I want to go upstairs a moment before Mrs. Manner is taken away."

"Of course," she said gently, and gave my fingers a squeeze.

Gregory rose and accompanied me to the door, murmuring insincerities in my ear about his sorrow at Mrs. Manner's passing. He detained me with a hand on my arm and said, "About your staying here, Jess — there is nothing in the will to prevent you from visiting London. Anita will be delighted to have you. She lives in a very elegant style. Such small and private diversions as our mourning allows will be a treat to lighten the gloom of winter. Think about it."

The only reply I gave him was a wary smile. He loved Anita, but he planned to marry me if he could. I had no intention of either visiting London, or inviting these two wicked sophisticates to visit Downsview. How long would I live, if I was all that stood between them and the fortune? Someone had already murdered two helpless ladies, and the idea was becoming stronger by the moment that it was Gregory.

I wondered, too, why Hettie had lied to Gregory about her will. Had he known the truth, he would have been making up to me all these years. Perhaps she preferred that he make up to her, to try to get her to change her mind, and make him the chief beneficiary.

THIRTEEN

When I went into the hallway, Juteclaw stood at the front door. "They've come for her, miss," he said dolefully. I knew he meant Mrs. Manner.

"She is not gone!" Gone, without my taking a proper leave of my dearest, best old friend.

"They're abovestairs right now."

I flew up the curving staircase at an unladylike gait. Four stout men were just carrying their burden down the hallway. The coffin was heavy. I could not ask them to put it down, or take it back to the room. I preceded them down the stairs and said my last goodbye to Mrs. Manner at the doorway, with no privacy and not nearly enough time to suit me. I felt cheated. Juteclaw and I watched from the door as they put the coffin on the flatbed and attached it with chains. In my mind's eyes I could see it jolting over the cold rutted roads of winter to Bath.

I would make a pilgrimage to her grave in the spring and plant some daisies, which simple wild things were her favourite flower. I disliked that she was to be buried so far away. Mrs. Manner had often spoken of Bath to me. Her main interest centred around the cathedral and ecclesiastical doings, but she also spoke of the Pump Room and the assembly rooms, the theatre and gardens, Milsom Street and the circulating library. She had assured me one could have a full and useful life in Bath. The prospect of London was overwhelming, but I thought I might make a place for myself in the quieter society of Bath when the business of Downsview was settled.

As the coffin disappeared around the bend in the road, we came back inside and Juteclaw closed the door. Felix appeared then and asked the butler to bring his coat and hat.

"I am going out, but I shan't ask you to accompany me on this nasty errand, Jessica," he said. "I am going to look for Duke. Not that I expect to find him alive, but I hate to think of him lying frozen in some ditch."

I was pleased with this unsuspected streak of sentimentality in Felix. He had never revealed any notion of it before. Yet an involuntary shudder seized me at the image his words called up. He reached out and held my arm. "Poor Jess," he said gently. "What a wretched position this will has put you in. I shan't pester you with an insincere assurance of my undying love and devotion, but I hope you know I have always felt a genuine fondness for you. I am here, if there is anything I can do to help you. Anything at all."

I could not remember his ever touching me before, except for the ritual kiss on the cheek when parting, and even that was not always done. I felt more sincerity in his simple words than in all of Gregory's ranting.

"Thank you, Felix. I appreciate that. Things are indeed difficult."

"You ought to go up to bed and have Cook take you a nice hot cup of cocoa. You look worn to the socket."

"That sounds tempting."

He gave a "tsk" of combined frustration and annoyance. "I suppose Greg has been at you to marry him."

"No, not quite."

"He must be cursing himself for having brought his mistress here."

The hint of satisfaction in his tone betrayed a deep-seated dislike for his brother. Felix had a spiteful streak, as seen when he mentioned Anita Rampling in front of Hettie. But I did not judge him too harshly, not knowing what past doings might have caused this dislike. Gregory was easy to despise. I left, and let Juteclaw see Felix out the door. I would do just as he had suggested—go up to my room and call for a cup of cocoa. I wondered where Otto and Horatio had gone, and what they were doing. As I passed the purple saloon I peered in and saw them standing before the grate, talking in what struck me as a conspiratorial way, with their heads together. The fire cast flickering shadows on their faces, lending them an air of diablerie.

Horatio looked up and saw me. "Ah, here she is now," he said. That suggested to me that I was the subject of their private chat.

"Speak of the devil," I said, entering.

"Nothing of the sort," Horatio objected. "An angel, more like."

"Doing it too brown, brother," Otto said.

As I advanced towards them, Otto turned and directed a long, measuring look at me. "We are honoured, Miss Greenwood," he said with an exaggerated bow. "Won't you come and give us a chance to endear ourselves to you by compliments and cajolery? Does Miss Greenwood not look particularly lovely today, Horatio? Black is so becoming in the young."

"I am well aware that I look like a carrion crow," I said testily.

Horatio looked confused, but said, "No, by Jove! You look dashed pretty—as usual." He examined me more closely as I accepted a seat and added, "A tad peaked, mind, and those smudges below your eyes—"

"Are completely charming," Otto said, in a silken and insincere manner.

I gave him a chilly look. These clumsy compliments were unlike Otto. If he had decided to make me an offer, he would have to do better than that. After we had settled in, Horatio cleared his throat and said, "Well, have you decided? I notice Greg rushed into the study before you had time to think. Daresay he's made his bid already."

"Surely not in front of Mrs. Rampling!" Otto said, and laughed. "He must curse himself for having imported her!"

"No, he did not quite offer," I said.

"He will before long," Horatio warned me.

"Why should he not try his hand?" Otto asked.

"True," Horatio murmured. "I expect it was what the old girl wanted, if the truth was known."

Otto just rolled his eyes at such witless innocence. "What she wrote in her will was that Jess should choose her husband from amongst the four of us," he pointed out. "Let us not forget Sir Felix. With his new eminence, he is not to be despised. Perhaps he is the dark horse in this race."

"Dark?" Horatio asked. "He is a redhead."

"And not actually a horse either, if we are to be mired in literalism," Otto said with a lazy smile.

"More like a fox," I added.

"A sly young fox," Horatio said, but I don't think he really meant anything. The word "fox" automatically triggered the word "sly."

I was surprised when Otto agreed with him so readily. "Yes, I rather think we have been overlooking the Reynard. He has a few tricks up his sleeve."

"What do you mean?" I demanded at once.

"To disparage the competition is the mark of the amateur—or a desperate man. I do not give up on winning you fairly, Jessica. Let Reynard remain in the race. We do not fear the competition, eh, Horatio?"

Horatio said, "The fortune actually came from our Uncle Aldous. It should, by rights, go back to the Farr side of the family."

"Then do your duty, man," Otto urged. "Don't leave all the courting up to me."

"You include yourself in this contest then, do you, Otto?" I asked.

"Certainly I do. Need you ask? Such a lovely heiress does not cross my path every day."

I was annoyed at his jesting manner. "I just thought your affections might be engaged elsewhere."

"I knew it!" Horatio exclaimed, turning to his brother. "Greg has been trying to spike your gun. Who did he say—"

"I did not say Gregory gave me the idea. I was merely asking Otto whether his affections were engaged."

"My affections are at liberty," he said. "You are welcome to try your hand at capturing them, if you are interested."

"Mine too," Horatio chimed in.

My new fortune lent me confidence to indulge this raillery in a bolder manner than I had ever employed before. "Surely it is for the suitors to try to capture the lady's affections," I said, "or why are they called suitors?"

"The art of flirtation is like the waltz, Jess," Otto informed me. "It takes two."

"And like the waltz, it is for the gentleman to lead."

He directed a long, penetrating look at me. It was as inscrutable as the gaze of the Sphinx. I could not tell whether it was devoid of feeling, or composed of a mixture of amusement, admiration, curiosity, disdain and even anger. What was lacking was love, or any sort of tenderness.

"Let us abandon that metaphor," he suggested. "The waltz

only goes in circles. If we are actually interested in getting somewhere—"

"There is no rush," I said at once. "I have a year to make my choice." Yet I felt that if I had held my tongue, I might have received an offer on the spot. An angry offer, with Horatio looking on in confusion.

"If you live that long," he said, and lifted an ominous eyebrow to bolster his meaning. A frisson shivered up my spine and lifted the hair on my arms.

"You're scaring her to death," Horatio scolded.

"Jessica has reason to be afraid. I hope you are taking precautions?"

"Against whom? That is what we must discover."

Horatio rubbed his nose and stared into the grate. "Where was Gregory when Mrs. Manner went out for her walk?" he asked. "Does anyone remember?"

"He went to order Aunt Hettie's tombstone," I said.

"Odd he was in such a rush to do it. She won't be buried till spring. I wonder if he did order it . . ."

He and Otto exchanged a questioning look. Horatio stood up. "Where is he now?"

"In the study with Anita," I replied. "Felix is out looking for Duke."

"Duke is dead," Otto said with no particular emphasis, but as if he were stating a well-known fact. "No, don't look at me like that, Jess. I did not kill him, but it stands to reason he was got rid of before Mrs. Manner was killed. Duke would not have stood by and let her be attacked."

"He might have hesitated while one blow was struck, if he knew the man. It would only take one blow. Duke was only a companion dog really. Weldon had not trained him to attack, or anything of that sort, though of course Duke would not stand still while Mrs. Manner was killed."

"Duke does know all of us," Horatio said. "Come to that,

where were we when she was killed, Otto? I was in the house somewhere, for I never left it all day. In the armaments-room, very likely."

With an air of vague annoyance, Otto said, "I spent some time writing a column for the *Clarion*. I was in and out of the saloon, but I did not leave the house all afternoon."

I said, "Felix was in the library most of the time, I believe."

"No offence, Jess," Horatio said, "but since you are the one who inherited the lot, where was you?"

Otto's lips moved in amusement.

"I was busy about the house. Any of you—of us—could have found time to nip out after Mrs. Manner. It would not take long. Say ten or fifteen minutes. She did say it was 'him' she saw loitering about the cheese-room door, however."

"She told this tale to no one but you, though," Otto said with a mischievous air. "Might her story have been different had she lived to tell it?"

I ignored this and said, "Gregory was out of the house for well over an hour."

Otto and Horatio exchanged a look. Horatio said, "Easy enough to see if he ordered that tombstone. Shall I do it, Otto, or will you? One of us ought to have a look about the meadow for Duke."

"You go, if you don't mind, Horatio. There is something else I'd like to do."

"What's that then?" Horatio asked.

"Jessica needs a protector."

"You mean to turn her up sweet while I am out in the cold! No, sir, by gad. You can inquire about the tombstone yourself. I shall guard Jessica."

"I do not require a guard," I said. "Good gracious, no one is likely to jump out and kill me in broad daylight."

Otto just shook his head. "If you really think a man who has killed twice will hesitate to strike again, then you are dangerously naïve. The disbursement of the monies must wait for twelve months—or until your marriage, or death. You are the impediment."

I sat stunned at what Otto had just said. I had not looked at the matter in this light, but of course Hettie's murder did suggest an urgent need, or at least desire, for the money. I was the obvious next victim. "I shall not be going anywhere more dangerous than to the purple saloon or my bedchamber."

"Hettie was killed in her bedchamber," Otto said. "And the hours of daylight are short in winter. It is the night that concerns me. If Duke had been properly trained, Mrs. Manner might be alive today. I plan to get Jess a proper guard dog."

"I don't want some fierce brute trailing me about. I don't even like dogs. I much prefer a quiet cat."

"A cat ain't much protection," Horatio said.

"The dog need not accompany you about the house," Otto explained. "What I had in mind was that he should guard your bedchamber door at night. Have you any idea where I might find such an animal, Jess?"

John Weldon was said to raise and train such animals, but I did not want one, and did not tell Otto. "I do not want a dog, thank you."

"You would prefer to be strangled in your bed, would you?" he asked sharply.

"I shall lock my door."

"Much good that will do, when it is plain as a pikestaff Gregory has got hold of the keys somehow. I do not mean to disparage your charms, my dear Jessica, but did you not find it odd that he took to courting you *before* the will was read? If he was able to get into Aunt Hettie's safe, I doubt he would have much trouble with your bedroom door."

"He didn't get into her safe. She had a copy of her will in her bedroom, and the door was not even locked."

"How did he know she had a copy in her room?" Horatio asked.

"She always took it to her room just before your visit. He might have guessed, if he did not know. I met him in the east wing when Mrs. Manner was resting yesterday. I think that was when he saw the will. At least that is when he first began his clumsy compliments."

Otto nodded in satisfaction. "I am relieved to see you have been bending your mind to what is going on here."

"I am not a complete fool, Otto. I can see a church by daylight."

"And a rogue. But I still say you need a guard dog, and I mean to find one. Weldon, I have heard, trains some of his dogs to attack." I knew he would remember that!

"What she ought to have is a pistol," Horatio suggested.

"Good God! Next you will say I require a platoon of Grenadiers. I am going to my room for a rest. I shall lock the door. I have every expectation that I shall see you both at dinner. Unless, of course, our murderer decides to kill you two as well. The fewer of us there are, the more money for each, when the year is up."

Horatio listened, thought for a moment, then said, "Then you don't mean to have any of us?"

"Precisely. Good day, gentlemen."

I rose and strode from the room, but not before casting a peek at Otto, to catch his reaction to my announcement. He looked well-satisfied, and I was furious with him. Even my fortune was not enough to incite him to a proper offer.

FOURTEEN

Once I was in my room, I realized that all I wanted was to lock the door, lie down, and be by myself to recoup my strength and arrange my thoughts. I locked my door and lay down on the bed in the gown I was wearing, pulling the counterpane over me. As I gazed with unseeing eyes at the familiar room around me, my mind wandered over the past days, trying to figure out who had killed Aunt Hettie and Mrs. Manner. There was no concrete reason to suspect one nephew more than the others. Soon I would know whether Gregory had indeed ordered the tombstone. But what would that prove? If he had not, then he might have spent the time with Anita Rampling. And if he had ordered it, that was not to say he had not also nipped into the park and killed Mrs. Manner. Nothing seemed to prove anything. He might have spotted her from the road as easily as the others could have spotted her from the house.

Gregory had the sort of ego that prevented him from realizing when a person disliked him quite thoroughly. He probably thought he had as much chance of winning my hand as any of the others. Would he kill me for one quarter of the fortune, when he hoped to gain control of the whole by marrying me?

Mrs. Rampling would not like that marriage, but then, if gossip was to be believed, she was already an adulteress. The fact that Gregory was married to me would not limit their pleasure. The possibility existed, too, that the ultimate plan might be for my untimely demise. Oh yes, that would surely be a part of it. But it was all based on Gregory's marrying me, and he could hardly do so if he murdered me.

The puzzle was like a game of snakes and ladders. One advanced a pace or two, only to come crashing back down. If not Gregory, then who? Felix? In all the years I had known him, I had never seen him betray much interest in money. He lived in a world of books. He had more money now than ever before, and he did not even bother to buy himself a new jacket. No doubt he would have been happy if Aunt Hettie had left her fortune to him, but I could not see him being sufficiently interested to murder for it.

Horatio? He had come looking for money, to be sure, but he was only short because of his generosity. An overly generous man would hardly murder to finance his generosity. And the sum required, a mere five hundred pounds, was not impossible for Horatio to beg or borrow elsewhere.

No, the two gentlemen who I felt were capable of murder were Gregory and Otto, and I turned reluctantly to the latter. This lawsuit in which Otto was involved must worry him considerably. The *Clarion* was as dear to him as any son is to his father. He spoke airily of "other gentlemen" being in on the slanderous article with him, but suppose their involvement amounted to no more than having incited him to write and publish it. What if, once the thing was done, they washed their hands of him? The suit was laid against the *Clarion*. I doubted he had any proof of anyone's involvement save his own. I could almost believe he would kill to save his journal.

He was certainly clever enough to have done it. Not that it had taken much cleverness to dispose of two unsuspecting old ladies. It required more daring than intelligence, and of them all, Otto took the palm for daring. He knew where the belladonna was kept. He might have seen the cold medicine in Auntie's room. It would have taken him less than five minutes to get the poison and put it in the bottle. No one's actions were so closely scrutinized that he could not have slipped away unnoticed for five minutes. The same with Mrs. Manner's death. Her walk through the park could be clearly seen from either the saloon or Otto's bedroom. If he knew she had seen him near the cheese-room, he could have run out after her to silence her. The weapon, a rock, seemed like a hastily arranged murder.

My "rest" was more wearying than performing my usual duties, and I decided to return belowstairs. Lunch had been sparse, and I hoped that tea would help to fill the hollow ache inside me. I would ask Juteclaw to have it served a little early today, as the others were probably hungry as well.

I met Horatio at the top of the staircase. He beckoned me and hissed in my ear, "He did order the tombstone—Gregory. A great, gaudy thing in pink granite, with an angel holding a cross. Hettie will love it."

Horatio seemed so much like his usual harmless self that I could behave naturally with him. I nodded and said, "He might still have had time to sneak into the park."

"Wouldn't have taken a minute to kosh poor Mrs. Manner on the head, the bounder. He and Rampling have gone out for a spin. Spotted 'em when I was in Littlehorn. They was going into a house, the one where she is staying, likely."

"She brought only a bandbox with her. She would be getting more clothes, I expect."

"I ain't sure it's wise to have her here. What I said about a pistol, Jess—not a bad idea. I have a dandy set of duelling pistols I got myself for Christmas. Happened to bring them with me. I was at Manton's Shooting Gallery trying them out just before I left London."

"Did you not tell me last Christmas that you had bought new duelling pistols?"

"So I did. A little weakness of mine. Cost me a pretty penny too. I shall fetch one of my new set for you to protect yourself."

"I don't know how to shoot a gun."

"I'll teach you. Nothing to it, really. We've time to do it now, before tea. I'll just nip up to my room and get them. Meet you in the armaments-room." I looked my disagreement, and he hastened on to convince me. "It is half an hour to tea-time. Felix is the only one in the saloon. I made the mistake of picking up the latest journal in Littlehorn. It has another review of his book. We'll have to listen to it if we go there."

"Very well," I agreed, and went to the armaments-room to avoid Felix. It was odd Horatio had not mentioned this new set of pistols as being responsible for his shortage of funds. Such things were expensive, and quite useless as Horatio was not the sort of man to challenge anyone to a duel.

The armaments-room is a spacious chamber as large as the purple saloon and entrance hall put together. It is situated at the rear of the house, across from the library. It was used to be in constant use when Aldous was alive, but since his death a dozen years before, it was largely ignored, even by the servants. I know Aldous only by rumour. He was gone before I came to Hettie.

The enormous stone grate, stained with black marks, was empty. The oak-panelled room was shadowy and cold. High up on the wall limp old flags, discoloured with age, stirred slightly in the draught from the door. Some of them had brown stains which Juteclaw had told me were the blood of Farrs slain or wounded in battle centuries ago.

Below, there were a dozen suits of armour ranged along one wall. One suit was so small it had been fashioned for either a child or a midget. They were all of an ornateness that belied their rough usage. One helmet was fashioned like a lion's head, with holes at the eyes for the wearer to peer out at his enemy. Some of the breastplates were works of art, with elaborate engraving and gold trim. There was also one set of horses' armour, as elaborate as the men's. A miscellany of old arms, from halberds and shields to muskets and swords and rapiers, was arranged in glass-fronted cases and on the walls. I felt a shiver to consider that I was now the mistress of these antique barbarities.

Other antiques used in ship navigation had found their way into the chamber as well. There were ornate cross-staffs, compasses and dividers, quadrants and astrolabes and other things that looked like the skeletons of hollow globes, whose function I could not even imagine. They were all coated in dust.

After a moment, Horatio returned carrying a flat black leather case. "I see you are admiring the antiques," he said. "A dandy collection. A shame to see it rusting here. That suit of armour you are looking at dates back to the Renaissance. Look at that tasset! A work of art. I should like to snap up this collection, if Downsview is sold."

I knew Horatio always visited the armaments-room when he visited Aunt Hettie. I had considered it a sort of escape for him, but I realized now that he coveted these ancient old things. The eye gazing at that embossed tasset was the eye of a connoisseur; the hand touching it was the possessive hand of a lover. It was a bothersome thought. Men have killed before now for inanimate objects.

"Is that the pistols you have there?" I asked, to push the troublesome thought away.

"Yes, here we are," he announced proudly, and opened the lid to display a handsome set of duelling pistols. The barrels were engraved with arabesques; the ebony handles had inlays of mother-of-pearl. These elaborate engines of death lay nestled in blue velvet, like a lady's jewelry.

"Very handsome," I murmured.

"The latest thing," he assured me. "They cost me a monkey, and worth it. A patented Forsyth percussion lock. It don't need priming powder. The hammer strikes the compound—potassium chlorate—and it explodes, firing out the cartridge."

"It sounds very dangerous!"

"Hair-trigger," he said, lifting one of the weapons by the barrel and handing it to me. It was heavy and felt extremely awkward in my hand. "I'll charge up one of them while you aim t'other at the grate, just to get the feel of it. Mind you don't shoot wide and destroy that breastplate hanging above. It's Italian, early-sixteenth century," he said.

"No, I don't want to shoot it in the house!" I tried to hand it back to him, but he was already loading the other gun, and did not take it.

"It won't go off until I load it, Jess. We'll do the shooting outdoors, if you like. Just heft it to get the feel. It's wonderfully balanced."

I did as he suggested. It still felt heavy and awkward, but well enough balanced, I daresay. "Let us go out and practise shooting at something," he suggested.

I was suddenly very reluctant to be alone with Horatio and a loaded pistol. In fact, I felt I hardly knew him. A love of weapons did not seem to suit the gentle man I had always taken him for. "There is hardly time for it," I prevaricated.

"We'll do it tomorrow morning. Keep the gun with you tonight. Even if you don't shoot him, just having this pistol will put a fright into him, you see."

I knew Horatio meant Gregory by this vague "him." Gregory was still at the top of my own list of suspects as well, but I kept thinking that he would not kill me until he was certain he could not win me by romantic means. I could ensure safety from that quarter if I let Gregory believe I might accept his offer. It seemed a sane, if underhanded, precaution for the short term—provided Gregory was the murderer.

From the doorway, the sound of approaching footsteps and

a peculiar clicking sound were heard. The clicking was the soft rasp of a dog's nails scraping the linoleum of the hall. "Duke!" I exclaimed. "He's come back!"

Otto appeared at the doorway, preceded by a fierce-looking bulldog held on a leash. It was tawny in color, with a huge, pugnacious jaw. Some black markings on the face added to the air of ferocity. It was squat, with short legs and massive shoulders.

"This is Jack, short for Gentleman Jackson," Otto said. "He's a scrapper, according to Weldon. Odd you did not direct me to Weldon, Jess," he added with a quizzing look.

"Weldon's bulldogs are notorious for their ferocity. He holds illegal dogfights with them in his barn."

"Does he, by Jove!" Horatio exclaimed with the keenest interest.

"A lap dog would hardly serve your purpose," Otto said.

"I do not want his dog. I refuse to have anything to do with him." Gentleman Jackson felt quite otherwise about me. He was sniffing at my skirts, straining at the leash. "This brute is more frightening than Horatio's pistols," I said, stepping back.

"If you are afraid of dogs and afraid of guns, how are we to protect you?" Otto said. He glanced at the pistols. "These are the new Forsyths you were telling me about, Horatio."

Jack seemed eager to eat the pistol I was holding, so I quickly handed it to Otto, who held it in one hand, while trying to restrain Jack with the other. The latter job required at least two hands. He tied the leash to a table leg and began examining the pistol in good earnest, while Horatio praised its "balance" and expostulated on its other marvels.

"It is a nice gun," Otto said. "We must give Jess a lesson in how to use it."

Voices in the hall announced the return of Gregory and his mistress. It was Anita's fluting voice that carried so well, but of course Gregory would be with her.

"Jessica! My *dear,* whatever are you *doing!*" she exclaimed, when she entered and saw the pistols. The guns were set aside.

Horatio narrowed his eyes at Gregory and said, "I am lending Jessica a pistol and teaching her how to shoot it. She will keep it under her pillow at night."

Anita gave a shudder. "I would as lief sleep with a *viper!* What is to stop it from going off in the night? It could blow her *head* off." She turned to me and added, "My dear, you must not *think* of such a thing."

Jack made a lunge at Gregory, who shuffled back, trying not to look frightened at the angry growl that came from the animal's throat. "I suppose this beast is also a part of Jessica's defense?" he asked with an air of injury. "Good God, if you are that frightened for her, the best thing is to get her out of here."

"Here she has me to protect her," Otto replied.

"And who is to protect her from *you?*" Anita asked pertly. The smile she turned on Otto suggested that any danger from him was of the romantic sort. Next she turned an ingratiating smile on me. "If you are *truly* frightened, my dear, why not let me share your bedchamber? A truckle-bed will do for me. I sleep like the dead."

"Then you will not be of much use in case of attack," Otto said.

Anita laughed and said, "Pooh! You are all making *much* too much of the danger to Jessica. The only danger *she* is in is the danger of unwanted offers of marriage. I daresay she can handle *that,* eh, Jessica?"

"She don't plan to marry any of us," Horatio said bluntly.

"Well then, where is the problem?" Anita asked brightly. "You have only to wait a year, then you all share the fortune."

"The problem is the intervening twelve months," Otto mentioned.

Gregory sneered. "That is only a problem for you, Otto. I am not in desperate need of my share. No one is suing me."

"No one is desperate," Horatio said, leaping to Otto's defense. "There is always the post-obit. The money-lenders would jump at the chance of earning a year's interest at some outlandish rate."

"But how much nicer to be able to pay cash, and save the interest," Anita said.

Jack growled again and began straining at the leash with such force that he dragged the table forward an inch or so. And it was a large table, holding some of the navigational equipment.

"If this is one of Weldon's curs, it is not safe to have in the house. They are trained to attack," Greg said, frowning at the beast. He moved towards the larger table where the pistols had been placed. I felt his real reason was to escape Jack, and I did not blame him in the least.

Anita joined him. They each picked up one of the guns. "Careful, one of 'em is charged," Horatio said.

"Which one?" Anita asked.

"Charged?" Otto exclaimed. "Horatio, what are you thinking of, to leave a loaded pistol lying around the house!"

"I was planning to shoot into the grate," Horatio replied.

"Someone could get killed." Otto reached towards Anita to remove the gun from her hand, perhaps because he felt a lady was less likely to handle a loaded gun with the proper care.

Jack took a pet at Otto's harsh tone, or perhaps the sudden movement he made towards Anita. He rose up on his hind legs and began straining forward, pulling the table behind him. Anita either lost control, or Otto's sudden movement caused her to pull the trigger. In any case, a terrific roar resounded in the room. The bullet whistled past my ear so quickly and unexpectedly that I did not even realize at first what it was. It missed me by not more than an inch. I could hear a faint whistling sound, followed immediately by a louder thud as it imbedded itself in the oak-panelled wall.

The room was silent for a second or two, then Jack began

howling and lunging so violently that the antiques on the table clattered to the floor. Anita screamed and dropped the gun as if it were a live coal, and the gentlemen all rushed towards me.

"Jess, are you all right?" Otto demanded. His hands gripped my shoulders so tightly they hurt. His face was white and strained.

The bullet had missed me, but I felt far from all right. I was badly shaken, and gratefully accepted Otto's help to a chair. It was a wretchedly uncomfortable straight-backed chair with no cushioning or arm-rests.

"For God's sake put those pistols away, Horatio," Otto ordered. "And someone get some wine for Jess." Anita flew off to get it.

"Is the other pistol charged?" Otto asked.

"No, just the one," a chastened Horatio replied.

Otto emitted a harsh expletive or two, and Horatio mumbled an apology.

The pistol shot brought Felix to the door. "What happened?" he demanded, his eyes large with curiosity.

"An accident," Gregory said. "Horatio left a charged pistol lying about. Demmed foolish thing to do."

"Not so foolish as you and Anita playing with them! Told you one of them was charged," Horatio shot back.

"Are you all right, Jess?" Felix asked me.

"A little shaken. That's all."

"What is Jackson doing here?" was his next question. Jack continued his howling.

I noticed that Felix recognized the dog.

I said, "Otto got him from Weldon as a guard dog for me. I refuse to let the beast near me. It was Jack's lunge that caused the gun to go off." But was it? Had Anita used it as an excuse to try to kill me? It might even have been Otto's hand that guided the shot. It had all happened so quickly I could not be sure.

Anita returned with the wine and I sipped it gratefully. I don't know why, but it flew into my head that she could have poisoned it, since she brought only the one glass, and not the decanter. I immediately began imagining it tasted bitter, and set it aside.

"Let us have tea," I said, as an excuse to leave it.

"Jolly good idea," Felix said, and assisted me from the chair into the hallway, and thence to the purple saloon. Gregory and Anita followed us, regretting the accident, and adding a few comments that hinted it was all entirely Otto's fault.

Horatio remained behind to put away the troublesome guns, and Otto took charge of Jack. I am not sure where he took the beast, but when he entered the saloon five minutes later, he was alone.

FIFTEEN

Anita did the honours of the tea-table, as I was too shaken to be trusted with the pot. It was a curiously unsettling interval. The air was dense with suspicion. Narrowed eyes glanced around the circle from face to face, asking tacit questions. *Is he the one? Did she fire that shot on purpose?* Long silences would be followed by a sudden eruption of two or three people into nervous speech at once, as if there were some desperate need to fill the silence. Only Felix seemed isolated from it all. He sat hunched close to the grate, staring into the fire, as if he were alone in the room. I thought it must be nice, at a time like this, to be able to lose oneself so completely in another world. Yet to judge by his pensive frown, his world was not without its own problems.

With the shadows of evening falling beyond the windows, the purple saloon seemed more funereal than ever. I would change those horrid old purple window hangings, and perhaps paint the aged panelling a brighter color. I was to be mistress here for a year, and there was nothing in the will that forbade my making a few changes.

Felix was the first to leave. "There is something I want to look at in the library," he mumbled, and left after one cup of tea. He had not eaten a bite.

"You had no luck finding Duke, Felix?" I asked, as he went towards the door.

"I'm afraid not. I shall have another look tomorrow," he said over his shoulder, and kept going.

"Demmed odd, Duke's disappearing," Horatio said, tugging at his ear.

Anita looked at Gregory, then turned to the rest of us and said, "I was just thinking—as Jessica has *definitely* decided not to marry any of you, would it not be possible for her to sign an affidavit to that effect and get the money distributed *before* the end of a year?"

Gregory leaped on the idea at once. I had a distinct impression he had put her up to it. "Now that is an interesting idea. You might speak to Ogilvy about it, Jess."

Otto gave him a knowing look. "You are a *little* interested in when you receive your share then, are you, Gregory?"

"A little interested, but not concerned," Greg replied. "It was just an idea. Jess cannot be looking forward to being buried here for another twelve months."

"It is a lady's prerogative to change her mind. She may accept an offer. I doubt very much if what you suggest would be permitted in any case," Otto said. "The terms of a will must be executed unless they are illegal or not feasible. It may be unfair to ask Jess to stay here another year, but it is neither illegal nor impossible."

Some desultory conversation ensued. Gregory said he thought we ought to look into the matter, but I did not encourage him. I rather wanted that year to weigh the situation before making any decision.

I disliked the idea of being alone in my room again, and sat on without adding much to the meeting. Eventually Anita went upstairs to see that the servants had done her unpacking as she liked. She had brought more clothes with her, as I thought. Gregory followed her out within three minutes.

"I doubt much unpacking will get done," Horatio grinned. "He'd have done better to leave her in Littlehorn, where they could meet in private more easily."

"What did you do with the dog?" I asked Otto.

"Cook tied him up outside. He is used to the cold. Weldon kept him outdoors."

"I hope you did not pay much for him. Will Weldon take him back?"

Otto shrugged. "I still think Jack will prove useful. Did you notice Felix recognized the dog when he came into the armaments-room? He asked if that was Jackson."

"He has probably been to call on John Weldon. They seem to be bosom bows. Felix used to call on his papa."

"Gentleman Jackson was kept by the kennel out back. An unlikely spot for a couple of scholars to discuss Plutarch, if Felix did visit Weldon."

"Weldon would have taken him out to see the dogs," I said.

"Very likely, for he has no real interest in—or knowledge of—scholastic matters. He ventured a word on Felix's translation regarding Julius Caesar breaking into tears when he heard of the conquests of Alexander the Great. Weldon thought it was Alexander who had done the sobbing. Alexander was dead two and a quarter centuries before Caesar was even born. Alexander had many talents, but clairvoyance was not one of them. Shortly after that gaffe I offered Weldon a lift. Felix was quick to detain him. He was afraid Weldon would display his ignorance. When I tried to discuss Horace with Weldon this afternoon, he proved mighty reluctant. Yet he visits Felix regularly to argue fine points of the classics."

"Perhaps Weldon is really trying to sell Felix a mount," I said. "He breeds them too, and now that Felix has some money, he could buy one. He bought a carriage and team."

"Don't see what Weldon has to do with anything,"

Horatio said, looking to his brother for elucidation. "There is no way Hettie's death affects him."

"I just thought it odd," Otto said. "Odder still, Felix himself occasionally makes a gaffe. He mispronounced Damon, if you recall, although Plutarch specifically tells us it should be pronounced with the first syllable short."

Horatio said, "Demme, Otto, the lad's head is full of nothing but Latin and Greek. You are up to your tricks again, trying to poke holes in a fellow because he has made a name for himself. Plain and simple jealousy because you fancy yourself a bit of a classic scholar. Felix has worked hard for his success, and I for one don't begrudge him his due."

"Hear, hear," I agreed. "Felix would not know what to do with Auntie's money if he had it."

"True," Otto said, "he is strangely free of the vice of greed, but for the meanwhile, I say we keep an eye on all our suspects, not just Gregory. I don't like this idea of Rampling throwing up a truckle-bed in your room, Jess. She might provide easy access for Gregory."

"Do you not think that just a trifle obvious?" I said.

"Yes, I do, but they are not subtle, as his quick dash out of here not two steps behind her testifies. In fact, her being in Littlehorn in the first place was hardly subtle."

"Nor was the duel, come to that," Horatio added.

"Actually I had no intention of letting her share my room," I said.

"We'll keep the dog," Otto said. "I plan to let Jack loose in the corridor tonight. That should prevent any unnecessary roaming about."

"You will do nothing of the sort! I forbid it!"

"Then I shall keep him in my own room, with his nose to the door. Or do you feel your guardianship of Downsview includes even what goes on in your guests' bedchambers?"

"As bad as Hettie," Horatio grumbled. "Not that it will bother me. Once I hit the tick, I am out like a lamp."

I said, "Now that I have announced my intention of not marrying anyone within the year, I think the troubles here are at an end."

"Despite Greg's efforts to get your signature on that affidavit, and my urgent need of five thousand?" Otto asked with a quizzing smile.

"Not urgent," Horatio said. "Post-obits. And in the worst case, you know, Papa would come up to scratch. He is pleased at your settling down, Otto, even if he don't say so."

"I plan to keep my eyes open in any case," Otto said. "I noticed today, for example, that Felix was not searching the park for Duke, as he told you he was going to do, Jess. I had a good look around. There are not that many trees that he would have been invisible. Where was he?"

"In some quiet corner, dipping into Plutarch," Horatio offered.

"That is possible," Otto admitted, "but we should not lose sight of the fact that Felix and Gregory are brothers. Felix might be concealing something, perhaps on the promise of remuneration." I gave him a disparaging look and he added, "Blood is thicker than water."

"You and me are brothers too," Horatio pointed out. "Not that I am concealing anything, nor you either, Otto."

If the best Otto could do was to imply Felix was an accessory to murder, I decided to leave him to his ravings. I left, but only went to the library to sit alone, gazing out at the park. The tree-tops stirred in the wind. I felt suffocated inside the house and wanted so very much to walk outdoors and feel that fresh wind on my cheek. It was not cold today. The ice had melted to puddles. Had Mrs. Manner felt like this when she took her last, fatal walk? This was no life; it was like being in prison.

Gregory and Anita had suggested that I should get away

from Downsview, and I began to feel they were right. But where could I go? Certainly not to Ireland with Anita. The gentlemen were all bachelors, and none of them quite free of the taint of suspicion. I was angry that Otto had managed to cast even a shadow on Felix. I paid little heed to his charge that Felix had made a few mistakes in his Latin. What were these mistakes? He had pronounced someone's name as "Damon" instead of "Dammon." But Latin was pronounced differently by different people. I remembered Hettie saying the papists used a different pronunciation than the universities. Even if Felix had forgotten a fact or two, what of it? The greater mystery to me was that he could carry all those quotations in his head.

More troubling was Otto's hint that Felix might be helping Gregory by remaining silent. If Felix had not been in the park looking for Duke this afternoon, where had he been, and why had he felt it necessary to lie about his destination? As I gazed into the gathering twilight, I saw a man coming through the park towards Downsview. He came from the direction of Weldon's farm. The only person I could think of was John Weldon, but this was not his sturdy build, not his swaggering gait. The man seemed to be stumbling, as if he were hurt. My heart began knocking in my chest. Not another one! Please, God, not another murder!

I threw open the door and ran a few feet forward, peering behind me to make sure I was not being followed. I recognized the struggling man as Felix, and went to assist him into the library. He hung heavily on to my arm, scarcely able to walk. His face was bruised, but his gait told me the greater injury was to his abdomen.

"Felix, you were not shot!"

"No, beaten," he gasped. "I went into the park for a breath of air." I helped him to a chair where he sat a moment panting, with his face buried in his arms.

"Who did it?" I demanded.

"I don't know. I couldn't get a look at his face. He came at me from behind."

"You must have seen him when he struck you in the face. You have a bruise over your left eye."

"No, I didn't see him. He threw something over my head, a bag of some sort, and proceeded to pummel the daylights out of me."

"I'll call Doctor Culpepper at once, and the constable."

He grabbed on to my arm. "No, Jess. Don't."

"But why not? You are dreadfully hurt! We cannot have a ruffian—or worse—lurking in the park."

He looked up then, with such a pale, worried face, and such a frightened look in his green eyes that my heart went out to him. Felix was younger than the other nephews. In fact, he was a year younger than I. At that moment, he looked like a boy.

"If you just help me upstairs . . ."

"Oh, Felix! Let me at least put a plaster on that cut."

"That might be a good idea. But can you do it discreetly? I don't want to cause a fuss. *Absit invidia.*"

I could hardly credit that he was spouting Latin at such a time. "What do you mean?"

"Let there be no ill will. No more ill will, I mean. I don't want everyone suspecting everyone else, as they were this afternoon at tea. We were used to have such good times here together. I am sure it was a stranger, someone just after my money."

"But he did not take your watch," I pointed out. His watch-chain was still in place. "Did he take your purse?"

He felt in his pocket. "My purse is gone," he announced. I knew he was lying, not only by his inability to meet my look, but because he kept his hand over his pocket to conceal the bulge that I felt sure was there.

I could only think of one person he would go to such lengths to defend, and that, of course, was his brother. But why would he defend even a brother who had done this to him? Had Gregory threatened him with death if he told whatever it was he knew?

"Do you think I might have a glass of wine? I feel rather faint."

He looked very pale. I ran off to get the wine and a plaster. I meant to see where Gregory was before I did anything else, however. A quick look told me he was not downstairs. Abovestairs, his bedroom door was open; the room was empty. The only place he could be was in Anita Rampling's room. I knocked sharply at her door. I heard a little bustle, then she said, "Come in." She had thrown on a peignoir, but as her evening frock was already laid out on her bed, I thought she was dressing for dinner.

I entered and took a discreet look around. If Gregory was there, he was hiding in the clothes-press, and I lacked the gumption to go and look. "Have you seen Gregory, Anita?" I asked.

"Not since leaving the saloon. What do you want him for?"

"It is nothing important. I'll speak to him later. Sorry to disturb you."

"My dear, you are welcome at *any* time. I was just dressing for dinner." She invited me in, which convinced me she was alone. I was too rushed to accept the offer. I asked Juteclaw to bring a basin of water, a plaster and basilicum powder to the library, and snatched up the wine decanter myself from the saloon.

When I reached the library, Felix had recovered somewhat. He was sitting upright, still pale, and still frightened. He accepted the wine and drank it down quickly, then he tilted his head back for me to clean his wound. The skin was hardly broken, but it had been a hard blow, and not through a layer of cloth either. The long, narrow purple welt that was rising had a sharp, clear edge. Felix knew who had done it; he must. It looked as if the blow had been administered by a stick of some sort, perhaps a cane or riding crop.

He did not speak while I tended to his wound. When I had finished, he sat up straight and said, "Jessica, this place is not safe. You should get away from here at once."

"It seems it is not safe for you."

"It isn't safe for any of us. He's insane."

I leaped on him. "Who, Felix? Who is insane?!

"Whoever did this," he replied evasively, but I was certain he knew. "You see what the villain is about. He means to finish us off, one by one, until there is only himself left to inherit the whole thing—money, Downsview and all."

I could no longer hold back the overwhelming question. I grasped his fingers and said, "Was it Gregory, Felix?"

"No! No, of course not. That is—I told you, I have no idea who it was. I daresay it could have been Greg, but I do not rule out the Farrs by any means. Where is Otto anyway?"

He quite ignored Horatio. "I don't know. He was in the saloon with Horatio, but they're not there now. I expect they are changing for dinner."

"Aye, he would be back by now. I don't want to frighten you, Jessica, but I do not trust Otto above half. Anita thinks he pushed her hand in your direction just before the pistol went off this afternoon. I heard her whisper as much to Greg. Which of us is in desperate need of money, when you come down to it? And Otto has always been unreliable, you know. His past is not spotless by any means. Hettie would certainly have cut him out of her will after that libel suit. She was furious with him. Very convenient that she was killed when she was. It did not do *me* any good, I can tell you. I don't doubt she would have given me Otto's share, or part of it. She was thrilled to death with my pending knighthood."

I tried to weigh his words objectively and had to admit there was some truth in them, though sentiment disliked to hear

Otto disparaged. As to Anita's claim that Otto had steered her hand—that must be taken with a grain of salt. "There is no place I can go. I have been thinking about it myself. Anita invited me to Ireland, but—"

"Good God, you don't want to get mixed up with that trollop. I have hesitated to speak, but I fear the time has come that I must override my scruples and offer for you myself. I know you don't love me. I don't know whether I love you or not. Certainly I like you as well as any lady I have met. I daresay we could hobble along as happily as most. If you would agree to marry me, I could take you away from here. To London, or wherever you like."

"That is very kind of you, Felix. I appreciate your offer, and I know it is sincere, but really I could not contemplate marrying for such a reason."

"Then get away from here at least. Go tonight, while everyone is asleep. I'll help you."

I felt the desperation in his words and knew he was not telling me everything he knew. "What is it, Felix? What are you not telling me?"

"I don't know," he said wanly. "It is just a feeling I have. A feeling of doom. This is no *brutum fulmen*. You are in danger. I know it. Go to an hotel in the countryside. I shall let you know when it is safe to come back."

I listened but remained unswayed, because I sensed that Felix was in a state bordering on hysteria. "Where were you this afternoon, Felix? Otto did not see you when he was in the park."

"I was in the park. I found Duke—dead. I was burying him."

"Why did you do that?"

"I didn't want you to know, Jess. It was horrible. He had been—his throat was cut. He had managed to crawl to the orchard to die." He looked nauseous at the memory.

"That is odd. There was no blood at the hollies, where Mrs. Manner was killed."

"Then whoever did it lured Duke to the orchard. Yes, I daresay he *was* killed there. There was a pool of blood." I shook away the image his words conjured up. "I buried him in the orchard, under the third tree in the third row, and covered the grave with leaves and branches. It is almost beyond belief that anyone could be so barbaric to a helpless dog. He could have just poisoned him. It was not necessary to butcher the poor animal."

I poured Felix another glass of wine and had one myself, for the image of Duke in a pool of blood kept recurring. Felix's story accounted for Otto's not seeing him. The orchard is not visible from the park. He pressed me a little more to either marry him or at least go and hide in a country inn. In the end I said I would think about it, because it seemed so important to him.

I felt I knew at last who was responsible for the murders. Felix was protecting Gregory, not through any sense of family loyalty, but from sheer terror. He had seen what Gregory had done to a helpless dog. Felix was equally helpless. I doubt he had ever held a pistol in his life, or anything more dangerous than a pen.

Before I left, Felix begged me to say his bruise was a result of accidentally walking into a door. I acquiesced to calm him, but I did not feel bound by it. The Farrs should be warned.

I went into the hallway to go upstairs to change for dinner. Gregory came out of the saloon and said, "I have just been trying to stir the fire into a blaze. I believe the flue needs cleaning. Anita said you were looking for me, Jess? I was in the wine cellar with Juteclaw, selecting some wines for dinner. What was it you wanted to see me about?"

He had changed into evening clothes. He seemed completely relaxed, his cheeks ruddy from working by the grate. He could not have got back from the park and changed so quickly.

And he would have fashioned an excuse that could not be so easily contradicted if he were not telling the truth.

"Oh, Felix found Duke, and buried him in the park."

"Did he, by God? Foolish thing to do, burying him, but that is Felix all over. I expect Culpepper will want to have a look at him for clues."

He didn't even bother asking what had happened to Duke. I felt he already knew. I ran upstairs to change for dinner. Again suspicions whirled in my head. There is a door in the cellar leading outdoors. Greg could have slipped out of the cellar unseen and attacked Felix to frighten him into silence. He might have gone to the cellar for that very reason, already prepared for his job. If he had worn a greatcoat and changed his slippers for boots, his clothing would not be soiled. Those rosy cheeks might be due to cold, not the heat from the grate.

At the end of the hall, Otto was just coming up the servants' stairs from the kitchen. The family seldom used those stairs, and I was surprised to see him. Traces of mud were on his top-boots, and his clothing was splattered with mud, as if he had been out in the park. What else could account for his condition?

I felt the colour drain from my face. "What's the matter?" he demanded at once. "You look as if you'd seen a ghost. Where is Felix?"

It surprised me that he was foolish enough to mention Felix's name. Why should he be interested in Felix all of a sudden, unless . . .

"I have no idea," I said. "Where have you been?"

He studied me a moment, frowning, before he answered. "Out sparring with Gentleman Jackson. His racket was bothering Cook. She asked me to quieten him down. I spoke to him quite civilly, but the dog is a cur. You are right. I'll sell him back to Weldon, or pay him to take the beast away, if necessary. Otherwise he'll have to be put down, and I dislike to do that to a dumb animal."

"I shouldn't think talking to a dog would make such a mess of your clothing."

"He's a savage brute. I had no idea how strong he was. His first lunge sent me sprawling on my back. I'd best go and change for dinner."

"Yes, I was just about to do the same."

We parted, Otto going to the west wing, myself to the east. Before I had gone two yards, I broke into a run. I could not wait to get to my room and lock the door behind me. Otto! Otto had attacked poor Felix, and put such a fright into him that he was afraid to open his mouth. What reason could he possibly have for doing such a thing, except a fear that Felix knew something dangerous? Had Felix seen him going after Mrs. Manner in the park? Why had he kept it to himself for so long?

Perhaps Felix had not been sure. Otto must have let some chance remark fall that gave Felix a clue. I felt desolate, not only that a man could be capable of such treachery, but that the man was Otto. For a decade I had secretly loved him. I had lived for twelve months at a stretch on his few crumbs of compliments, that meant no more to him than a pat on a dog's head.

He had made a point of professing his love for dogs, to suggest he had not harmed Duke. I would ask Cook if she had complained to Otto about Jackson's howling. *I* had not heard it. Tending to Jackson could be a mere excuse to get out of the house without giving rise to questions. And of course it made a fine excuse for his disarray.

Or it could have been Gregory, as I first thought. Or even Horatio—I had no idea where he had spent that important quarter of an hour.

It could not have been a planned attack, because when Felix left the saloon early at tea-time, he had said he was going to the library. If only he had stayed there! The attack made unpleasantly clear that we who were innocent must be on guard every minute.

SIXTEEN

I was surprised to see another black gown, an evening gown, hanging in my room when I went to change for dinner. Mrs. Maherne had said something about sending me a gown she had been fashioning for a customer who had since become *enceinte,* and could no longer fit into it. I had not replied to her note, but obviously she had sent the gown along for my approval.

A new evening gown was usually a great event in my life, occurring once annually, like spring. This silk gown of unrelieved black was fashionably designed with black bugle beads its only ornament, but it brought no pleasure. It was cut low at the bodice. It looked like a headless woman, hanging there so stiffly. But I had urgent need of such a gown, and would keep it if it fit properly.

Of course I did not have a dresser. As the mistress of Downsview I might appoint one of the servants to this task now if I wished. I rang for Mary, not because I really wanted her help, but because I was nervous alone. I also wanted to ask some questions without alerting the household to what I was up to.

I knew by the maid's spontaneous "Cooo!" when I spoke to her that she was surprised and happy to be the chosen one.

"But miss, to have to be wearing black in front of all the gentlemen! What a pity it is, though the gown is handsome in its own way," she said, examining it. "There was talk below about whether you'd want a personal servant, like," she said, lifting the gown down. " 'Not she!' says Cook, but I thought to myself, why not? She's queen o' the castle now. I'd do it if it was me."

She assisted me into the black gown, which fit as if it had been fashioned for me, and looked well. It clung tightly to my waist and flared flirtatiously below, if a black skirt can be said to flirt. While she worked at the buttons, I said, "How is everything in the kitchen, Mary?"

"As good as can be expected," she said dolefully.

"That dog Mr. Farr brought did not cause too much bother, I hope?"

"Lord, it's worse than a banshee for wailing, and us a house of death. You could hear it howling three fields away."

"You should have told Mr. Farr the dog was bothering you."

"Cook did! That is to say she told Juteclaw, and he dropped Mr. Farr the hint. 'Twas comical to watch Mr. Farr dealing with the brute. Cook gave him a bone as big as the jaw-bone of an ass to feed the brute. The hound leaped on poor Mr. Farr and tried to wrestle the meat out of his hand. Mr. Farr went sprawling in the mud. Lord, it was better than a raree-show."

I duly noted this confirmation of Otto's story, while checking it for snakes and ladders. "Mr. Farr came rushing right back into the house, I fancy?"

"Devil a bit of it! He got hold of the rope around the brute's neck and headed for the stable, planning to take the dog back to Weldon, but he was back inside of a quarter of an hour. The hound was such a handful he couldn't manage both him and his mount, so he just tied Jackson up in the stable, and says he'll make Weldon come and fetch him. Mr. Farr is the third gent Weldon's sold that brute to, knowing full well he'd be back. We could of told Mr. Farr if he'd asked. Nobody can handle Gentleman Jackson except Mr. Weldon."

A quarter of an hour was long enough to attack Felix, especially as Otto had been at the stable, with access to a mount. Aunt Hettie kept a gentle bay mare for general use. I rode it at times, and occasionally a footman was allowed to get astride in an emergency. Otto might have taken the bay mare. That bruise above Felix's eye looked very much like a mark from a riding crop. And if Otto wanted to proceed at a faster pace than a trot, he would need to use a crop.

There was one other statement to question, and I said, "Mr. Chapman found the wine he wanted, did he, Mary? He mentioned he was in the cellar."

"Found it and took a dozen bottles to his room!" she said angrily. "He bribed Juteclaw with a bottle of the good Madeira to get the keys out of him. Juteclaw developed a little weakness that way, you know, miss, when the gout got hold of him last fall. Cook says the gout's gone, but he's stuck with the cure. Mind you, Juteclaw never helps hisself to the *good* wine. He only nips Cook's cooking sherry.

"Mr. Gregory was in the cellar for the better part of half an hour, nosing about, and when he come up he had six bottles in either hand. Lord, he was dust from head to toe from mucking about them dusty old racks. He went up to dress for dinner, and took the bottles with him without so much as a by your leave."

Then I was still in doubt. Gregory might have been rooting about the wine cellar, or he might have been out attacking Felix. To account for everyone, I said, "Was Mr. Horatio Farr also in the wine cellar?" I knew he was not, but wanted to learn if he had been seen by the servants during that important interval.

"No, miss. *He* is a gentleman. He was in the armaments-room, playing with the war toys. I happen to know, for he caught Juteclaw with the Madeira, and asked for a bottle to be sent to the armaments-room."

But he was not in the armaments-room when I went to the library. The door had been open, and the room empty.

Mary proved adept at arranging my coiffure. She lifted my hair high on my head and secured it with pins. Between the coiffure and the new gown, the lady gazing back at me from my mirror looked like an elegant stranger—a stranger with a haunted look in her eyes.

"What do you say to a touch of rouge?" Mary suggested daringly.

"I don't have any, Mary. My aunt did not approve of it."

"Mrs. Manner used it. She'd not begrudge it to you, miss."

It was eerie—I did not want the rouge of a dead lady on my cheeks. I looked at "my" ring. That was different. I had never taken it from my finger since the moment I put it on. It was a constant reminder of my old friend.

"I think not."

"I'll pinch your cheeks before you go down. It works well, but it don't last. Still, it's first impressions that count."

"I am ready to go downstairs now."

Mary gave my cheeks a pinch. "You look fine as a star, miss," she assured me. "It's none of my affair, but have you decided which of the gents you favor?"

"Perhaps none of them."

"Pshaw! We all know which one we want as master of Downsview!" I looked a question at her, already knowing the answer. "Mr. Otto, miss. I'm sure I don't know how any lady could resist him. What a laugh we had when Jackson sent him sprawling, and he merry as a grig. That's a good sign in a man, that he ain't too toplofty to enjoy a laugh at hisself."

"Yes, he is always good-natured," I agreed, and escaped.

No doubt it is a sad reflection on my character, but I was

concerned for the impression I would make in my new gown when I entered the saloon. My first thought was that I was entering an empty room. Only one lamp was lit, and there was no one around the grate, where we usually huddled in that draughty chamber. I glanced around, and saw, in the far corner, Anita and a gentleman. The corner was dim, but I could see she had one arm around his neck, and one hand cupped under his chin. Their foreheads were nearly touching. The black of his sleeve stood out in stark relief against the light violet of her gown. She is snuggling with Gregory, I thought with annoyance. They might at least choose a private place for it.

"Don't let me disturb you," I said satirically.

They had already leaped apart. Anita stood up and began patting her hair and skirt into place. When the gentleman rose, I recognized Otto, and could hardly believe my eyes. He walked forward, into the light, and stared at me as if he would like to run me through with cold steel. A frown pinched his brow, and drew lines from his nose to his mouth.

For a long moment we stood, eyeing each other like gladiators. I could think of no words to say. Felix's warning came back to me. "I do not trust Otto above half . . . He has always been unreliable . . ." But he had always kept his vice out of this house at least. Carrying on under my roof with a light-skirt — and his cousin's light-skirt at that — was really the outside of enough.

"This is not what you are thinking, Jess," he said in a cold, angry voice.

A burst of embarrassed laughter came from Anita. "You are only making it worse, Otto," she said, tapping his forearm with her white fingers. "Jessica already knows I am no provincial, and the whole of London knows *your* wanton ways." She turned a conning smile on me. "It was nothing at all, my dear. I was frightened in this *horrid* house, and Otto was trying to allay me fears. You must not say a *word* to Gregory."

I said in Arctic accents, "I may be a provincial, Anita, but I try to remember I am a lady. I do not carry tales."

What really vexed me to no small degree was that Anita had never looked more enticing. She wore another mauve gown whose only token of half-mourning was its color. In style, it was a very dashing, low-cut evening gown. Her mohair shawl was around her shoulders for warmth. Her eyes sparkled, and her hair gleamed in the lamplight.

While we three stood trying to conceal our embarrassment, Horatio appeared at the doorway. We greeted him and tried to assume a nonchalant air as he entered and began pouring sherry.

Anita looked at my stylish black gown and gave a little cluck of sympathy. "I know a modiste in London who can do things even with mourning-clothes," she said. "Once you get away where no one knows you, there is really no need to drape yourself in black crape."

I could find no suitable reply to such an outré suggestion. Horatio said, "She ain't going away. She's staying here."

He brought me a glass of sherry, and before long we were joined by Gregory and Felix. Anita looked at me nervously, wondering if she could trust me to keep her secret. The plaster over Felix's eye caused a welcome diversion. When asked about it, Felix turned pink and said he had walked into a door.

"Whilst walking with your nose stuck in a book," Gregory laughed.

"Something like that," Felix replied with a weak smile. His eyes just flickered to mine. Of course I did not reveal his secret either, but I could not keep myself from thinking about it. Which of these smiling gentlemen around the grate was the vicious brute who had attacked him? My instincts ruled Horatio out. At the moment, I was ready to believe any crime of Otto. And there was Gregory, Felix's own brother. Of course it was Cain who slew Abel.

I was conscious, while we drank our sherry, that Otto kept staring at me as if he would like to say something. I made a point of ignoring both him and Anita. When Juteclaw announced dinner, I went in on Felix's arm. Otto rushed to the seat on my right side, where he was ignored by me throughout dinner.

Gregory spoke of the liquid treasures in the cellar. He did not mention that he had availed himself of a dozen bottles. Horatio talked about his new pistols, and Otto regaled the company with some stories about Gentleman Jackson—the dog, that is. Anita and I listened without speaking much.

"I have written to Weldon asking him to come and take Jackson away," Otto said. "I shouldn't think he would come before tomorrow."

"There was no need for that," Felix said. "I will be calling on Weldon once more before I leave. I'll take Jackson with me."

"Are we free to leave, then?" Gregory asked, with joyful hope shining in his eyes.

"I am to deliver a lecture in London the day after tomorrow," Felix said. "I plan to leave by noon tomorrow. I wrote to let Croton know. He did not deign to reply, but he knows where to find me if he needs me for anything. Croton is not taking much interest in the affair. We have not even seen Culpepper all day."

"You won't want to take Jackson to Weldon's in your carriage," I told him. It occurred to me that he only wanted the dog for safety's sake.

Felix said, "I'll tie him to the carriage door and let him trot beside me. It is not far."

"I paid three guineas for the dog," Otto said. "I would be happy to sell him back for half of that."

"He won't pay you anything," I said icily. They were the first words I had said to Otto since leaving the saloon, and I only said them because they were unpleasant. "The servants tell me selling Jackson is a sideline business with John Weldon. You have made a bad bargain."

"That pleases you, no doubt."

"It is a matter of indifference to me, so long as you get the animal away from Downsview. I intend to maintain some minimal standards here, you must know."

He coloured up at the angry sting in my voice. He knew it was not only the dog I meant—and so did Anita. She began smiling and suggesting we two put our heads together over the fashion magazines after dinner.

It seemed strange, sitting at the head of the table, surrounded by four young gentlemen, with Anita pandering to me as if I were a queen. When dinner was over, we left the gentlemen to their port and retired to the saloon.

We were no sooner seated in front of the grate than she began apologizing and explaining once more about her and Otto. "I feel such a ninny-hammer! It did not mean a *thing,* Jessica."

"Then let us not discuss it any further," I suggested.

Then she started to harp at me about going with her to London, to Ireland, to Tunbridge Wells—anywhere, just so she had me under her wing.

"I fear for you, *alone* here, my dear," she said in an urgent voice. "Look at what happened to Felix! Do *you* believe that story about walking into a door? *I* do not. Someone *attacked* him. Who will be next? It is all to do with the money, of course. If the Farrs could eliminate you and the Chapmans, they would have the *entire* estate to themselves. I do not want to *frighten* you, Jess, but when that pistol went off this afternoon, I had a very strong impression Otto pushed my hand in your direction. It is *my* belief Horatio and Otto are in on it together. Why did Horatio load that gun when he was in the house and could not fire it?"

"He meant to fire into the grate. Horatio, you know, is not terribly sensible."

"I agree that Otto is behind the scheme," she said at once, putting her own interpretation on my words. "I shouldn't be surprised if he imported that dog for *no reason* but to attack you. He wants the *next* murder to look like an accident, you see. You were wise to refuse to accept the dog."

I did not accept her troubling remarks holus-bolus, but naturally they gave me reason to worry. She watched me like a hawk. After a moment she said, "Did he offer for you? Otto, I mean? Is *that* why you are so out-of-reason cross with me?"

"He made some facetious remark that he included himself amongst my suitors. Something of the sort."

"He would marry you in a minute if you'd have him."

"What of the lady he is betrothed to in London?"

"It is not actually a betrothal. He has been seeing Lady Mary, but you know Otto. Her dot does not *touch* yours. Did you see how *angry* he was when you caught us flirting? Really there would be no hurry to kill you, if he could convince you to marry him. He would have the handling of the money, and could dispose of you at his leisure."

"What an ideal marriage it sounds, to be sure."

"Marriage is never ideal," she said rather sadly. "If *I* were in your shoes, I would do just as you are doing, and not marry anyone. Though it is a shame to split up the fortune when you *could* have the lot."

There was more talk of Ireland and Tunbridge Wells, and when I expressed not a jot of interest, she discussed Brighton, though winter was not the season for this fashionable seaside resort. Anita was familiar with all the fashionable pleasure haunts. Her life was one long, desperate search for pleasure.

I was thoroughly fatigued by the time Gregory and Horatio joined us. I noticed Felix and Otto did not come into the saloon with the others, and inquired for Felix, though it was Otto I was really curious about.

"Felix has decided to pay his last visit to Weldon tonight," Gregory explained.

I was nervous for Felix's safety. When I saw him putting on his coat in the hall, I went out for a word.

"Must you go out alone at night?" I asked him.

He peered nervously into the saloon. "This is the best time to go, while they are all here. And I shall have Jackson with me."

"You won't have him with you on the way home. And Otto is not in the saloon. I don't know where he has gone."

"He just stepped upstairs for a moment. Something to do with the *Clarion,* no doubt."

He accepted his hat from Juteclaw and said, "Thank you, Juteclaw. That will be all. I shall let myself out."

He waited until Juteclaw had returned to his cubby-hole before saying more. "Have you thought about coming with me tomorrow, Jessica? I would feel much easier in my mind if you would come. You could stay with friends of mine in London. My old professor of philosophy is retired and lives with his wife in a pleasant cottage on the Thames. You would be safe there. No one would know where you are."

It was more appealing than Anita's offer, but hardly ideal either. Hettie had entrusted Downsview to me. How could I run it from London?

"They will all be gone soon," I said. "Then I shall be safe."

"Will you? If it were me, I would be worried every time I stepped out of the house. All it would take is one shot. There are so many trees in the park. Any one of them would provide excellent cover for a good marksman."

"That is certainly a frightening prospect. It makes me see that we must find the murderer, not run away from him, or I shall never feel safe."

After a frowning pause he said, "Perhaps you are right."

"Felix," I said urgently, grabbing his hand, "who was it who beat you this afternoon? You did see him. You must have."

He gazed into my eyes and said, "On my honour, I did not, Jessica. Do you think I would stand idly by and let a murderer run loose? No, I did not see him."

"Did he try to murder you? How did you escape?"

"It was sheer luck."

"But if he went after you with the intention of killing you, surely he must have had a weapon—a gun or a knife. He had your head covered. Why did he not finish the job?"

"I don't know," he said, frowning harder. "Perhaps he saw someone coming. Just when I was sure he was going to kill me, he let go and rode away."

"He was mounted, then?"

"He must have come on a horse. I heard a horse whickering in the distance. I think he whistled, and it came to him."

"You didn't see if it was Aunt Hettie's bay mare?"

"I had a bag over my head. By the time I had wrestled it off, he was gone."

"Which direction did he ride? Was it towards Downsview?"

"Yes. The man didn't speak—not one word. I have been thinking about all this. He did ride towards Downsview and the fact that he did not speak makes me wonder if it wasn't someone I know." His eyes slid to the saloon.

"Well, at least you are no longer pretending it was an unknown robber."

"It might have been that, too. I must go now."

I saw his carriage waiting at the front door. With a driver and Gentleman Jackson trotting alongside, I hoped he would be safe, but for one awful moment I feared this was the last time I would ever see Felix alive. Something came over me, and I reached up and placed a chaste kiss on his cheek. He looked very surprised, then he smiled and returned a warmer kiss, just missing my lips.

"My dear!" he said.

There was such a look in his eyes! I knew at once he had misread my intention. "That was just for good luck!" I said.

He gave an embarrassed smile. "Thank you." Then he left at once, leaving me feeling foolish and gauche, and still concerned for his safety.

When I turned, I saw Otto. He was coming down the staircase. His gait was stiff, and a cynical smile curved his lips.

SEVENTEEN

I must rearrange my bet! It seems the dark horse is pulling into the lead in the marriage sweepstake," Otto said, advancing. An angry light glowed in his dark eyes as he studied me.

Far from being ashamed, I was thrilled to death that he had seen me kissing Felix. I tossed my head and replied coolly, "I was merely warning him to be careful."

"A kiss is not usually considered a warning, but an encouragement."

"Is that what you were doing with Anita, encouraging her? No doubt you know all about that, Otto."

A light blazed in his obsidian eyes. "I fancy I know more about it than—but comparisons are odious. You must judge for yourself."

He swept me into his arms, there in the public hallway where anyone might have seen us, and assaulted me with a violent, angry embrace. Before I could prevent it, his strong arms crushed me against him. The stiff silk of my gown emitted a squeak, echoing the muffled protest that sounded in my throat. He paid no heed to either sound, but continued his attack, his hot lips firming to passion as I struggled to free myself. The harder I tried to escape, the harder his arms bound me to him. I felt as helpless as a kitten caught by a tiger.

A hot anger welled up in me that he dared to treat me as he had no doubt treated that trollop, Mrs. Rampling. I do not know when, or how, the anger was transmuted into something else, but as the kiss bore on and my struggles proved in vain, a more languorous feeling invaded me. A sensation of golden ease washed through my limbs, turning them to water. Otto was like an alchemist of yore, turning lead to gold. What had begun as an outright attack grew gentler as I ceased to resist, yet its effect was stronger.

I felt the heat of his lips inflaming mine. The flame spread to my chest, warming my whole body with its strange radiance, until I was glowing with an unknown euphoria. It was not love, at least not the sort of tame, unrequited love I had always felt for Otto. It was something entirely different—wilder, ecstatic, insatiable. Common sense abandoned me entirely. I forgot we were embracing in a public hallway. I could scarcely remember my name; how should I think of propriety? The only thought in my whole body was Otto, Otto, Otto!

When he had me suitably subdued, he slowly released me. I read the smile of satisfaction on his lips and despised myself, and him. My little triumph was that he was shaken too. There was a wild confusion in his eyes, though he tried to conceal it.

I wrenched away from him with a glare. "Is one assault a night not enough for you?"

"I did not assault Anita Rampling!"

"In her case, there may well have been compliance. If you are quite finished molesting me—"

"For the time being," he said, turning cynical again. "Just a word of caution, my pet, as you are so obviously a novice at this game. Next time a gentleman takes into his head to molest you, I would advise a little less cooperation on your part, or you will give him the notion you enjoy it."

"I assure you I did not enjoy it for one second."

"Ah well. I cannot hope to compete with the amorous Felix. I felt, myself, that it was one of my more successful efforts. Of course I lacked a wound. There is nothing like a wound to raise a lady's pity, and pity is akin to love, if we are to believe common gossip. I wonder if that is why Felix did it."

"Are you suggesting he wounded himself? Don't be absurd! He could hardly strike himself on the forehead."

"It would require more fortitude than I possess, but then Felix is a horse of another colour—a darker colour, as we have already established. I wager he did not walk into a door, in any case."

"Of course not. He was obviously attacked."

"And yet he has the courage to go out alone at night. A veritable hero—or a fool. Or perhaps a scoundrel," he added pensively.

"There is a scoundrel in the house, true enough, but it is not Felix Chapman."

"No, he is not here, at the moment. I suppose he has made you an offer?" His voice was almost bored, but his sharp eyes betrayed his interest.

"A lady does not boast of an offer unless or until she has accepted it," I parried.

"So he did offer."

"I did not say so."

"You did not say no. I should like to have heard him trying to do the pretty with a lady. What quotation did he bethump you with? *Amor omnia vincit?*"

"Nothing so pedestrian. French, not English or Latin, is the language of love, is it not?"

"*Je crois que oui, ma chère. Parles-tu français?*"

I knew at least that "*tu*" suggested greater intimacy than "*vous*," and said, "We spoke plain English."

His brows lowered in annoyance. "I would not rule young

Felix out, when you are counting up scoundrels, Jess. He has as much to gain as any of us by marrying you."

"What he would gain from marrying me is only money. That means nothing to him."

"Then he is unique in all the annals of mankind. Even a scholar might covet a more handsome presentation of his own *oeuvre*. Fancy Egyptian leather, gilt trim, perhaps. If he is any sort of scholar at all, he must have a hankering for a rare and expensive collection of books. Old Lord Arnoldson has his library up for sale, I hear."

"That is arrant nonsense! He does not care—"

"Does he not? Before you offer up his shiny jackets as a defense—"

"There is no need to defend the innocent."

"Surely you are mistaken! Is it not everyone's duty to defend the innocent?"

"You know perfectly well what I mean!"

"I am afraid I do. You mean Felix is considered above suspicion."

That was not exactly what I meant, but I accepted it. "Let us return to the saloon. They will all be wondering what we are up to."

"No, they won't. Anita has been peering round the doorjamb. She is bound to tell them. She lacks your ladylike quality of knowing when to remain silent and content herself with angry glares. You did a formidable job over dinner, my pet. I congratulate you. Hettie herself could not have mounted a higher horse. How I longed to topple you from your perch!"

I looked over my shoulder, but saw no one. "Are you saying Anita was spying on us?"

"Tit for tat. You spied on her."

"I did nothing of the sort. You were carrying on in public—and you knew perfectly well she is Gregory's mistress, too."

"Much safer to dally with either a wife or a mistress. If you can call it dallying."

"I did not notice much dallying to be sure. I expect you got down to business in a hurry."

"She wanted me to talk you into signing the affidavit to free up Hettie's money. Flirtation is the only weapon she is aware of, when dealing with a man."

"And the most likely to appeal to *you!*"

"Do you know, you are beginning to sound marvellously jealous, Jess?"

I ignored it. "Why should she think I would listen to you, of all people?"

"Why indeed, when you have such luminaries as Felix to whisper in your ear, but so it is. I am richer than the others, and will have a title one day. Such gents are considered the better *partis,* and ladies will often listen to a gentleman—until they have got him shackled."

"I have no intention of marrying you."

Glancing back to the saloon door, I thought I discerned some motion there. "She has been peering round the door-jamb all the while," Otto said, biting back a grin.

"You mean she really saw us!" I gasped, and felt myself blush.

"I fancy she did. She has a sharp eye in her head. Mind you, she is in no position to complain. A case of the pot calling the kettle black."

"This is intolerable!"

"Yes, isn't it?" he agreed. Without a single sign of shame he put his hand under my elbow to lead me back to the saloon. I did not see any sign of Anita, and thought he had only said so to annoy me. He lowered his head and said in an intimate way, "Next time we shall arrange our tryst more privately."

"There won't be a next time."

He drew to a stop. "Now there you are very much mistaken, my pet. I take leave to warn you, you have only whetted my appetite by that niggardly little kiss."

I gave a mental gasp at what he considered a niggardly little kiss. "It is odd this appetite only revealed itself after the reading of Hettie's will, Otto."

"On the contrary. I planned to speak to you before Hettie was killed. You recall I told you there was something I wished to say to you? But our drive was cancelled."

"You must take me for a fool. You had no intention of offering for me."

"It was always my intention—no, let us say hope, for intention is too presumptuous—to marry you."

"And for a decade you delayed? How very dilatory of you."

"I could hardly offer for a girl sixteen years old!" he shot back angrily. "To be fair, I was not really certain we would suit until three years ago. I was still wet behind the ears myself. It was not until I had done some mental comparing with other ladies I met in London that I realized—" He stopped, just when I hoped to hear him say he loved me.

"I was completely tied up with my journal by then. My finances were uncertain, and I could not give that degree of attention to a bride that she deserved."

My pride listened to all this with a satisfaction bordering on glee, but common sense prevented me from believing it. "If you did love me, you would have come more often than once a year."

"I wrote to Hettie about seeing you. She forbade it. She said I was welcome to marry you, but she would not have me turning your head and putting off other suitors until I was in a position to offer. Of course she hoped to palm Greg off on you. She also wrote some rather unpleasant things about my trying to wring a dowry out of her by the offer, to squander on my journal."

It sounded exactly like Hettie, but there was something in his pretty speech that did not ring true, and I soon pin-pointed it. "How did you feel you were in a position to offer this year, with a lawsuit for five thousand pounds hanging over your head?"

"I am thirty-one years old, Jess, and you are not exactly a deb. If we waited until our path was entirely smooth, we might be old and grey, for there is always something to cause a delay. You were not accustomed to luxury. If some skimping and cheese-paring are necessary, I felt you would not object. It seemed time to make my offer."

"Five thousand pounds would require more than cheese-paring."

He batted it away as if it were a midge. "That will come to nothing. It is a tempest in a teapot."

"A mere tempest!"

He pokered up then. "If you choose not to believe me, then I have nothing more to say. It is entirely possible Hettie saved my letters. You might have a look for them among her papers."

"I am hardly that interested," I lied, and we returned to the saloon in stony silence.

Anita turned a sharp eye on us. "Wherever have you been, Jessica?" she demanded. I could not tell whether she knew, or if it was only my absence that annoyed her.

"I was just seeing Felix off. He has gone to call on Weldon."

She suggested a game of whist. Horatio seconded it. Everyone seemed agreeable, but I had other things on my mind. I wanted to search through Hettie's private papers and see if I could find those letters from Otto.

"You have four people without me," I said. "I really do not feel like cards this evening. I have still not written all the death notices. I shall be in Aunt Hettie's study if I am needed."

"Why do you not write them here, where there is a fire and company?" Anita suggested.

"If there is not a fire in the study I may do that," I said, and escaped, with one last scalding look from Otto.

There was a small fire in the study. Felix spent so much time there that Juteclaw kept it going. I went to the desk and rooted through a welter of bills and letters. Everything was in a terrible jumble. Looking over her correspondence was like reliving the past ten years of my life. I found the letter Mama had written to Hettie before she died, asking if Hettie would take me. There were others letters from Mama, arranging the details.

"You will find Jessica a good girl. She will give you no trouble, and she is a willing worker. She is my greatest treasure, Hettie. Please be kind to her."

Hettie had fulfilled Mama's last request. She had been kind, but her last generosity had brought more trouble than she ever thought. I could not find any letters from Otto, but that did not mean he had not written. I wanted very much to believe he had. Gregory, I knew, wrote often, and none of his letters were here either. She had either destroyed them, or they were in her bedchamber. I would have a look there before retiring.

I felt upset, and looked for the wine decanter that is usually on the desk. It was not there, but I soon espied it on top of a bookcase just inside the door. Juteclaw must have been in a hurry. I had a glass of wine to settle my nerves. I thought it would be sherry, which was what Hettie drank, but it was Madeira. I found it too sweet, and only drank half a glass, then threw the rest on the fire.

From the hallway, I noticed the whist game was proceeding quietly. I did not disturb them, but told Juteclaw I was retiring, and he might tell the others so if they asked. I also asked him to let me know when Felix returned, for I was worried about him. "You can tell Mary. She'll inform me."

"That I will, miss."

As I mounted the stairs, I suddenly realized how very tired I was. It had not been a physically active day, but the mental and emotional strains were fatiguing. The search of Hettie's correspondence could wait until morning. I locked my bedroom and lay down on the bed. I would wait until I heard Felix was home safely before undressing. Before I knew it, I was asleep.

EIGHTEEN

In my dream, I wandered through a tractless void of fog, with nothing to guide me. My eyes could not see, but I felt with my heart a trembling fear, as of evil lurking in the mist around me. It advanced on soundless feet, creeping closer, closer. I ran, heart pounding, until I could run no more. As the fog receded, I found myself in the centre of a large circle, surrounded by black-jacketed gentlemen with eyeless faces. Each man carried a gold band between his teeth. Each set of lips was lifted in a frozen smile, but behind the smiling, eyeless façades lurked danger. The circle began to move withershins around me. There was no exit from the circle, no way out.

The eyeless men increased their speed until they were whirling recklessly, their tailcoats turned to a cloud of flowing skirts. I watched helplessly as the teeth holding the golden bands lengthened, grew to a wicked point, then began advancing on me, like a pack of mad dogs. I shrank to the ground, trying to protect my vulnerable throat from those menacing fangs. From the lurking fog beyond the circle, a bloodied canine beast slouched forward, then rose up on its powerful hind legs and lunged. Droplets of cold blood bespattered my face. I tried to shout, but terror constricted my throat. Only a muling whine issued from my lips.

I was aware of hands seizing me, shaking me, thrusting me into the maw of that canine beast. I leaped up from my pillow, bathed in perspiration, to see Anita Rampling bending over my bed. She had a bowl of water in her hand, which she was sprinkling in my face. Behind her, Felix watched in mute horror.

"Thank God she is all right," he gasped, and brushed past Anita to grab my two hands while I looked on, trying to distinguish reality from nightmare. Felix held no ring between his teeth; his eyes were not only where they ought to be, but were full of sympathy. A shudder of relief washed through me.

I gazed in bewilderment from one to the other, then past them to the closed door, like the closed circle of my dream. But here the closed space felt safe. I knew, at some deep level of consciousness, that what I was looking for was Otto.

I sat silent a moment to collect myself, then asked in a weak voice, "What happened? What time is it?"

"It is only half past ten," Anita said. "Juteclaw sent Mary to tell you Felix was back. When she found your door locked and she could not rouse you, she told Juteclaw. He let us in. Jessica, my dear, I fear it was no normal sleep. Did you take laudanum?"

"Of course not! I never take it."

"That is what Mary said. We believe, Felix and I, that you were poisoned."

"But that is impossible! I only ate what the rest of you ate. Are the others all right?"

"No one else was poisoned," she said, and stared at me with unblinking eyes to reinforce her meaning. "*Think,* Jessica! Was there nothing you took before coming upstairs? A cup of tea, a glass of wine . . ."

I remembered then. "Yes, a glass of Madeira when I was in the study looking for—for some note-paper," I said, because

I had no intention of telling them I was looking for Otto's letters. "You recall I had some letters to write, Anita."

"Madeira?" Felix asked. "But it is sherry that is in the study. I had a glass this afternoon and felt no ill effects."

"No, it was Madeira," I insisted.

"She is still raving," Felix said quietly aside to Anita.

"Go to the study and see, Felix," Anita said. "I'll stay with her. Mind you don't tell the others." Felix left.

"Then Ot——the others don't know?" I asked.

"We did not tell them. Juteclaw told Felix, since it was him you were concerned about. I had come up to my room for a shawl, and asked him what he was doing at your door. Jessica," she said, crouching on the edge of my bed and leaning her face into mine, "you really *must* get away from here. It isn't safe. No one can watch every bite one eats, and everything one sips. I have been *distracted* with worry about you."

"I think you are right. I really must get away."

"The best thing is to marry. *That* will settle the troublesome terms of your aunt's will. Now I *know* you are not interested in a real marriage, and I think I have got the answer. Marry Gregory. It will be a marriage in name only. He won't bother you in *that way*," she said. I knew what way she meant.

"No, really—" I protested weakly.

"It would suit *perfectly!* We could all have such a *jolly* time together. Gregory is not greedy. He would not expect to control the whole fortune. Say an even split, fifty-fifty. You are *both* ahead, for if you do not marry, you only get a fifth of the money."

"No, I could not—"

She saw the doubt in my eyes, and continued her urgent persuasions. "You are afraid he would murder you," she said bluntly. "He is not so brave. All you have to do is make a will bequeathing your half of the fortune to someone else, then there would be no advantage to him in killing you."

Even in my state of confusion, I could see some merit myself behind her thinking. Within a few moments, I also saw that while I lived, Anita and Greg could not marry. If he killed me, however, he could marry Anita and still have half the fortune. Was it Anita and Gregory who had doctored that Madeira? Having failed at murder, were they trying to get the money by this new ruse? I remembered thinking earlier that if I pretended to go along with marrying Gregory, he would leave me alone for the present at least, until I could get away.

Or was her plan even deeper and darker than this? She had been embracing Otto earlier this same evening. If she got me married off to Gregory, then she and Otto . . . But my mind was too disordered to see any financial advantage to her in that scheme, except that she could always whistle Gregory back, and pick his pocket by means of smiles and kisses.

"It is certainly something to think about," I said.

"We could get a special licence tomorrow," she urged.

"I feel so very weak, Anita. Let us discuss it in the morning." I lay back on the pillow and closed my eyes, hoping she would now leave me alone.

Felix was back inside of two minutes, holding the decanter of wine. "It is sherry," he announced. "I tasted it. Here, see for yourself." He handed the decanter to Anita.

She removed the stopper, sniffed it, and passed it under my nose. It was indeed sherry, but there had been a decanter of Madeira there earlier.

"I really should get back to the whist table," Anita said. "They will be wondering what is keeping me. Are you all right now, dear?"

"I'll stay with her a moment," Felix said.

"Be sure you leave the door open," the model of propriety advised.

"I am fully dressed, Anita," I said, and got up from the bed to remove any taint of lechery, in case anyone should pass the door and see us.

She gave my arm a squeeze and said in a conspiratorial manner, "We shall talk about it tomorrow. Everything will be all right. *You'll* see."

She whisked off downstairs to tell Gregory the news. I noticed she was wearing her pretty mohair shawl, the same one she had been wearing all evening. She had not come upstairs to get a shawl. She had seen Mary and Juteclaw in excited conversation, and come to investigate—perhaps to see if her plan had succeeded.

Felix was obviously ill at ease being alone in a lady's bedchamber. "You gave us such a fright, Jess," he said. "Why do I not get Mary to sleep in your room tonight? I shan't sleep a wink myself for worry about you."

"Felix, there was a decanter of Madeira in that study," I said.

"Then someone switched it before I returned."

"Gregory took a dozen bottles of Madeira up from the cellar this afternoon," I said. I did not accuse him outright, but let the words speak for themselves. A puzzled frown seized his face. I thought about what had happened and said, "Actually Gregory had no reason to think I would be in the study. You are the one who usually works there. Felix, that laudanum was meant for you! When he failed to kill you in the meadows, he resorted to poison."

"But Greg knows I dislike Madeira," he said simply. He did not deny that it was Gregory who had attacked him that afternoon, however.

"Oh." That brought me to a halt. "Does Anita know?"

"I have no idea. We are hardly on close terms." After a slight pause he said, "What were you doing in the study, Jessica?"

I found I could not tell the truth, even to Felix, so I spoke of what I had found, not what I was looking for. "Reading some letters from Mama. I mean to keep them, for sentimental reasons."

"I don't think it is Gregory who is behind this latest trick," he said. "He is not a subtle man.

"That is odd—Otto said the same thing." Perhaps they were right. It was hardly subtle to come right out and suggest a marriage of convenience. His only subtlety was to use Anita as his negotiator.

"There is subtlety afoot here," Felix said. *"Ars est celare artem.* True art is to conceal art. Perhaps the doctored wine was not meant for me, but put in the study to incriminate me—or to cause confusion, to distract us from the one who is truly at danger. You. All they think of is money, and you are the key to the fortune. Did the Farrs know about Gregory taking the Madeira? This could be a trick to aim the finger at him."

"Horatio did. He had a bottle taken to the armaments-room. He might have mentioned it to Otto."

"They used that bottle to fill the decanter they put in the study."

"That is possible. I might have died had I drunk a whole glass, or say two. I only took half a glass."

"Thank God for it! Why was that?" he asked. "I thought ladies liked a sweet wine."

"I don't. Hettie always served sherry, and I have come to prefer it."

"I still feel it was intended for you. I am pretty sure the Farrs know of my aversion to Madeira. Gregory took some bottles from the cellar, you say?"

"A dozen bottles, according to Mary."

"Then we cannot rule him out either, but who would want to incriminate me?" I said nothing, but I remembered Otto had made disparaging remarks about Felix on more than one occasion. "It was either Gregory or the Farrs," he continued. "I feel sure the decanter was destined for your chamber. If it was not put in the study to incriminate me, it may have been just a handy place to leave it for the nonce."

"It is odd, you know, but it was not on the desk, as it usually is. It was on top of the bookcase just inside the door."

Felix listened, nodding. "They all knew I was going out this evening, so if it was meant for me, why put it in the study? Why not take it to my bedroom? It would be interesting to know what happened to the bottle that was in the armaments-room, and also to know how many bottles are still in Greg's room."

"Yes, that would be interesting," I agreed.

He peered out the door, then darted off. He was gone for several minutes. When he returned he said, "The bottle is gone from the armaments-room. Mary tells me the servants did not remove it. Gregory's door is locked."

"That sounds suspicious—why lock his door?"

"It is not necessarily the Madeira he wants to keep secret. I saw him putting that pretty little Sèvres box in his pocket, the one from the table in the saloon. He is picking up a few knick-knacks to pawn when he returns to London."

I gave a "tsk" of annoyance. "He must be in a tight financial corner if he is sunk to petty pilfering."

"I chided him for taking it. He said Hettie intended to give him five hundred pounds, and he means to take five hundred pounds back to London with him, one way or the other. *Zonam perdidit*. He is without funds, as usual. Of course he is not the only one in urgent need of funds. They all are, really. We can trust no one."

"And when you leave tomorrow, I shan't even have you to—to talk to," I said, stumbling over the last words."

An anxious look seized his face. "You must come with me. Please, Jessica! I shan't have a moment's peace for worrying."

"It would be difficult to get away."

"All you have to do is get into the carriage. You need not tell anyone you are going. Except perhaps Juteclaw or Mary, or the others will raise an alarm and say I have abducted you."

It was a strong temptation to do as he suggested. Tomorrow Gregory would post over to the bishop to procure a special marriage licence. How was I to put him off?

"I shan't leave unless you come with me," Felix said firmly. "I won't leave you here unguarded. I dare not. You must come with me."

I was aware of a shadow at the door. I put my finger to my lips to caution Felix. He turned towards the door just as Otto stepped in. I wondered how long he had been listening. He was wearing his cynical face again.

"This goes from bad to worse!" he chided, shaking a finger at me. "Stolen kisses in public doorways are one thing, but really, my dear! When did you take to entertaining gentlemen in your boudoir? And why was I not told?" he added with a reckless, angry grin.

I noticed his eyes making a hasty tour of my toilette, to see if my hair or gown was disturbed. I lifted a hand to tidy my coiffure, which had become tumbled during my nightmare.

"That gesture is more telling than a ripped bodice," he informed me. He retained his cynical demeanour, but there was real anger glinting in his eyes.

"I wish you will get your mind out of the mire," I snapped. "I asked Juteclaw to send Felix to me for a moment when he returned. We have private matters to discuss."

"Indeed! Then might I suggest you go down to the study and discuss them like respectable folks, for you set the household a poor example by doing your 'discussing' in your boudoir."

"You, no doubt, would recommend the saloon?" I said, to remind him of his own indiscretion.

"I was just leaving," Felix said. I disliked that he truckled so easily to Otto. A lady's protector should have more bottom.

"And so, I trust, is Mr. Farr," I said, with a commanding look at Otto.

"After you, Sir Felix," Otto said. He made a flourishing bow and let Felix precede him from the room.

Otto remained behind a moment at the doorway. "You look like the wrath of God," he said, raking me from head to toe, then lifting his eyes to study my face at greater length. "Has that pup been frightening you with more Gothic tales? What was it this time—chased by a bogyman as he rode home?"

"If he was, he did not mention it."

"I noticed all the dashing upstairs as soon as Felix returned. Juteclaw, Mary, Anita, Felix—all running around and whispering. Then Felix dashed down and went back up with the wine decanter. Did you have a fainting spell?"

"No. You certainly kept a sharp lookout on what was going forth. It must have created havoc with the game of whist."

"Not much attention is required when playing with amateurs. It left me time to wonder just what you had been doing in Hettie's study. Did you find my letters?"

"What letters do you mean, Otto?" I asked, as if I had forgotten all about his writing to her about me.

"You know the letters I am referring to. If they are not in her desk, try her bedroom. They must be around the house somewhere. She never threw anything out."

"So you thought I would go darting off in search of these imaginary letters, did you?" I asked with a sneering smile.

"I was, shall we say, hopeful? If you had not even bothered to look it would have been a blow to my pride."

"Your pride is strong enough to withstand a few blows."

His jaws moved in anger. "There is more of Hettie in you than I realized. I did write the letters, Jessica," he said. "But enough of diverting me from the more interesting matter. Just what, exactly, happened here tonight?"

"I fell asleep. Mary could not rouse me, and became concerned."

"Why did she not tell me? Why Felix?"

"Why should she tell you?"

He silently ground his teeth, then said, "Like that, is it?" When I made no reply he turned, said, "Lock the door," and left without saying good night.

I locked the door, and was left to conjure on what he had told me. He knew, or strongly suspected, I would go to the study to look for the letters. Was that why the decanter of Madeira had been placed there? It was obviously the remainder of Horatio's bottle he had got hold of. He must have been in a hurry. He had not had time to put it on the desk, but only stuck in his arm and put it on top of the bookcase.

That would explain his keen interest in the commotion abovestairs. He must have been on thorns to know whether I had drunk the Madeira, and what effect it had. After I left, he had no doubt made an excuse from the card table to get rid of the Madeira and fill the decanter with sherry. There was little doubt in my mind that I must leave Downsview. Without even Felix here to help me, I was alone. Gregory or Otto—one of them was out to murder me. Or perhaps even Horatio, though he came lower on the list. Gregory might be staved off for a few days by my ruse of accepting his offer, but if Otto got wind of that, he would step up his efforts. A marriage to Gregory would deprive him of any hope of inheriting anything.

Fleeing was only a temporary solution, but I would put that drive with Felix to good use. I would weasel out of him what he knew. He must surely know who had attacked him in the park. Once he was free of Downsview, he might tell me. In London I would make further plans. Visit Bow Street, perhaps, and let the police seek the murderer. I could not handle the situation alone.

NINETEEN

I awoke in the night with my throat parched. I dared not even take a sip of water to ease the ache lest someone had put poison in it. But who? All through those long, sleepless hours I wrestled with the question. It all boiled down to money. What a wretched reflection on mankind that people would kill their own kin for gold. I would gladly give up any claim on Hettie's fortune if I could lay down this heavy burden of fear and suspicion. It weighed on me in the darkness of the night like a physical presence.

Had the doctored Madeira been meant for me? It still seemed more logical that Felix was the intended victim. He had already been attacked once. He was the one who regularly used the study. Otto could not know I would go there to search for his letters. But of course he did know. He was clever; he must have known for years that I harboured a tendre for him. I was seduced into a memory of that scalding, stolen kiss by the doorway. After that, he knew I would look for the letters. Perhaps that was why he had kissed me, to heat my passion. To think that evil could seem so sweet as that kiss! I could not bear to think of it.

I had no proof Otto was the perpetrator. It might be

Gregory, egged on by Anita. It was she who pressed on this idea of marriage. A lady who would scheme to sell her lover off to another lady was surely capable of anything. But Anita had not been here when Hettie and Mrs. Manner were murdered.

Horatio? His manner was awkward, but he was no fool. He had the wits to put himself forward as a suitor at the first opportunity. He had no management of his money. He might be in a worse financial bind than we knew. He had been at that gambling den, Mrs. Hennessey's, was it? He said he had seen Gregory there. Horatio would not have gone as a mere observer. And Horatio's bottle of Madeira was missing from the armaments-room. He admired the armaments-room so much—he had mentioned hoping to keep the antique armaments if Downsview was sold.

Felix, I thought, would not kill for the money itself, but Otto had mentioned some library that was for sale. That might lure him. That, or a more handsome presentation of his own books—also suggested by Otto. Otto frequently cast slurs on Felix. He had suggested Felix's scholarship was wanting, when the whole critical world was praising him to the skies. Otto probably was jealous, as Horatio said. There had been a certain jealous strain in his attitude when he saw Felix in my room earlier. My "boudoir" he called it, as though he had caught us in flagrante delicto. Otto and Anita—what was afoot there?

I enjoyed a few moments' contemplation of how he would act when he discovered I had gone to London with Felix. That would put him in a pelter! Just how we were to get away was a matter for deep scheming. My throat began to ache so wretchedly that I thought I must have one small sip of water, even if it was poisoned. I would have just one tiny sip, to wet my tongue. I reached for the carafe on my bedside table, fumbled in the darkness, then decided to light a lamp after all. If the water looked cloudy, if there was any precipitation in the bottom of the glass, I would not drink it.

I used the tinder-box to ignite the lamp. As I poured the water—-clear water—into the glass, I heard a slight sound outside my door. It was so slight I was not sure I had not imagined it. I sat bolt upright, ears straining. It came again, a light rustle, like the susurration made by a skirt when a lady moves. There was someone outside the door! Anita? Or a gentleman in a dressing gown? My breath caught in my lungs as I sat staring at the door, wondering if I should extinguish my lamp. But I feared the darkness. The lit lamp would warn the presence beyond the door that I was awake. My hope was that it would deter him—or her—from trying to enter.

The sound stopped. I sat for what seemed a long time, scarcely breathing. I was surprised to see that I held the glass in my hand, with a small quantity of water in it. It looked perfectly clear. I tasted it, just a drop. It tasted normal. I took one minuscule sip, then set the glass down on the table and sat staring at the door. I don't know how long I sat there, immobile, but when the silence continued for what seemed eons, I finally extinguished the lamp and lay down, rigid as a frozen rag.

After another indefinite period of time, I heard the sound again, the soft whisper of moving silk. As I lay staring at the invisible door, I heard the doorknob turn, heard the soft jarring sound as the door was tried, and found locked. My heart knocked so hard against my ribs I was sure the whole house could hear it. I waited, ready to screech my head off if he tried to get in, but nothing happened. He did not try to force the door open, or insert a key in it. The noises stopped then, and after a long time, I finally fell into a fitful doze.

When I awoke in the morning, the incident in the night seemed like a dream. Downsview was old. Old houses made random noises, especially at night. Mrs. Manner used to complain of it. Hettie said it was the rafters contracting as the house cooled after the fires were allowed to burn low. I half convinced myself I had imagined the whole thing.

But I had not imagined the doctored Madeira. Mary came tapping at the door at eight o'clock to help me dress. She brought a trace of everyday life with her.

"How are you feeling after last night, miss?" she asked.

"As well as can be expected."

"Fancy Mr. Felix hinting it was Mr. Otto as put the laudanum in your wine, miss. As if he would do such a thing to you! We all know who took a dozen bottles from the cellar, and one came down from his room empty this morning," she said with a sage look.

"I see!"

"Mind you, there's nothing unusual in that. Many's the time in the past we've taken two empty bottles away from Mr. Gregory's room of a morning. Is it to be the bombazine gown again?" she asked with distaste.

"The bombazine. I have only the one mourning gown for day wear."

"Cook says to tell you you may eat your breakfast without worry, for she's not let anyone next or nigh her larder. What you must do is only eat what everyone else eats. That way you're safe as a church. And if you fancy a bite between meals, I'll bring it straight from the kitchen myself, miss."

I entrusted Mary with the secret of my departure. I asked her to pack a small bag of necessities and have it smuggled into Mr. Felix's carriage.

"You're never leaving us, miss!" she exclaimed in shock.

"Only for a short while. I have some business in London. Mr. Felix will be driving me. You must not tell anyone except Cook. After breakfast I mean to come up to my room and steal down the back stairs, out to the carriage. I shall tell the guests I feel poorly and am staying in my room. Mrs. Rampling is likely to be the most persistent in inquiring for me."

"And that's a fact!"

"We must put her off somehow."

"Why don't I sit in your room myself? I'll draw the curtains and tell her you're sound asleep."

"That is an excellent idea, Mary. At lunch, Juteclaw may tell the others where I have gone."

Mary was sharp enough to grasp my plan at once. "They'll never be able to catch up with you after such a head start. Can you tell us where you're going, in case anything comes up?"

"I shall discover the address of Mr. Felix's friend and leave it with you, but don't tell any of our guests, Mary. Don't even write it down, but just keep it in your head."

"For fear they hunt you down like a fox and kill you," she said. "Lordie, what a way to live. You can hardly call it living at all, can you? Whoever thought it would be such a curse having money."

"It is more bother than it's worth."

"I really ought to go with you, miss. I hate to see you strike out alone."

How I would have loved to have her. "I shall ask Mr. Felix if his friend can accommodate two people."

"If I'm to go, though, who will put off Mrs. Rampling when she comes nosing about? There's no trusting Meg with such an important chore."

"I shall think of something. I would really like to have you with me, Mary."

"Oh, and I'd love to go, miss. It's like walking across the firing-line, living here. You never know who'll be next."

That was exactly how I felt as I went downstairs. The others had already assembled at the breakfast table. The gentlemen rose and greeted me.

"How are you this morning, Jess?" Anita asked.

"I am feeling a little tired. In fact, I plan to go back to bed as soon as I have had breakfast."

"You should not have come down. My dear, I would have been happy to take a tray upstairs and keep you company. I shall take a copy of *La Belle Assemblée* to your room after breakfast. We shall spend a quiet morning quizzing all the new fashions."

"That is very kind, but I have a touch of megrim. I mean to draw the blinds and try to get a little sleep."

When I went to the sideboard to choose my breakfast, Felix rose and joined me.

"I plan to leave at nine-thirty," he said in a low voice. "Have you thought of a way of joining me without being seen? I will not go without you, Jess."

"It is all arranged. I shall go out by the kitchen and get into your carriage before it is brought around. I shall hide myself under a blanket so no one suspects I am there, if they happen to look out."

His tense face relaxed into a smile. "Excellent!"

"I must have the address of your friend in London."

He gave me the address on the Chelsea Embankment, and the name of his friend, Doctor Evans. I committed it to memory and said, "Would he be able to put up a servant as well? I would like to take Mary with me."

"The Evans live in a small way," he said with a worried frown. "I hope I have not misled you. Really it is only a cottage. I dislike to impose on them, but if you feel you must have a servant . . ."

"No, that is all right. It was just an idea. Actually it will be easier for me to get away by myself, and Mary has a few things to do for me here."

We could not prolong our conversation without arousing curiosity. Otto was already directing curious stares in our direction. We returned to the table and I tried to eat something. I found myself looking along the board, wondering which of these people had been outside my door last night, and why. Had he—or indeed she, for I also suspected Anita Rampling—planned to sneak in and murder me? How had he planned to do it? A quiet kind of death would have been necessary. A pistol shot would not do. A pillow rammed against my nose and mouth?

I studied their expressions as I fiddled with my breakfast. Gregory and Anita looked smug, so she must have told him I was not averse to their plan. Horatio's whole interest was ostensibly concentrated on his gammon and eggs. Yet he wore a frown that was surely not caused by Cook's excellent food. Otto was pale and stiff and angry-looking. The paleness might be due to a lack of sleep, if he had been at my door in the night. The stiffness and anger were due to my conversation with Felix at the sideboard.

Otto was the first to leave the table. He excused himself curtly. Felix was the next to leave. Soon Horatio rose, said, "I shall be in the armaments-room if you need me, Jess," and left.

It was the signal for Anita to begin having at me about the marriage licence. Strangely, Gregory did not push the idea at all. I had the feeling he was not so keen for the plan. I soon slipped away and went upstairs. Mary was in my room, waiting to learn her fate. When I told her she was not to come with me she took it without sulking, and promised she would put Mrs. Rampling off if she came to my room. My outer garments and bandbox had already been slipped out to Felix's carriage. There remained nothing to do but to join them.

As I went down the hallway towards the servants' stairs, I noticed Aunt Hettie's door was ajar. My first thought was that it was Gregory, picking up some trinket. I peeked in, and saw Otto. He was at her private desk, rummaging through her papers. As I watched I saw him remove something from his inner jacket pocket and insert it in a yellow folder she kept in her desk. My curiosity was aroused, and I slipped back to my room to wait until he left. I intended to see what he had put into that folder.

I was no sooner in my room than a light tap came at the door. I had Mary answer it. Over her shoulder she said, "It's Mr. Otto, miss, wanting a word with you."

I went to the door. "What is it, Otto?" I asked.

He said, "I thought we might have a look through Aunt Hettie's papers to see if we might find those letters we spoke of last night."

I knew at once what he had been putting in the yellow folder. I went along with him to confirm my suspicion. He was too clever to pounce at once on the yellow folder. We wasted five minutes sorting through boxes containing her personal mementoes—concert bills, dance-cards, letters from her late husband and such things. When I purposely avoided the yellow folder, Otto was forced to open it himself.

"Here we are!" he exclaimed, and handed me two letters written in his own hand.

He had made some effort to age the paper by rubbing it until the first crispness was removed. The ink had been watered, to give the look of fading. I glanced at them. Of course he had written what he told me he had written. The first one asked if there was any possibility of Hettie's sending me to London for a visit, to stay with his parents at their house. Presumably she had said no. The second asked if he might come to Downsview at Easter, and went on to reveal a "long interest in Jessica."

How thrilled I would have been had the letters been written when he claimed they were. But as a ruse to trick me into marriage, they left me feeling ill.

"Very interesting, Otto," I said with a sneer.

"This proves I was telling the truth. You see they are written on my own stationery."

He obviously carried it about with him, as he had a deal of correspondence to write regarding the *Clarion*. "It does not prove when they were written," I replied.

"They are dated!" he said, pointing to the upper corner.

I stared hard at him. It was the first time I had ever seen Otto discomposed in just this way. I had seen him angry before, and bluffing his way out of a tight corner. I had seen him put on a charade of uninterest when Hettie hinted that Gregory was her favourite. I had even seen him bluster up at Hettie on my behalf, but I could not remember ever seeing him afraid to meet my gaze before.

"And the paper well-rubbed too," I added angrily. "This was a shabby trick, Otto. It is beneath you."

His brows drew together. "You are highly suspicious, ma'am. Are you saying—"

"Cut line, Otto. I saw you put the letters in this folder. You should have made sure the door was closed."

His shame quickly rose to anger. "So you have sunk to spying on me! Demme, I had to do something to bring you to your senses. I won't let you marry that weasel. I did write to Auntie. These are not the letters, but they are as close as I can remember the words. The meaning is the same. I was not trying to deceive you as to my feelings, and their duration."

"Forging letters is a poor way to convince me of your honesty. Good day, Otto. I mean to stay in my room today. Please don't come disturbing me."

"Have you given Felix the same orders?"

"Felix, you recall, is leaving us this morning," I reminded him.

"Thank God for that!" he said, and strode angrily from the room.

I waited until he had turned the corner, then I went quietly down the servants' stairs and out to Felix's carriage, wearing just my day frock. Mary had my bonnet, gloves, pelisse and reticule there waiting for me. I put on my pelisse, hid myself on the floor and pulled a blanket over my head.

TWENTY

It seemed a long time I waited in the cold darkness of the carriage, with the sounds and pungent reek of the stable all around me. Horses whickered and moved restlessly in their loose boxes, annoyed that Felix's team was getting out when *they* must stand idle. I had plenty of time to think, and mostly I thought about Otto's low stunt in trying to prove he had written to Hettie about marrying me. Surely she would not have been so cruel as to deprive me of marrying Otto years ago, when she knew in her heart I cared for him. Love and a cough cannot be hidden. Was that why she had written such a bizarre will, to make it up to me? She preferred that I marry Gregory, but she had not insisted. But no, those letters were merely a ruse to deceive me. And they might very well have done so, had I not seen Otto put them amongst Hettie's papers.

Eventually the carriage gave a lurch, telling me that the groom had mounted the box. We lumbered out of the stable and around to the front door. I heard Felix saying his adieus to Gregory, who had come to the door to see him off. Felix entered the carriage. He reached out and patted the blanket to make sure I was there, but he did not say anything. Until the front door was closed and we were a few yards down the

driveway, we both sat with bated breath, half-expecting someone would come out and force us to return.

As we drove beyond view of the house, Felix drew back
the blanket and said, "It's all right, Jessica. They can't see you
now. We're safe."

I felt as if the weight of the world had fallen from my
shoulders. I looked out on the bleak countryside and imagined
it was beautiful. Actually it was a cold, sullen day. The sky was
a dull pewter, with long clouds piled one on top of the other at
the horizon. Naked branches of oaks and elms were a tangle of
dark-grey limbs etched against the dreary sky, punctuated at
intervals by black firs frosted at their tips. The horses' breaths
spouted like steam from a kettle in the cold air.

We were approximately sixty miles from London. The
gentlemen spoke of a journey of five or six hours, but in Felix's
light carriage, with only one team to draw us, a more realistic
duration would be eight hours. The ride seemed endless already,
and we were not yet half-way to Littlehorn. We would jog
along all day in this cold, bumpy little rig, and still be driving
when night fell. Hettie's carriage was old but it was well-sprung
and the squabs were of velvet. Felix's carriage had black leather
squabs of an uncompromising hardness. The inferior springing
made one aware of every rise or depression in the road. It was
extremely dreary to contemplate the long voyage, and I thought
of how we might amuse ourselves. I would not rush into quizzing him about his beating in the meadows. First I would cement
our friendship and gain his confidence.

"Tell me about Doctor Evans and his wife, Felix," I said.

"As I warned you, they live simply. They do not have a
carriage, alas, but of course I shall put mine at your disposal when
I do not require it. Doctor Evans is like me—*Arcades ambo.*
Rural people, really, but civilized rurals. They will have plenty
of books."

"I am afraid we will arrive quite late."

"They will be at home. They seldom go out—that will suit you, as you are in mourning."

"Yes indeed," I said dutifully.

I was used to being house-bound, but I had anticipated going about a bit and seeing the sights of London This was to be my first visit, and I had heard so much about the metropolis. "Perhaps you and I could go to Bond Street and see the shops?" I ventured after a longish silence.

"Certainly, my dear. Doctor Evans is no *censor morum,* and you will no doubt require a few items for your toilette."

I essayed a few more suggestions, but met with so much Latin that I gave up and just sat silently looking out at the dismal countryside, shivering. Felix opened a book and read, despite the poor light and jiggling seat. The treacherous thought darted into my head that this visit would have been a deal livelier if it were Otto who was whisking me off to London. His well-sprung chaise would have a fur rug, and hot bricks to warm the feet. Despite our being in mourning, he would have arranged a few discreet outings for my visit. Then the image of him slyly inserting those letters into Hettie's yellow folder darted into my head to restore me to sanity. Better an honest dullard than a charming scoundrel.

Felix looked up and smiled gently. I was ready to try to like him, until he said, *"A natura rei,* I would say—"

I turned off my ears. Silence was preferable to trying to converse in an unknown language. I closed my eyes and pretended to be asleep. I would put my questions to him over lunch, when, presumably, he would stop reading. We hit a bad patch of road, and the carriage lurched uncomfortably. Suddenly something snapped, and the carriage tilted to one side, throwing me against the window.

"What on earth has happened!" I exclaimed.

"These unmetalled roads! They must have broken a

wheel," he said, and struggled out of the carriage to inspect the damage.

The groom hopped down from his perch and joined Felix. I bundled myself up in the blanket, wondering how many hours this would add to our journey. The groom would have to walk to Littlehorn, unless he could borrow a nag from a farmer. A worker would have to come and take the wheel to the stable-yard. Or perhaps he could make the repair on the spot if it was not too serious. I got out to see how much damage had been done.

"The axle has broken," Felix said, and gave a weary sigh. "There is nothing else for it, I shall have to send John Groom back to Downsview to borrow Gregory's rig."

"Gregory's! But surely the whole point is that no one knows I am with you."

"I told Gregory you were coming with me," he said. "It was the Farrs I did not want to know."

I did not trust Gregory by any means. And how had Gregory accepted it so calmly, when he planned to send off to the bishop for a special wedding licence that same day? Gregory did not want to marry me; that was the fact of the matter. Anita was trying to goad him into it. It was clear that the Chapman brothers were scheming together behind my back. This trip might be Gregory's idea for all I knew. I no longer felt it was such a good idea to go to London with Felix. What was to prevent Gregory from following us, and doing his mischief there?

"Can you not get your axle fixed in Littlehorn?" I asked.

"That could take hours. You know how they are. We are closer to Downsview. Run along, Ransom, and see if my brother will help us out. There's a good fellow."

The groom said, "If you say so, sir," and darted off, leaving me alone with Felix.

"We might as well get back inside. It will be warmer there," Felix said.

I was in such a pucker I declined. "The carriage is frigid. I shall walk to keep the blood flowing."

"Suit yourself."

He got into the carriage and I walked up and down the road for a minute, trying to decide what to do. I took my decision to go and tell Felix I would return to Downsview. I gave a look of disgust at the broken axle. It was a stout affair, about three inches thick. The carriage was new, and the road not that rough. How had the axle broken? I went and examined it. It had snapped close against the rear left wheel. I thought at first that it was not broken at all, but the wheel had just come loose. I took a closer look, and saw the break was perfectly smooth on half the surface of the axle. The other half was jagged. It had been sawn half-way through.

A shiver of fear trembled up my spine as I stood in the cold, gray air, looking at the source of the planned accident. Gregory was the only one who knew of our trip. He had not even told Anita, as he was bamming her he planned to marry me. Gregory had done it, then. For what possible purpose? It would suit him for me to vanish, if he did not want to marry me. Was it to keep us from reaching London? But we could hire a carriage if he refused to lend his to Felix, or take the mail-coach, for that matter. If we hurried, we could just make it.

I went to tell Felix about the sawn axle, but I did not suggest his brother as the culprit. He would not believe it. I suggested we take the coach. "We could borrow the Clancys's gig and drive to Littlehorn. They live less than a mile further along the road. We'll have to hurry."

"Nonsense!" he declared, in the maddening way of a gentleman when discussing horses or carriages with a lady. He condescended to examine the axle, and found an innocent reason for its having broken. "The flaw occurred at the coachworks. Someone began sawing it here, you see," he said, fingering the break, "then realized he had made it six inches too short, and just made another cut at the proper spot. Shoddy workmanship!"

"In any case, we could catch the coach if we hurried."

"I cannot leave my new carriage unguarded on the roadside. John Groom has gone to Downsview. I do not fancy making you walk a mile to the Clancys's place in this raw weather. Come into the carriage. I shall keep you warm," he said, with a conscious smile that was trying to be dashing and failing miserably.

A carriage appeared in the distance, coming from the direction of Downsview. "There, you see. Gregory has come to our aid already," he said.

"There has not been time."

I peered into the distance, trying to make out whose carriage it was. The team were bays, high-steppers like Otto's, but he drove greys. So did Gregory. Horatio, then.

My heart lifted. I trusted Horatio more than any of them. Him and Felix I considered fairly safe. Felix had betrayed me to Gregory, but I felt that was due more to naïveté than anything else. He would not have told Gregory of his plan if it were Gregory who had given him that beating in the park. Felix either truly did not know who had assaulted him, or he knew it was not Gregory.

Horatio's carriage drew to a stop when he spotted us. He stuck his head out the window and said, "Jessica, I did not know you had gone for a spin. I thought Felix was going to London this morning. I see you have met with a spot of trouble. Nasty day for a breakdown. Can I give you a lift home?"

Horatio's frown told me he was trying to make sense of my being with Felix at this time. He would soon work it out. I had lost my enthusiasm for London. Gregory was aware of our destination, and now Otto would know too, for Horatio could not be trusted to hold his tongue. There was no safety when all my suspected murderers knew where I was going. A decent carriage could overtake us before we were half-way there.

"Thank you," I said. "It is frigid here. Please take me home."

"Hop in," he said, and got out to hold the door for me.

I retrieved my bandbox and told Felix I had changed my mind. He was quite upset at first, but eventually accepted it. "I am surprised it was not Otto who dashed to your rescue," he said curtly. "I begin to wonder if you were not right about someone having damaged that axle on purpose. Of course Otto is sharp enough to send Horatio to do his errand for him. Take care you are not hopping from the frying-pan into the fire, Jessica."

"This carriage is no frying-pan. It is more like an ice-house," I retorted.

"I did not realize you had become accustomed to luxury so quickly!" he retaliated. "Just remember what I said. Do not put all your faith in the Farrs. They are not your real family, as Gregory and I are. You may tell Gregory I shan't use his rig after all, but wait until mine is repaired. I only asked for it for your comfort. I shall just drive his to Littlehorn and send it back to him. I expect he will have a few pointless errands to run today."

His insolent tone and sharp look told me he knew all about the plan to get a special licence. As he called it a "pointless" errand, I think he also knew that neither Gregory nor I had any intention of getting married.

"Have a safe journey," I said, trying to damp down my anger.

"*Absit invidia*, Jessica. *Vive, vale.*"

"If that means goodbye, then the same to you."

He just smiled a cool, cynical smile, then he lifted his book and ignored me.

In Horatio's carriage I wrapped myself in a cosy fur rug, placed my frozen feet on a hot brick and breathed a sigh of relief when the carriage lurched forward. His groom had turned the horses back towards Downsview while I took my unhappy leave of Felix.

"Was you making a bolt for it, Jess?" he asked bluntly.

"Yes, I was."

"Why, if you don't mind my asking?"

"Because I was afraid."

"Can't say I blame you, but me and Otto will look after you, never fear."

"How did you happen to be driving this way today?"

"Otto asked me to take a run into Littlehorn and pick up the latest journals. He was doing a bit of writing himself. I'll send my groom into the village for the papers after I get you home. If you wanted to get away, Jess, you should have told me. I would have taken you wherever you wanted to go."

"I have no place to go, Horatio. That is exactly the trouble. Felix offered to take me to stay with friends of his, Doctor Evans and his wife. He is a retired professor."

"Maybe he is, and maybe he ain't. I'm not calling Felix a liar, but once he got you alone in London, he could have done what he wanted with you. Did you ever think of that?"

"I don't think he wanted to do anything except bore me to tears. If you are thinking of a forced wedding, or something of that sort—"

"I was thinking of murder, actually," he said calmly. "Him and Greg, close as inkle-weavers. Greg would not have been a day behind him. And the Rampling as well. She would have lured you off somewhere . . ."

"I wish you will stop this! You're making my flesh crawl."

"Thing is, go to Mama. You'll be safe as a bug in a rug at Cleremont."

I had never been to Cleremont, but I had met Horatio's parents a few times when they called at Downsview. Lord Kidd was a kindly old gentleman, and his wife was a good-natured widgeon. Whatever I feared from Otto and Horatio, I would indeed feel safe with their parents.

"Do you think they would have me?" I asked.

"Delighted. Ought to have taken you there in the first place. I'll set it up."

I accepted with trembling joy. I felt some apprehension regarding how I would cope with the magnificence of noble life, but none for my safety. Once I was within the stone walls of Cleremont, my troubles would be over.

TWENTY-ONE

From the road we turned left through Downsview's gateless stone arch, shaped in a similar manner to the Gothic windows, into the park. Gregory's carriage was just coming out. The grooms exchanged a wave and each continued on his way. The road to the house was a gently curved sweep. As we progressed, the sombre walls and irregular roof-line of Downsview appeared through the trees. It was the first time I had examined it in any proprietary way. It was mine for the next year, and until I died, if I married one of the nephews.

I have described it as a "hideous monstrosity," and indeed that was the impression it had made on a lonesome, frightened young girl ten years before. I discovered now that over the decade my perception had changed. I had come to accept Downsview as home, and even to love it. It was gloomy inside, but the lancet windows and pointed arches lent a graceful touch to the design. In a more benign season, the trees and grass and shrubbery softened its austerity, but even in winter it was impressive. In a lady, its particular quality would be called "countenance." It held its chin high, truckling to no one; it knew its place in the world, and was proud of it.

As my secret journey was no longer a secret, we went into the house by the front door, with Horatio carrying my bandbox. It chanced that the purple saloon was empty. No one except Juteclaw saw me enter. He looked surprised but did not make any comment. I ran straight upstairs to remove my pelisse.

"Miss, you're back!" Mary exclaimed. "Whatever happened?"

"The carriage broke down. Has anyone been calling at my door?"

"That Rampling creature," she said with a sniff. "I told her you was indisposed. She was bound and bent she was getting in but I told her you was sound asleep. She said she'd be back after lunch. Will you still be here, miss?"

"I have returned for good, Mary."

"Oh, miss!" she exclaimed, in a tone that was half joy, half fear for my safety. "Have you decided to accept an offer then?"

"I have not made any decision yet. You may go back downstairs, Mary."

"You've only to give that bell a ring if you need me," she said, pointing to the bell-cord by the bed.

"I shall bear it in mind."

She left, and I went to the mirror to remove my bonnet and tidy my hair. I scarcely recognized the angry lady staring back at me. Some new iron had entered her spine. She stood taller, straighter, the defiant tilt of her chin lending her a new air of authority. Determination and anger had finally imbued me with enough countenance to do credit to Downsview. I was mistress now, and it was up to me to bring order to the chaos that engulfed us. What had possessed me to turn tail and run from my duties? The household depended on me, and it would be pusillanimous to shirk my duties. Hettie had expected better of me. I would make mistakes at first, but I would grow in stature until I filled the role thrust on me: Mistress of Downsview. I thrilled to the unspoken words, and all they implied.

Hettie would not have sat with her tongue between her teeth while a murderer was allowed to run loose. She would have harried and hounded Croton until he installed a man in the house to protect us, and uncover the murderer. That was his job; not mine. I had quite enough to do running my house.

I strode downstairs and went straight to the study to write a note to Croton. As soon as it was dispatched, I would begin to sort through Hettie's business papers and contact her man of finance to help me arrange affairs. I must have monies to run the house.

Juteclaw stuck his head out of the doorway as I passed. "Oh, it's you, miss," he said.

"You must call me Miss Greenwood, Juteclaw," I said severely. "And a butler does not speak until spoken to," I added, in very much the accents of my late aunt.

"Yes, miss. Miss Greenwood. Could I get you a cup o' tea?"

Well, at least he had called me Miss Greenwood. And I found I did want a cup of tea very much after my chilly morning. "In the study, at once, thank you."

He darted off, and I opened the door into the study. There at the desk sat Otto. He held the waste-paper basket in his hands and was sorting through its contents. The surface of my aunt's desk was littered with papers. It flew into my head that he was looking for the letters he had written to Hettie about me. Of course a second thought soon told me he would not expect to find them in the waste-basket, if they even existed.

His face was a mask of anger as he looked up at me. "A lady has just entered the room, Otto," I said, staring back in the same bold way, until he rose to his feet. His anger dwindled to surprise at my new air of authority. "We have servants to empty the waste-bins," I said. "May I ask why you have taken it on yourself to do their job for them?"

"I was looking for something," he said, tucking a crumpled sheet of paper into his jacket pocket.

"So I gathered. You are not likely to find much of interest there. Felix is the only one who has been using this room lately."

"I am aware of that." He swept the papers from the desk back into the waste-basket with one swipe of his hand and placed the basket back on the floor. "Did you wish to see me?" he asked.

"Not in the least. I wished to use the study, if you are quite finished with it." There was no air of supplication or apology in my words, but rather a suggestion that he leave.

"Yes, madam." He stood behind the chair and gestured me into it with a flourishing sweep.

I liked the sound of that "madam." It had more dignity than "Miss Greenwood." Spinsters of consequence often adopted the title of madam. I decided I would do so in future.

I said, "Thank you," and took up the indicated seat. "Was there anything else, Otto?" I asked coolly.

His brows drew together. "The Hindus have a theory of reincarnation," he said musingly. "Are you familiar with it?"

"Certainly not. I hold Christian beliefs."

"So do I, but if I did believe such things, I could believe Hettie had slipped into your body overnight."

"What interesting secrets she could tell me," I said, challenging him with a bright stare.

He met the stare, but not the challenge. "I expect you are going to begin cleaning the Augean stable here. Do you require any help? I am at liberty this morning."

"That is odd. Horatio told me you were too busy to go to Littlehorn for the journals, and sent him instead."

"I have finished my business."

But he had not been writing an article for the *Clarion*. He had been rooting through the rubbish. I said, "I can manage by myself, thank you."

"I did not realize you were an expert on investments. You will have a portfolio of tens of thousands of pounds to scrutinize. Consols, mortgages, stocks, bonds . . ."

"That is why Hettie hired a man of business. I must make an appointment with Walgrave. Meanwhile, I am quite capable of writing to Croton myself, and demanding to know why he has not appointed a man to guard Downsview." As I spoke, I drew a sheet of paper from the upper right-hand drawer and reached for a pen.

"You have become quite the lady of affairs," Otto said, chewing back a smile.

"Some are born capable of managing affairs, and some have affairs thrust upon them. I fall into the latter category."

"I trust you will manage Hettie's affairs more successfully than your own."

I knew what that bold grin meant—a love affair between Felix and myself. "We were speaking of business affairs, Otto," I said. "I assume Horatio has been speaking to you?"

"You may be very sure he reported your efforts at running away. I approve of your going to Cleremont, by the by."

"Thank you, but it is your mama's approval that I must have." I had forgotten all about Cleremont. My place was here.

"There is no necessity to wait for that."

"Actually I may not go at all. I shall see what Croton has to say. If he thinks I would be safer away until he catches the murderer, I might make a short visit. If your mama approves, that is to say."

"Demme, Jess, you must go at once."

"No, Otto. I must do as *I* think best."

"You are as stubborn as Hettie."

"Thank you, but I call it determination, not stubbornness. I have not found taking other people's advice to be in the least helpful. In future, I shall make my own mistakes." That did not come out quite as I planned.

"So the worm has turned," he said pensively.

"What a delightful turn of phrase!"

He leaned across the desk and stared deeply into my eyes. "Just remember where Hettie's 'determination' got her," he said in a menacing tone.

The blood rose to my cheeks and pounded in my veins. It was partly fear, and partly outrage. "Is that a threat, sir?"

"Call it a warning. And don't expect Croton to save you. He cannot have his man everywhere at once. He will hardly appoint someone to guard you for twelve months. Until the year is up, or until you marry, you are a prime target for murder. In fact, even marriage is no guarantee. You would really be much better off at Cleremont."

A new idea was beginning to take hold of me. What guarantee was there that my murderer would not stalk me within the walls of Cleremont? Both Otto and Horatio had complete access to it.

I schooled my voice to civility and said, "Do you spend much time there, Otto?"

"As much as I can. Of course my journal keeps me pretty busy, but weekends, perhaps . . ."

What a fool I was, to think Cleremont was any safer than Downsview. Nowhere was safe for me until this business was cleared up.

Juteclaw appeared at the door with the tea-tray. "Here is your tea, miss," he said, ignoring my orders, as he had always ignored Hettie's.

"Just put it here on the desk. I would ask you to join me, Otto, but I am really extremely busy," I said.

He took the hint and left, wearing a frown of dissatisfaction. Juteclaw turned to follow him out.

I said, "Would you ask Mary to come to the study, if you please, Juteclaw."

"Yes, miss."

While awaiting her arrival, I took a peek to see what Otto had found so interesting in the waste-basket. It was just what you would expect from Felix—bits of translations, with the name "Horace" or "Virgil" scrawled across the top. If there had been anything here, Otto had beaten me to it. He had found one sheet of sufficient interest to keep.

Mary soon came tapping at the door. I asked her to step in and close the door. "Whatever is it, miss?" she asked, eyes like saucers.

"Mary, I don't want you to spread this beyond these four walls, but Mr. Felix's carriage had been tampered with before we left. Someone sawed the axle nearly in half to ensure that it would break down. He must have got the saw from that cupboard at the back of the kitchen. I want you to see if you can discover who took it. Try to find out if any of the guests or their servants were at the stable either late last night or early this morning."

"Why, I already know, miss. 'Twas Bonham," she said, naming Otto's valet. "I saw him myself at six o'clock this morning. He was in the kitchen when I went down to stoke up the fire for breakfast. He was poking about the tool cupboard. Said he was looking for a screwdriver to tighten something on Mr. Otto's carriage."

"A screwdriver? What on earth is that?"

"It's some new tool folks in London are using, miss. I told him we didn't hold with such contraptions. He said in that case he'd use the blunt edge of his hasp-knife. He left the door of the tool cupboard ajar, and when I tried to close it, the end of the saw was holding it open. The saw wasn't put back in its proper place."

"And did he go to the stable?"

"He'd already been, hadn't he? He must of. The back door was unlocked. We keep it locked at night. He'd been out and back, mark my words, the bounder! You ought to report him to Mr. Otto."

I assumed he had been doing Mr. Otto's bidding. What I did not know was how Otto had known I would be in that carriage. Unless he had overheard Felix and me discuss it the night before, when he was loitering outside my "boudoir" door. Otto wanted to keep me here, that was clear. Or better, he wanted, if possible, to get me to Cleremont, where an "accident" could be arranged at his leisure. The law would not perform any scrupulous investigation of Lord Kidd's family or premises.

I dismissed Mary and sat conjuring with this discovery over tea. Otto had sent Horatio to Littlehorn that morning to verify that the carriage had indeed broken down, and to bring me back. And while we were out, he had been searching Hettie's study. He had been sorting through the waste papers when I came in, but he must have heard me in the hallway. The waste-bin had been a ruse. What he had really been doing was trying to discover how Auntie's fortune was tied up. How much cash he could hope to get his hands on immediately, in other words. Selling Downsview would take time, and that part of her monies that was in mortgages would also be difficult to realize quickly.

Hettie kept her investment portfolio in the lower left-hand drawer. I drew it out, and could see signs that the papers had been hastily stuffed in place. They were not as tidy as Hettie kept them. As I sorted through them, I noticed they were not in the right order. The ones on top dealt with consols and stocks that could be turned to cash immediately. The long-term investments were at the back. He must have been doing a quick calculation to determine whether his share would be enough to pay off his lawsuit. That was the paper he had stuffed into his pocket.

I returned the portfolio to its drawer and started to write requesting an immediate interview with Sir Aubrey Croton.

TWENTY-TWO

I had my reply from Sir Aubrey Croton's office by lunch-time. His secretary informed me that Sir Aubrey was at a horse auction in Grimstead, and not expected back before late evening. He had business in Littlehorn the next morning, and the secretary would ask him to call at Downsview on his way there, around ten o'clock. Meanwhile, I must not hesitate to avail myself of either Doctor Culpepper's or the constable's services if I had any problems. Problems indeed! Constable Hodgkins was about as much use as an old scarecrow in solving my problem, and Doctor Culpepper had his own practice to keep him busy.

The remaining guests assembled for lunch. Anita honoured me with so many grimaces and raised eyebrows and squinty looks that Horatio, never the soul of subtlety, asked her if she had got something in her eye. Gregory was not a party to her tacit questions. He seldom opened his mouth except to put mutton in it. His sole conversation was to complain that Felix had been sold a shoddy carriage.

"Demmed shame," he said. "He paid a pretty penny for it, too."

Otto looked the soul of innocence when this subject arose,

which convinced me he was guilty. An overly concerned look settles on his face when he is trying to conceal his misdeeds.

"Two hundred and fifty," Horatio said. "What he paid—told me. Not including the team, of course."

Otto did not speak as much as usual. He seemed distracted. "Where is Felix to speak this evening, Gregory?" he asked once.

"I'll be blessed if I know," Gregory replied. "At some scholastic society or other, very likely."

"At Rideau Hall," Horatio said. "To a bunch of schoolmasters called the Friends of Antiquity. They are trying to get Latin put into the curriculum of free schools, the scoundrels. They've no business to go lumbering healthy young minds with such stuff. I told Felix so."

"Did you see it advertised in the journal?" Otto asked.

"Eh? No, he told me so—at great length."

Anita took no interest in Horatio's speech. She turned to me and said, "I shall visit my friends in Littlehorn this afternoon, Jessica. Will you come with me? It would do you a *world* of good to get out of the house."

I was aware, throughout the meal, of Otto's dark eyes on me. I knew he was listening for my reply. Was he wondering if this outing would leave me vulnerable in some way, and planning how to exploit it? "I am afraid I have too much to do, Anita. I am writing to Hettie's man of business to tidy up her affairs."

She looked annoyed at my reply. She turned to Gregory and invited him to join her. He agreed. As soon as lunch was over, I went back to the study to do exactly as I had said I must. Before I got pen to paper, Anita's head appeared at the door.

"Well, Miss Greenwood!" she exclaimed angrily, demoting me from the former Jessica. "That was a shabby trick you played on me and Gregory. Slipping off to London with Felix. You had no intention of marrying Gregory."

"Nor he much interest in marrying me. It did not seem like a good idea, after I had considered it."

"Did a runaway match with Felix strike you as ideal?" she snipped. "Good God, if you are going to marry anyone, why not take Otto?"

"Why, I seem to recall your telling me Otto was already taken. And it was not a runaway match with Felix." Of course she already knew it.

"You might stand a chance with Otto. He is not *entirely* impervious to flirtation. He is here, and you have a larger dot than Lady Mary. Not that I am encouraging you to marry *anyone*. There is something to be said for independence after all."

"So there is. I shan't keep you, Anita," I said, looking at the letter-paper and lifting the pen.

She ignored my hints. "Have you made any arrangement for someone to replace me?" she asked. "I cannot stay buried in the country forever."

"That is something I wish to discuss with my advisers. I intend to hire a respectable older lady as soon as possible."

"If I am to stay past tomorrow, I must ask to be reimbursed," she said. "I have been put to considerable trouble and expense coming here."

"Certainly, Mrs. Rampling. In fact, I prefer it that way. Shall we say ten pounds?"

She looked pleased with this, and left with a smile on her sly face. I was relieved to make Mrs. Rampling an employee; it removed the onus of treating her like a friend. I assumed Gregory would return to London with her. I did not think Croton would prevent them from leaving. He took his duties lightly.

With Felix and Gregory and Anita gone, that would leave only the Farrs, and I had no intention of being alone in the house with them, with only an elderly lady for companion. If Croton would not install a guard, I would hire one until the Farrs left.

And when they left, I would be virtually alone at Downsview. The aftermath of the annual New Year's visit was always a particularly dreary time. This year, I would not even have Hettie and Mrs. Manner to help alleviate the gloom.

I finished my letters and gave them to Juteclaw to have delivered by a footman. My mind had been full of memories of Hettie and Mrs. Manner as I wrote. I felt tears stinging at the back of my eyes, and decided to go to my room to mourn in private. I also had to do some deep planning about the rest of my life. I could not stay alone at Downsview for a whole year. No one could take so much solitude and retain her sanity. I must get away, meet people, make new friends. I thought of Bath. It had always shone like a beacon to me. What I ought to do was look for a companion willing to accompany me to Bath. Eventually I would meet some gentleman who could love me for myself, and marry him, and we would set up a house of our own.

None of this could be undertaken until the mystery at Downsview was settled, however. Yet I knew everyone was eager to get away, and I could not count on Croton to detain them. How was anything to be settled if all the suspects dispersed? A man who has killed twice was not likely to cease his efforts only because I had removed to Bath. I would never know around what corner danger lurked. A shot from a doorway, poison put into my food, a sudden push in front of a moving carriage . . . The means of murder were infinite. Until the year was up, I could not call my life my own.

"You are wishing your life away," Hettie used to say, when I expressed a wish that some hovering event would hurry up and arrive. I would gladly have given away one year of it to find peace and safety.

I closed the study door behind me and went up the beautiful curved staircase to my room. The brass of the banister beneath my fingers was cold; the steps were grooved by the tread of my predecessors. As I turned towards the east wing, I saw

Otto just coming out of my bedchamber. A tide of anger swelled up at his impertinence. I strode briskly along to the door and demanded in a voice of fury what he thought he was doing.

"Trying to save your life," he growled.

"Indeed! And how is your spying around my room to accomplish that? For that matter, how did you get in? I had locked the door."

He held up a key. "With this," he said. "It is the key to my own bedroom. It fits yours as well. The same key opens all the bedchambers."

"A pity you had not known that last night, when you were outside my door," I said. Anger robbed me of discretion. "Yes, I heard you. If you had tried to get in, I would have raised such an outcry you would have been caught before you could stick a knife between my ribs."

He looked as if I had struck him. His mouth flew open and he stared in disbelief. "Well, upon my word! That is the thanks I get for losing a night's sleep trying to protect you! I did know last night that my key fit your door. I could have entered had I wished. And so could the murderer. I advise you to push a dresser in front of your door, until you remove to Cleremont."

"I have no intention of removing to Cleremont."

"Then you are extremely foolish."

"If you already knew that key fit my door, what is your excuse for being here now?"

"There is more than one way to skin a cat, and more than one way to enter a lady's bedchamber. As the situation now stands, it is possible your room will be broken into from outside the house. I was investigating the window."

"No one is likely to climb up a steep wall and break in via the window."

His nostrils pinched in annoyance. "You have heard of the ladder? Your window has no lock." The lower portion of the arched windows opened like a double door. The upper, arched part, was stationery.

Such spurious concern for the security of my room told me that any attempt from Otto was not likely to come while I was there. That left the rest of the huge house—and the rest of England, for that matter.

"It has a catch on the inside." I went to examine the window, with Otto following me.

"The catch is quite loose," he said, jiggling it. It did not strike me as impossible that he could shake it open. "Only to be expected in an old house." He reached over my shoulder, pulled two newly cut pieces of wood from between the windows and the bottom of the frames and opened the windows. "The pins are on the outside," he said, pointing to them. "All he has to do is quietly remove a pin and lift out the window while you sleep. He could get in with no trouble."

"It seems to me he would have the trouble of holding a large window while he balanced on a ladder. He could hardly drop it without raising the dead."

Otto was unhappy with this display of common sense from a mere female. "He could quietly set the window on the floor inside. It would help if you had been fed a drink of laudanum first, of course. There would inevitably be a little noise."

"What were those pieces of wood you removed before opening the window?"

He held them up. "I made them to stop the window. The windows open inwards. With that loose lock, it seemed a sensible precaution. I am not entirely happy they are stout enough to do the job. Metal would be better."

"What is the point of that, if he could lift the window from the hinges?"

"Removing the window would be a last resort. I am not even sure it could be done. I merely pointed it out as a precaution. Let it not be said I have been lacking in my efforts to save your life."

"And who do you imagine plans to get at me through the window, Otto, when those who would benefit from my death are already in the house?"

"I would not like to accuse anyone without more proof than I have managed to collect thus far."

"I doubt it is Horatio you have in mind."

His black slash of eyebrows rose in irritation. "He was never mechanically inclined," he replied.

"That only leaves one man, does it not? I am assuming you exclude yourself."

"That, at least, is a safe assumption. Safer than some of the others you are making."

"I am not making any assumptions, Otto. I realize there is also a lady who might be involved. I keep an open mind and a sharp eye on all my guests at all times."

"You are not watching them while they are away."

Was he suggesting Gregory and Anita were up to some mischief at Littlehorn? I don't know why, but the idea of an abduction popped into my head.

I accompanied him to the door. He seemed inclined to linger. "How is the accounting going?" he asked in a friendlier tone.

"I have not got started on it."

"You realize I must return to London very soon. When the Prince honours one with a lawsuit, it would be poor manners to fail to appear in court."

"I am sure Croton will have no objection to your leaving. He let Felix go to make his speech."

"It was not Croton's objection I was hoping to hear of, but yours, Jess. Don't let this come between us."

He used his honeyed courting voice. His eyes glowed with passion as they moved about my face, lingering on my lips. If I did not know better, I might easily be led to believe he was serious.

I replied in a mocking voice that showed my opinion of his performance. "Naturally the Prince of Wales must take precedence."

He left with a snort of annoyance, and I closed and locked my door. I thought of all that Otto had said. "Let it not be said I have been lacking in my efforts to save your life." That was what people would say, if I was killed. Otto would point to the pieces of wood in the window and shake his head, telling the others he had told me to lock my door. Obviously the man who was taking so many pains on my behalf would be above suspicion. Otto was always the clever one.

TWENTY-THREE

The interview with Otto had one beneficial effect. It lifted me out of the mournful mood that had caused the trip to my bedroom. I no longer wanted to cry; I wanted to strike someone, or throw a vase against the wall, or break a window. How dare Otto, or anyone, create such a dreadful situation! To take two human lives, and turn my own into this hell of frustration. He would not get away with it. The next time death came calling, I would be ready for it. I would not eat one bite that did not come directly from the kitchen, and be poisoned like Hettie. I would not leave the house alone, and be struck down like poor Mrs. Manner. I would have a locksmith change the lock on my bedchamber door, and I would carry a weapon on me at all times.

Not one of Horatio's dangerous guns with the hair-trigger. What, then? A knife. A good, sharp knife of a size that fit into the pocket of my skirt. I did not bother locking my door when I left. What was the point? I went down to the kitchen and borrowed a small vegetable paring knife from Cook, under the pretext that I required it to remove some hardened mud from my slippers. I did not want to alarm the servants.

Next I went to Juteclaw and asked him to send for the

locksmith to bring a stout lock and install it on my bedchamber door that very day. He must have sensed the new iron in my voice. He said, "Yes, Miss Greenwood." I would wait a little to become "madam."

When Hettie's man of business called—an eminently sensible man of middle years and neat appearance—he dealt not with an uncertain miss, but a lady determined to take the reins.

"I shall require a mature lady of sterling reputation to bear me company for the next year, Mr. Walgrave," I said. "Not too old, mind. Somewhere between forty and fifty. It is possible I shall be spending some time in Bath. Will you advertise, check the references, and bring me such replies as you deem suitable?"

We discussed the lady's remuneration and working conditions. After the terms of employment were clear, he mentioned he had a widowed sister living in Bath whom he would like me to meet. If we rubbed along, my problem might be solved. "She is just turned fifty. She has lived in Bath for three decades. She knows the place well by now." Walgrave was not only sensible but good-natured. If his sister was like him, she was just what I required. Before he left, it was arranged that she would pay him a visit next week, and he would bring her to tea at Downsview, for us to meet.

"Better than hiring a stranger," he said. "Letters of reference can be forged, and if the ex-mistress is dead, there is no way of corroborating them. I always have a suspicion when the ex-employer has passed on."

"Your sister sounds suitable. If she is wise as yourself, Mr. Walgrave, my problem is solved."

As I was seeing him out the door, Gregory and Anita returned from their drive. Gregory asked if he might see me alone in the study for a moment. There was no avoiding it, and we had a brief, rather unpleasant conversation.

"You know Hettie was planning to give me five hundred, Jessica," he said.

"Yes, to avoid cutting that stand of oaks that is already cut," I reminded him. "You systematically lied to her and in a way cheated her for over a decade, Gregory. I do not think it fair to give you five hundred and give the others nothing."

The murderous expression that leaped to his face was enough to make me reach for my knife. I did not draw it out, but it felt good to know it was there.

"She meant for us to have the lot," he said, growing red. "You know perfectly well she thought you would marry me."

"Perhaps, but she never for one moment imagined we would set up a *ménage à trois* with your mistress."

"Demme, it is Hettie's money! I was always her favourite."

"Actually it is her late husband's money. Farr money, in other words. She did feel genuine affection for you, and you deceived her at every turn. I am sorry, I cannot give you five hundred, but I will give you half that sum, provided you return the small objects you have stolen since arriving. It is true you had a special place in her affections."

"Two-fifty?" he asked. He did not even have the grace to blush at being called a liar and a thief. "Done!" he said, and jumped up with alacrity. "I shall put back the gewgaws, but Aldous's watch was meant for me. She did not put it in her will, but she always said so."

I had not realized he had rummaged through the box of mementoes in Hettie's toilet-table. Really, the man was unconscionable. His foraging might account for the light I saw in Hettie's room the afternoon Mary and I found Mrs. Manner in the park. "You may keep the watch," I said.

He was all smiles when he left. "Very kind of you, Cousin. About the wine cellar, if you want to sell it off before the end of the year, I know a chap in London who will give you top price for it."

"I don't believe Hettie meant for me to pillage her estate. We shall each get our fifth at the end of the year."

"Then you have definitely decided not to marry?" he asked eagerly.

"Let us say I have not definitely decided to marry."

"It is the same thing—oh, I see."

He frowned when he had worked out the difference. At the door he stopped and turned back. "Do you happen to know where Otto has gone? I saw him driving out of Littlehorn—heading away from Downsview, not towards it."

"No, I have no idea."

"Odd. He is not escaping to London, for he only had two horses, and he came with four. Oh well, probably courting some lady. You know Otto."

He gave a debonair laugh and left. I sat on alone, wondering what Otto could be doing on the far side of Littlehorn. No reason occurred to me, unless he did indeed know a charmer there. I also wondered why Gregory had told me. Gregory was certainly *not* a subtle man. He had blurted out about seeing Otto right after I told him I had not definitely decided to marry. Was he afraid I might succumb to Otto's blandishments, and was trying to blacken his character? This seemed the sort of petty thing Gregory would do. He was petty in both his behaviour and his desires. Two hundred and fifty pounds had put a smile on his face. It occurred to me that he was not the sort of big thinker to envisage a scheme to get the whole of Hettie's fortune. I realized it must have been Anita who had tried to push him into marrying me. Slipping gewgaws into his pocket was more his style. He was petty even in his sins.

The locksmith arrived quite promptly. I accompanied him upstairs and showed him which door was to get the new lock. Within half an hour I was called to approve it. It looked very stout and safe. He gave me the two keys and I put them in my pocket with my knife.

It kept nagging at me, what Otto was doing on the far side of Littlehorn. I decided to see if he had confided in Horatio. I ran Horatio to ground in his favourite spot, the armaments-room. He was not admiring the war toys, but sitting at the window holding a telescope to his eye, and gazing out at the park.

"I am afraid we are not entertaining you very well, Horatio," I said, advancing towards him.

"Nothing of the sort," he smiled. "I have been having a dandy time. A fox has got into the park. Don't I wish Hettie kept a pack of hounds and we could hunt Reynard. If we had brought our hunters, that is to say."

I noticed he had had another bottle of the Madeira brought up from the cellar. He noticed me noticing it, and blushed. "Don't worry, I ain't foxed. I never have more than a glass or two, though the last bottle I had here disappeared on me."

"I wonder who took it," I said, hoping he might know.

"The servants," he said vaguely. "I must keep an eye on—on Reynard." I felt he had been about to say something else. He lifted the telescope and turned it towards the park.

"Is that all you are watching?" I looked out the window. There was nothing to see except empty parkland. Weldon's place was beyond the park, but not visible from here.

"I am keeping an eye out for Weldon's dog as well. Otto tells me he has sold that brute of a Jackson again, to the butcher in Littlehorn. I thought I might see him fetching him home. He is little better than a thief, with his selling the beast over and over."

"He would not be bringing Jackson home through the park but by the road, Horatio."

"True." He set down his glass and looked sheepish. "I was chatting to Greg. Told me about the two-fifty."

"I plan to give you two-fifty as well. Sorry I could not make it the five hundred you need."

"Very kind of you. I feel like a dashed beggar."

"Please don't. The money belongs to us all."

"It is yours, for a year."

"Did Otto happen to tell you where he is going this afternoon?" I asked, making it sound as casual as I could.

"Eh?" A guilty look came over his face. "Otto? He went out, I believe."

"Gregory saw him leaving Littlehorn, driving away from Downsview, not towards it."

"Is that so?"

"He did not tell you where he is going, then?"

"Ah! Matter of fact, he did say something about having a word with the local M.P.—Skelling, is it? For the *Clarion,* you know. That could be it."

Skelling did live just beyond Littlehorn. I felt the question had been answered. "Very likely." As I turned to leave, I noticed Horatio's pistol case was still, or again, in the armaments-room. It was on the table with the astronomical implements. The open lid revealed only one pistol in the case.

"Where is your other pistol, Horatio?" I asked.

"Eh? Why, it is . . ." He looked flustered.

"Don't tell me it has disappeared! Someone has stolen it!"

"Nothing of the sort. I had my groom put it in the pocket of my carriage as a precaution. Mean to say, with a murderer loose . . ."

"Is this one charged?"

"No. It's as safe as may be. Would you like to have a practice shot now? There is time before dinner."

I thought Horatio was nearly one hundred percent safe, but still I did not want to be alone with him and a pistol. "Another time. I must go now."

I left Horatio to his fox-watching and returned to the study to attend to some personal letters. I would require more mourning-clothes, and I wrote to Mrs. Maherne asking her to let me know when it would be convenient for her to call. There were notes to neighbours thanking them for their attentions at the time of Hettie's death. My activities helped to keep more unpleasant thoughts at bay. Someone was trying to kill me. The gentlemen were eager to resume their normal lives; there were not many more days when I would be so easily available to them. The next attempt might come soon. Very soon.

Horatio's manner had seemed—uneasy, was the closest I could come to pin-pointing it. I felt he was prevaricating, both about what he was watching in the park, and about where his pistol was. And even about Otto's destination. All those "eh's?" suggested confusion, yet my questions had been straightforward enough.

Soon Juteclaw called me to tea. "Tea's on, miss," he said in his old style.

"Miss who?" I asked, to remind him.

"Why, yourself, miss," he said, looking around to see if he had overlooked someone.

Juteclaw was too old for his duties, but it would be a cruelty to retire him. He loved answering the doors and making his announcements.

"Of course," I said in a benign mood. I must not let my misery vent itself on the servants. "Has Mr. Otto returned, Juteclaw?"

"Never a sign of him, miss. He'll miss his tea, but he'll be back for dinner. Mary tells me his valet is in the kitchen this minute pressing up his black trousers. Oh, he's a demon for style, is Mr. Otto."

"You should not gossip about the guests, Juteclaw," I said, but my heart was not in it.

"Sure if we did not gossip, what would we have to talk about, miss? I always like a good gossip myself."

He held the door and I left, bested by my butler.

TWENTY-FOUR

Tea was a quiet affair, served in the purple saloon. As it came hot from the kitchen, passing directly from Cook's hands to Juteclaw's, I could eat without worry for my life. Gregory and Anita sat on a sofa a little apart from the rest of us, discussing their return to London. Horatio and I carried on a desultory conversation, mostly about Cleremont. Having learned from Otto that I did not intend to go there, he outlined its manifold charms to tempt me. I knew it was a marvel, but the features Horatio discussed were not those that interested me. Neither shooting nor hunting nor fishing were in my style. I was in deep mourning and could take little part in the social life, but that was what I really wanted to hear about.

As if by mutual consent, we all left the purple saloon as soon as we had finished our tea. "Back to the armaments-room for me," Horatio said.

"It is coming on dark. You won't be able to spot the fox," I pointed out.

"True. Would you mind if I took Hettie's mount out for a bit? I am skittish from sitting all day."

"Go ahead, but be careful. The park is full of rabbit holes. They will be hard to see at twilight."

I envied him his freedom. How I would have enjoyed a ride, but I dared not set myself up as a target. I remembered Felix's attack and said, "Do be careful, Horatio."

"He's not after me," he replied, which told me he was thinking of my danger, even if he did not often mention it.

I passed the time until dinner in my room alone, with the door locked. The new lock gave me a sense of security. The turbulent emotions of the day had fatigued me. I actually dozed off for an hour, and awoke feeling refreshed. Mary came tapping at the door at six-thirty to help me prepare for dinner.

"You've gone and got your skirt all wrinkled, miss," she said. "Why don't you wear a coloured gown? Sure it's only family. They won't mind if you're not all in black. You don't want the Rampling creature to outshine you entirely."

"No, I shall wear the black silk. Has Mr. Farr returned?"

"Indeed he has. He was asking after you, miss. He was pleased as punch to see you'd got a new lock installed on your door. He asked me if Cook had the extra key."

"Did he? And what did you tell him?"

"I told him I didn't know what you'd done with it, but you hadn't give it to Cook. What did you do with it, miss?"

"I kept both keys myself."

"Maybe you'd ought to give me one, for safety's sake."

I felt safer with both keys in my pocket. Otto could wind Mary round his thumb. She was wonderfully fond of him. "They are quite safe in my pocket." I transferred them, along with the small knife, to my evening gown before going downstairs. The pocket was small, but I managed to get them all in.

"I'll just tidy up your room, miss," Mary said. "If you leave me a key, I can lock up when I leave."

"There is no need." I began to wonder at her persistence. Had Otto set her the task of getting one of the keys? It was not the room I was concerned about, but myself. I would be sure to lock the door before retiring.

Otto and Horatio were in the purple saloon when I went downstairs. They both rose and bowed when I entered.

"You look very nice, Jess," Horatio said.

"I shall have a few more gowns made up soon."

Otto watched and listened, then said, "It is a pity your first foray into elegance must be hampered by mourning gowns. Pray do not take that as a slur on your former toilette. I meant only that you would look well in brighter colours."

"A nice scarlet or yaller," Horatio said, gazing at me through squinting eyes.

Otto's eyes twinkled. "Do you see yourself as a scarlet lady, Jess?" he asked, drawing me towards the sofa.

"The primary colours are too savage for me."

"And too *déclassée*," he added. "I am happy to see you got a new lock for that door. You have both keys safely put away?"

"Yes," I said curtly.

He did not ask me where they were, but he looked as if he would like to. Horatio stopped squinting and asked his brother how the interview with the M.P. had gone.

"I wanted Skelling's views on the Luddites, but one questions a politician in vain. He always wiggles into a defence of the Tory's policies if he is a Tory, or lambastes them if he is a Whig. Mr. Skelling is a Tory. I shan't waste space in the *Clarion* on his views."

Anita arrived next, looking very dashing in another violet gown, not the one she had worn the evening before. She really was extremely elegant. And she did not have a dresser with her either. She had arranged that intricate coiffure by herself. She fawned on Otto, was polite to me, and ignored Horatio, who picked up a journal and ignored us all.

Gregory joined us just before dinner was called. Otto took my arm and said in a low voice, "I wonder what kept Gregory. He was already upstairs dressing when I returned three-quarters of an hour ago."

"I expect Mrs. Rampling could tell you."

"Why, Jessica! Are you implying you know what real lovers do? I doubt he was boring her with Latin quotations."

"I should think even true lovers occasionally do other things than make love."

"But I did not say true. I said real."

"Is there a difference? I meant they were probably discussing their remove from Downsview."

I expected an argument on the nature of love, but he only said, "Did you get a reply from Croton?"

"He is to call tomorrow at ten."

"I must leave by tomorrow at the latest. I think you should go to Cleremont. Horatio can accompany you."

"What is the danger, when everyone has left?"

"Who is to say they won't return?"

We had reached the dining-room. I took my seat at the head of the table without making a reply, but I was perfectly aware that what he said was true. Gregory sat at the foot of the table. Anita complained that the board was too long; we should all sit at one end. When no one paid her any heed, she moved down and sat beside Gregory. It was not a pleasant meal. The mutton was underdone for my taste and the fowl was dry. Or perhaps I was just not hungry. I noticed the others were only pecking at their food too. There was an air of uneasiness in the room. As before, conversation would cease for a noticeable length of time, then two or three people would speak at once, just to break the ominous silence.

Otto kept casting glances out the window, or perhaps he was looking at our reflection in the glass. He really could not see anything beyond, for it was pitch-black out. I was eager to escape and leave the gentlemen to their port. When we ladies retired to the saloon, Anita decided she was my friend again, and resumed calling me Jessica. She repeated her offer to stay with her in London, or go with her to Ireland if I preferred. She did not dredge up the old idea of a *ménage à trois,* for which I was grateful.

The gentlemen soon joined us, but had hardly taken a seat before Otto excused himself, saying he had work to do. He would give Skelling a few paragraphs after all.

"Make them suitably flattering. It would stand you in good stead with Prinney," Gregory suggested. He was always ready for ways to turn a situation to one's advantage. It was second nature to him.

"My principles are not so elastic," Otto replied.

"For God's sake, don't rip up at Skelling at least," Horatio said with a frown.

It seemed Horatio was not so sure the lawsuit would be dropped. As Horatio took his opinions from his brother, then Otto must be in real jeopardy of having to pay the five thousand and losing his beloved journal. That, I felt, was the only thing that might drive him to murder. It was certainly not an excuse. Nothing could excuse such a heinous act, but it was a motive.

Anita suggested a game of whist. When no one showed any interest, she did not pursue it. We sat about, talking desultorily for half an hour. Gregory picked up a journal; Anita opened one of the fashion publications that she had brought with her. Horatio decided to write to his mama, and went to the library to do it. I remained in the saloon long enough to show my goodwill, but when the others kept reading, I decided to get a book from the library and read it there, to bear Horatio company.

I was not really surprised to see he had been lured into the armaments-room. I went to the library and read, feeling secure to know he was across the hallway from me, within shouting distance. And of course I still had the knife in my pocket. At ten o'clock I went upstairs to bed.

I stopped at the top of the staircase and looked along the

corridor leading to my room. There was no one there. I looked towards the west wing and saw Otto at the far end of the hall. He came pacing towards me.

"That window was open an inch at the bottom," he said in some excitement. There were square windows at either end of the hall for light and ventilation. They were not mullioned windows, but opened by raising the bottom half. "Surely Hettie did not keep it open in winter?"

"No, of course not. The servants must have done it. Young Almond, one of the footmen, will sometimes leave it open and sneak in that way when he has been out late. There is a stout vine growing up the wall there. Almond is seeing a young serving wench from Weldon's. He chooses the west wing as it is usually empty."

"A girl from Weldon's, you say?"

"Yes, Jeanie Pughe. They plan to marry in the spring."

"I closed the window and fastened it. Let young Almond wake Cook to get in. He should not be sneaking around behind her back."

"I thought you would be more sympathetic to young lovers, Otto. By all means leave the window fastened if it will make you feel better."

He accompanied me to my room. I could see the door was ajar and a light burning within, telling me that Mary was on guard.

Otto said, "I want to hear your key turn in the lock before I leave."

"Would you also like to see that the window has not been removed?"

He defeated my attempt at satire by giving me a serious reply. "You would notice that, though you have been singularly unobservant in certain other respects. Will Mary sleep in your room?"

"That won't be necessary, with the precautions I have taken."

"I shall wait until she comes out," he said, and leaned against the wall to do just that.

"She will be out at once. I am accustomed to doing my own dressing. Good night, Otto. I hope you sleep well."

"I shan't sleep. If you hear a sound outside your door in the night, don't be frightened. It will only be your faithful hound, watching out for your safety."

"How reassuring," I said in a thin voice.

Otto bit back some sharp reply and said, "You are welcome, Jessica."

I went into my chamber, closing the door behind me. Mary had been helping with the cleaning up in the kitchen. She said she would press the bombazine and have it in my room by morning. I sent her off and locked the door behind her.

As it was early, I did not undress at once, but prowled the room for a few minutes, trying to shake off the uneasiness that bothered me. All Otto's talk of opened windows and guarding my door had filled me with nervous apprehension. He had Mary now to testify that he was taking every precaution for my safety. Well, tomorrow he would be gone, and tonight I would be perfectly safe, with the new lock on my door. I went to look out the window, in case there should be a mysterious ladder in the vicinity. I noticed the wooden strips Otto had made were not there. I could not remember seeing him replace them after he had taken them out to show me.

I did not think the window a likely means of access by any means, but I was curious what had happened to the wood strips. I found them in the waste-basket beside my desk. Perhaps they had fallen, and Mary had picked them up. I jiggled the windows. The catch did seem very loose. Telling myself I was obsessed with caution, I jammed them back in at the window.

Remembering last night's attack of thirst, I looked at my

water decanter. That was one danger that attended having left my door unlocked. I rang and asked Mary to bring me up a fresh decanter of water, straight from the kitchen pump. She was happy to oblige me.

"Mr. Otto will be glad to hear you're being so cautious, miss. Are you sure you don't want me to sleep in your room?"

"Quite sure, thank you. You will sleep better in your own bed."

"No, miss, on the floor in Cook's room," she replied.

"I am taking no chances with my life."

When she returned with the water, she wanted to help me undress. I let her, as she was so eager, but first I removed the keys and small knife from my pocket, hiding the latter from her in the palm of my hand.

"Now look at that!" she said, examining the black silk. "You've gone and got a rip at the pocket." The keys and knife were heavy. A few stitches had come undone. "I'll take it to my room and fix it up for you, miss. A stitch will make it good as new."

It was an unaccustomed luxury to have these chores done for me. I never much cared for sewing, and was happy to let her do it. I was finally alone, with the door locked, the windows protected, with safe water in case I should need it in the night, and with the knife under my pillow. So what could account for the morbid sense of misapprehension that hung about me? It was just nerves. Every little squeak and squawk that sounded in the old house became an assailant creeping up on me. I heard sounds under the bed, in the clothes-press, from the doorway, and from every corner of the room.

I resolutely blew out the lamp, lay my head on the pillow, closed my eyes, and thought of Bath. I would go to Bath with Mr. Walgrave's widowed sister as my chaperone, and all these foolish fancies would evaporate. I would not let myself become a laughable spinster, looking under her bed at night. After the year of mourning was up, I would register my name at the assembly rooms and meet some people my own age.

Anything is bearable, as long as one has something pleasant to look forward to. My heart stopped racing, my eyelids fluttered, and eventually I fell into a fitful doze.

TWENTY-FIVE

I awakened in the dead of night with a convulsive leap that felt as though my body had gone on a dream trip and returned to bed with a jarring thump. Thoroughly awake, I lay quiet a moment, trying to remember what I had been dreaming that caused my whole body to give that start. As I lay in the dark with my heart gradually slowing to normal, I heard a squeak from the far corner of the room. I was accustomed to the usual night sounds of my room. This one was different, not the complaint of shrinking wood, but a definite sound of movement.

My body tensed as I lay waiting to hear if it came again. The next noise was different, the soft, furtive rustle of silk. I could not imagine what made that sound. Then it came again, more noticeable now, followed by a slower, measured sound as of cautious movement, there in the far corner. What was there? Not the door, not the window, but the clothes-press. My clenched heart relaxed. Mary had left the door of the clothes-press ajar. The slight squeaking sound was the door swinging on its hinges, the rustle was my gowns, disturbed by a vagrant breeze. I listened again, and heard nothing.

My eyelids closed once more and I soon returned to that

somnolent state that precedes sleep; not quite waking, not quite asleep. It was a different sound that roused me from the threshold of sleep. Something moved in the hallway beyond my door. It was just one short, sharp complaint from the floorboards. Otto? He had told me not to worry if I heard him prowling the halls. That was like telling a chicken not to worry if the fox came to visit the coop.

I stared towards the door. The door is an aged, dark-panelled piece of wood. Its rectangle was easily distinguishable against the lighter wallpaper. I would see if it moved, but first I would hear if he tried to insert a key. He could not possibly have a key. I was safe, and tomorrow he would be gone. That was hardly a cheering thought either. Otto's annual visit had been the emotional lodestar of my life for so many years that I could not imagine life without it. There hardly seemed any point in existing.

As I lay thinking these morose thoughts, I was seized with the absurd idea that I was not alone in the room. It is impossible to describe the sensation, for it has no basis in physical reality. I did not hear a sound, or see a moving shadow, or smell a different smell. It was just a *feeling,* but so strong a feeling that it became a certainty in my mind. Someone was in my room, and I lay rigid with fear, afraid to breathe. My heart throbbed heavily, and a cold perspiration bathed my brow. Rational thought was impossible. He was here, in my room, peering at me through the concealing shadows, waiting to pounce.

He had found a way in after all. Was there a secret panel I was unaware of? A priest's hole, a trapdoor in the ceiling? After ten years of occupancy, I knew there was no such thing. He had somehow got hold of a key. I remembered his trip beyond Littlehorn, supposedly to speak to Skelling, but the locksmith also lived beyond Littlehorn. He must have gotten in while I dozed.

That was my last semi-rational thought. It was cut off by

the soft, padding sound of unshod feet rushing from the corner by the clothes-press. Once he decided to move, he moved with the speed and certainty of a jungle cat leaping on its prey. There was no time to seize my knife. In the split second that I realized what was happening, I reached under the pillow for it, but it was not there. It had slipped, or shifted beyond my grasp. I tried to rise, but before my head was off the pillow, a man leaped onto the bed and seized my shoulders. With his full strength, he pressed me down against the mattress.

I could not see his size or shape or grasp any idea of his face. He was a brute force, too strong for me to overcome. His legs straddled my body, pinioning me to the bed, and suddenly he was pushing a softly suffocating pillow against my face. I turned my head aside and screamed as loudly as my condition allowed. The muffled scream was weak, even to my own ears. No one beyond the room could possibly hear it.

He didn't speak, not a word. The silence was worse than threats. It seemed inhuman. The only sound was his laboured breathings, and the almost inaudible scuffle of our bodies wrestling on the feather tick as I fought for my life. His dead weight sat on my stomach, making it impossible for me to use my legs to any effect. My arms flailed, trying to dislodge his hands from the pillow. He moved one hand to seize my wrists. I managed to pull my head free from the suffocating pillow and shouted, a little louder this time. Desperation lent me strength. He had a firm grip on one arm, but I kept the other from him.

I heard a sound from the next room, Mrs. Manner's room, that had been vacant since her death. In my disordered mental state, I thought for a moment that it was she, back from the dead to save me. Anything seemed possible that moment. The laboured breathing above me deepened to an angry, inhuman growl. The dead weight shifted upwards, and I felt his chest press against my face as he grappled to get hold of my head. His fingers were in my hair, wrenching my head back under the pillow. I struggled with all my force, but there was a sinewy strength in his arms.

At some instinctive level of consciousness my mind was struggling to learn who was killing me. A person had the right to know that, at least. Gregory, Horatio, Otto . . . I fought the awful knowledge, but there was no denying the truth. It was Otto who had been lurking about my room; Otto who was in desperate need of money; Otto who had tried to lure me into marriage by forging letters. Having failed in that, he had come to kill me now, while he had the chance. I hardly had the heart to go on struggling, but the instinct for survival is an overwhelming force. A cornered rat will attack a dog fifty times its size.

I wrenched my hand free from his groping fingers to seek a weapon on the bedside table. The lamp, the decanter, my Bible—anything I could pick up to aim at his head. He seized my hand just as my fingers closed over the neck of the decanter. I managed to hold on to my puny weapon, but he saw, or sensed it, and pulled it from me. It slipped, hitting the lamp. A jarring crash ensued as the lamp rattled to the floor. I was caught off-guard a moment, and the man's hands now found their way around my neck. He was finished with the subtlety of a pillow. He was going to strangle the life out of me with his bare hands. The ends of his hot fingers pressed into my throat. I felt the blood throb against those pressing fingers, measuring my last heartbeats.

While consciousness remained I fought back. My fingernails clawed at those strong fingers squeezing the breath of life from me, but they clawed in vain. He had the strength, and the endurance, of desperation. I heard faint echoes of falling footsteps in the distance, a slamming door, and realized dimly that help was on its way. But I feared it would be too late. Already life was stealing away. My lungs felt as if they had collapsed, or burst. Darkness fell like sudden nightfall over my mind, softening the horror of it all. Just when it should have been over, the man's hands relaxed on my throat. I took a rasping, painful gulp of air, and heard the door to the hall rattle on its hinges.

An overwrought voice called, "Jessica! Jessica! Are you all right? Let me in." It sounded like an hysterical echo coming from far away.

My assailant finally opened his mouth to release an ugly flow of profanities. I still did not recognize the voice, but it matched its owner's ferocity. Anger lent it a harsh, barking tone. He leaped from the bed and made a dash for the window. I was too weak to try to stop him. I lay gasping against the pillows. I was still conscious, however, and heard my door being kicked and battered down. Across the room, my assailant was yanking the draperies from the window in his haste to escape by the only other exit.

As the draperies fell, moonlight flooded the chamber, showing me the slender silhouette of Felix Chapman, his face distorted with fear, wide eyes staring at the door, which was giving way. He stood a moment in indecision, then began trying to wrench open the mullioned window that I had fastened with the strips of wood. The irony of it escaped me at the time—that I should have trapped my murderer in the room, rather than keeping him out.

He was still there, trying to pull the mullioned windows open, when Otto stormed in and made a flying lunge at him. I was too spent to do anything but watch and listen as Felix was thrown against the window. The pane shattered in a noisy explosion. Shards of glass flew about the room. After a moment I remembered my knife, and felt around until I found it. During my restless sleep, it had worked its way across the bed to become lodged under the edge of the pillow on the far side. I seized it, but already I could see it would not be necessary to use it. Felix was easily overcome. His life amongst the classics had not prepared him for a physical contest with someone like Otto. I almost felt sorry for him as he cowered in the corner, whimpering, with his hands raised to protect his head, or perhaps to hide his face for shame.

Anita, sleeping in the east wing, heard the ruckus first and appeared at the door with a lamp. She did not speak, but just stared in astonishment as she walked slowly in, her eyes moving from Felix to Otto to me. Otto pulled a pistol from his waistband and handed it to her. "Watch him," he said. "If he moves, shoot the bastard."

She took the gun warily and stood pointing it at Felix while Otto came to me. I pitched myself shamelessly into his arms. Tears were streaming down my cheeks.

"I thought—Otto, forgive me, I thought—"

"I know, darling. It's all right. It's over now." His hands were gentle, and his soothing manner calmed me.

He cradled me gently against his heart, crooning tender words of endearment until I had stopped sobbing. I wished I could remain safe in his arms forever. The fear dispersed in a moment, but the sweeter relief was to lay down the burden of suspicion and open myself to the joy of love.

Horatio was the next to arrive. He stepped promptly in and removed the pistol from Anita's fingers. "Hair-trigger," he said. I knew now why the second pistol had been missing from the case. He had given it to Otto.

Anita came to me to see if I was all right. "You watch her, Anita," Otto said, meaning to watch me. "Horatio and I must take Felix out of here."

"We should tell Gregory," she said.

"Let him sleep. Turning his brother over to the law is no fit job for a man to have to perform."

I think he overestimated Gregory's sensitivity to his brother's plight, but it was a kind thought. The Farr brothers led Felix away. At the door he stopped and turned to me. "I am sorry, Jessica," he said in a dull monotone. "But it was necessary. *Necessitas non habet legem.*"

I could find no words to reply. He left with his head hanging low.

"How very like Felix!" Anita said angrily. "Spouting Latin at a time like this." She sat on the edge of my bed and demanded to hear what had happened.

I wanted to talk about it, to exorcize the demons of that ordeal in the dark. We both bundled up in blankets against the cold draught from the shattered window. She was all curiosity and sympathy, and when we were talked out, she suggested we go downstairs to wait for Otto and Horatio. She helped me into my woollen housecoat, which was more concealing than a gown. It was not an occasion to insist on the formalities of proper dress.

Juteclaw had been awakened, and was also wearing his dressing-gown. On his head sat a handkerchief knotted at the four corners to form a nightcap. Wisps of white hair stuck out in front and back. He looked at me as if I were an apparition from another world.

"Oh, miss!" he exclaimed when he saw me. "It's a miracle, that's what it is. Sit you straight down by the fire and I'll fetch a nice cup o' tea."

"Thank you, Juteclaw," "miss" replied gratefully.

He stoked up the fire in the grate while waiting for the water to boil. Anita and I sat huddled beside the blazing grate, for the house was cold.

"I shall take Gregory away until the talk dies down," she said. "Ireland, perhaps."

I hardly listened. My mind had more important matters to consider. I had yet to learn why Felix had turned to murder, but I could not believe love of gold was the cause. He had performed unforgivable acts. He had murdered two ladies and had tried to kill me, and it was hard to admit that my major sensation at that moment was untrammelled euphoria. I was alive. There was a parting in the dark clouds that had hung over Downsview. One day the clouds would pass and be forgotten. And in the meanwhile, I was alive, I was safe. Otto was free of suspicion, and best of all, I thought he truly did love me.

TWENTY-SIX

An effulgent sunrise crimsoned the purple sky, heralding a new day, when the Farrs returned, sober but triumphant.

"You must tell us all about it, every *word!*" Anita demanded of them.

"A glass of wine to wet my whistle first," Horatio said. The tea had grown cold long since, and I had sent Juteclaw back to bed.

Anita poured us all a glass of wine, and Otto said, "I can almost pity the poor devil." He sat beside me and grasped my hand in a tight grip, as if he were afraid to let me go. "Almost," he added, peering at my throat, which was bruised from the attack.

"Why did he do it, Otto?" I asked. "Surely not for the money."

"Not really for the money, but to save his reputation. It seems large parts of his *magnum opus* were lifted verbatim from Weldon's father's unpublished translation of *Plutarch's Lives*. Doctor Weldon lent it to Felix just before his death. Felix assumed John would demand it back, but when time passed and he didn't hear from him, Felix hatched the plan of passing the work off as his own, and began talking up *his* translation. John is no scholar, but he did at least know what his father had been working on. When Felix's work made such a stir everywhere, John began rooting around his papa's study and found the rough draft. He knew what Felix had done, and threatened to expose him if Felix did not pay him off. Felix did not have as much money as you might think. A work of that sort sells well over the years, but the money does not come gushing in all at once."

"You noticed Felix's scholastic lapses," I said.

"I first suspected when I told him he should be ashamed of himself for writing so well. It was a quotation from Plutarch. If Felix had slaved over the translation, he would have recognized it. I tested him on a few other points, as you may recall, and caught him up on a few things."

I said, "Felix said he was lending John a copy of his Cicero translation, but in fact I saw the book in the library after Weldon left. I wondered about that."

"John Weldon has no more interest in Cicero than he has in metaphysics," Otto declared. "Felix invented the excuse of lending him a book to keep me from quizzing Weldon. He had to have some excuse for Weldon's visits, so he pretended they were discussing the classics. Of course Weldon was putting the screws to him to raise the money. Felix says it was Weldon's idea that he kill Hettie. Greg had given him the notion the fortune was to be shared amongst us. Weldon was ready to settle for ten thousand—but he was *not* willing to wait a year. When he learned the terms of the will, he began urging Felix to either marry you or murder you, Jess."

"He did propose, but in a very half-hearted way."

Anita listened closely and said, "I wonder if Weldon had not assaulted Felix. I never believed that story about walking into a door."

"Yes, Felix says Weldon did it." Otto nodded. "And warned him that was just a sample of what was to come if he did not produce the money. It was also Weldon who butchered Duke, to show Felix what he was capable of in the way of ferocity."

"He was there when Felix murdered Mrs. Manner?" I asked.

"Yes. Felix learned Mrs. Manner had seen him going up to the cheese-room, so he felt he had to be rid of her as well. Felix says Weldon haunted the park at that time, to see that Felix did not try to escape to London. Not much danger of that, when Weldon had proof that the *Plutarch* translation was plagiarized. It was Weldon who had sold Duke to Hettie, so when he whistled, Duke went to him, leaving Mrs. Manner undefended. Felix handled her; Weldon butchered the dog."

I gave an involuntary shudder at the image his words conjured up.

Otto continued, "It was Felix's idea to bury Duke. Pretending to look for the body gave him an excuse to go to the park. What he was really doing, of course, was arguing with Weldon, trying to make some arrangement to delay payment."

"There are queer twists in the lad," Horatio said, shaking his head. "Too much bookwork will do it, I fancy."

"It was insufficient bookwork that caused Felix's problem," Otto said. "He knew himself to be only a second-rate scholar. Anyone who had read his Cicero must wonder at the sudden improvement in his work. One critic used the words 'almost unbelievable.' I felt the same way myself."

"All a hum, about Felix giving a lecture at Rideau Hall," Horatio said. "That was the next step in his plan to kill you, Jess. Who is speaking is that old bore of a Coleridge. Otto asked me to pick up the journals and see if it was advertised. That is how I came to be on hand to drive you home, you see. Killing two birds with one stone. Otto knew the rig would break down, after he had Bonham saw the axle."

"You had your valet saw the axle?" I asked Otto. He nodded. "How did you know . . ."

"A little eavesdropping gave me the clue, and a little gossip with Mary confirmed that you were planning a flit. Don't be hard on her, Jess. I knew you were putting too much trust in Felix, and gave Mary a hint to keep an eye on you. If she had not told me . . ."

"You might have warned Jess about Felix," Anita chided.

"I tried to, but she was strangely immune to my hints," Otto said, fixing me with a stare that still held some anger.

"And to think, Jess, you actually set out in a carriage alone with him to go to London," Anita said. "He had no intention of taking you to that professor friend he spoke of."

"The plan was to murder her en route and claim a high-wayman attacked them," Horatio said. "We got the whole story out of him. It would be dark before they reached London. That boiler of a Weldon was to do the deed, wearing a mask so the groom would not recognize him."

Otto added, "I took a drive beyond Littlehorn this afternoon to inquire at the toll booths if Weldon had set out for London, and returned."

My insides shrank to think how close I had been to disaster that day. "I knew you were fudging about that interview with Skelling! And of course it was Felix who Horatio was hoping to spot in the park this afternoon with the telescope, when he claimed to have spotted a fox."

"You called him a fox yourself," Horatio reminded me.

"Otto had the right name for him. He was the dark horse," I said, giving Otto's hand a squeeze."

Otto continued. "My scavenging in the dustbin added a bit of confirmation as well. Felix had left a sheet of ciphering behind. He had been sorting out Hettie's investments, and dividing them by four. That said pretty clearly that one of us was not to share in them. And we all know which of us was holding up the disbursement of the monies for a year."

"Yet in spite of all your sleuthing and precautions, Felix still got at her," Anita said. "He obviously sneaked back here instead of going to London, but how did he get into Jessica's room without anyone seeing him?"

"By the upstairs window at the end of the west corridor," Otto said. "Weldon followed Felix's carriage towards London. He was riding, not driving, as his role was to be a highwayman. He spotted the carriage at the stable in Littlchorn and gave Felix some signal that they were to meet up farther along the road. That is when Weldon told him about the window that the footman left open at night. Weldon gave Jeanie Pughe, his servant, the night off. Naturally she notified the footman here, and naturally Almond made sure the window was left open for him to sneak in late at night. Unfortunately Felix got in before I closed the window."

"He must have been hiding in that closet for hours," I said. "Mary was in and out of my room. It is odd she did not see him, or hear him."

"He hid in an unused room until he found his chance to get into your bedchamber unseen, not long before you retired for the night. I had Horatio on the *qui vive* in the armaments-room, thinking Felix would come from Weldon's. I knew he would hide his carriage there, as he did. I was also on the lookout myself, but he managed to get through despite us. I thought you were safe when you got the new lock for your door, Jess. Your arguments about the window showed me that was an unlikely route. What I never suspected was that he was already hiding in your closet, waiting, as you had obligingly left your door un-locked."

His fingers tightened on mine until my hand ached, and a shadow of lingering fear darkened his eyes. It was sweeter than a declaration of love.

Horatio shook his head. "If old Hettie had only made a sensible will, none of this would have happened."

"Speak no ill of the dead," Otto said. "It was Felix's pride and Weldon's greed that did the work. Weldon is being locked up as well, of course. I asked Croton to send a couple of men with the constable. Weldon could overpower Hodgkins with no trouble."

Anita sighed in disbelief. "It is inconceivable to me that a man would kill only to conceal that he had falsely claimed to have translated a book."

"Yes, and the fact is, very few would have listened to Weldon," Otto said. "It is not uncommon for some crackpot to come forward and claim authorship of a popular work. It would have been a tempest in a teapot. But Felix's conscience was troubling him too. He knew the work was beyond his skills, and thought that others would believe Weldon's claim without hesitation."

Anita rose and stretched her arms. "Well, it is a great pity, but at least it is over. We will be able to go to London now, I should think?"

"We'll hear from Croton in the morning," Horatio said. "There will be a trial and all that, but we need not stay here in the meanwhile. We are not criminals, after all, but only witnesses. Nasty business, trials, especially in the family. Of course Felix is only a connection of ours, not real family."

"Gregory will feel it," Anita said with a speaking glance that hinted money would ease his suffering. Of course I would give him something more than the two hundred and fifty pounds. His fifth, perhaps, and the same to Horatio. Anita bid us all good night and went upstairs to comfort her lover.

Horatio topped off his glass, leaned back and said, "About the doctored Madeira you was fed, Jess, that was Felix's work too, though it was my bottle he stole from the armaments-room. Wouldn't want you to think I did it. He was planning a peaceful death for you, but hadn't got around to giving the wine to you yet. He had it standing by in the study, where he usually works."

"I don't think Felix wanted to murder anyone," I said. "He is not violent by nature. I am sure he hated every moment of it." Still, as I remembered that fight for my life in the dark, I could not find much sympathy for him.

Otto cast a commanding eye at his brother. "Isn't that glass empty yet?" he asked impatiently.

"Eh? Why are you giving me that evil eye? Do you want to be alone with Jess?" Horatio asked.

"That would be nice," Otto said.

"Can take a hint. Before I go I would like to say—we'll have to take Jess to Mama, Otto. She will want to get away from Downsview for a while. Bound to have nightmares in that room. The clothes-press and all . . . Shocking. Well, I am off then. No point going to bed. Wonder if Cook is up and about yet."

He wandered from the room talking to himself, and at last I was alone with Otto.

"I'm sorry I thought it was you," I said. "When I saw you putting those forged letters in Aunt Hettie's folder—"

His fingers touched my lips, stopping my apologies, and sending a thrill tingling up my spine.

"That was foolish of me. Let us not begin apologizing or we shall be here all day. I was desperate to prove that I had loved you long before the infamous will was read. I did write to Hettie, though I doubt I shall ever prove it. It seems my letters alone were considered worthy of the dustbin."

"I wager she destroyed them to ensure I never saw them."

"That is possible. I came here this year determined to carry you away with me. What I wanted to discuss with you on that ride we never took was my lawsuit. I was afraid that might dissuade you. I knew Hettie would make a meal of it, forecasting penury, the loss of the *Clarion,* and disgrace at court."

"Oh, Otto! As if I care for that!"

He smiled fondly. "Mere bagatelles! What an excellent wife you will make. You know what is important and what is not. Actually the scandal will all be swept under the carpet to keep the rest of Prinney's sins company. It was a bluff that did not work."

"And even if you do lose the case—we will have Aunt Hettie's money. I mean—that is—if you still . . ." I looked at him, suddenly embarrassed.

A soft smile lit on his lips and spread up to light his eyes. "I do, still, despite your thinking me a liar and a murderer, and the rest of society thinking I married you for your money. For better or for worse, you know, as the marriage vows say."

"It could hardly be worse than these past days."

"Let us begin the New Year right. Good God!" He stopped and looked surprised. "This is the last day of December. Tonight will be New Year's Eve. If we hurry, we can spend it at Cleremont, as I had planned. Well, not quite as I had planned," he added ruefully, "but we shall celebrate our betrothal all the same."

As he drew me into his arms for a long, sweet embrace, his lips, without saying a word, spoke volumes of a bright future. Time, which heals all wounds, would soften the harsh memory of this past week, leaving the happier times to conjure with in an idle hour. We would return in the spring for Aunt Hettie's interment. I would go to Bath to visit Mrs. Manner's grave, but we would also come back to Downsview from time to time. Hettie did not want it sold, and despite the wretched happenings of the past week I was reluctant to part with it. Perhaps we would come at the end of each year for a visit.